Anne Wyn Clark was born and raised in the Midlands, where she continues to live with her husband, a sweet-natured cat, plus a chinchilla with attitude. She has three now grown-up children and six grandchildren. Much of her formative existence was spent with her head in a book, and from an early age, she grew to relish the sheer escapism afforded by both reading and writing fiction.

She has a love of antiquity and a penchant for visiting old graveyards, often speculating on the demise of those entombed beneath.

The Secrets of Mill House is her third novel.

You can follow her on Twitter @EAClarkAuthor

Also by Anne Wyn Clark:

Whisper Cottage
The Last House on the Cliff

The Secrets of Mill House

ANNE WYN CLARK

avon.

Published by AVON
A division of HarperCollins*Publishers* Ltd
1 London Bridge Street
London SE1 9GF

www.harpercollins.co.uk

HarperCollins*Publishers*
Macken House, 39/40 Mayor Street Upper,
Dublin 1, D01 C9W8, Ireland

A Paperback Original 2023
1
First published in Great Britain
by HarperCollins*Publishers* 2023

A catalogue copy of this book is available from the British Library.

ISBN: 978-0-00-861411-9

The Little White Horse by Elizabeth Goudge (Lion Hudson), reproduced by
permission of David Higham Associates

Typeset in Sabon by Palimpsest Book Production Ltd, Falkirk, Stirlingshire

Printed and Bound in the UK using 100% Renewable Electricity
at CPI Group (UK) Ltd

This book is produced from independently certified FSC™ paper
to ensure responsible forest management.

For more information visit: www.harpercollins.co.uk/green

For my much-missed grandad, Sidney Thomas Fry,
whose stories will always stay with me.
"Give us a kiss and lend us a bob"
xxx

‘But a hare, now, that is a different thing altogether. A hare is not a pet but a person. Hares are clever and brave and loving, and they have fairy blood in them. It’s a grand thing to have a hare for a friend.’

Elizabeth Goudge

Prologue

Stretmore, Halloween 1975

The pavements were still slick from the afternoon's rainfall. Stretmore looked even bleaker and greyer than usual, the grim high-rise flats on the outskirts of the estate looming threateningly against their charcoal backdrop. It would soon be dusk, and the plastic-encased bulb over the doorway of the scruffy grocery shop at the end of Ostleton Road was burning, though the streets were still just light enough. A clumsily carved, grinning pumpkin, a candle already flickering within, had been placed in the grubby window behind the store's faded posters advertising Ty-Phoo Tea and Lyons Cakes.

Lights had begun to blink on in the windows of some of the tall, terraced houses lining the avenue. It had just turned five o'clock, approaching tea time for many, and the streets were all but empty. A couple of laughing youths, hair dripping, their parkas sodden from the recent downpour, were kicking a ball to one another from opposite sides of the road as they weaved their way down the hill towards the gasworks and the muddy playing field beyond.

The man pulled up alongside the kerb, just a few feet from the shop. He looked from left to right, then switched off the engine and undid his safety belt, settling himself in his seat to wait. Initially, he'd been worried his shiny blue Daimler Sovereign would look conspicuous. If he had been superstitious, he might have thought it unwise to tempt fate on All Hallows' Eve; even to leave the safety of his house. He wasn't familiar with this neighbourhood or indeed the area, but it appeared rundown; some of the houses were boarded up and the glass from the phone box he'd just driven past lay smashed to smithereens beside it. The pavements were strewn with litter and discarded chewing gum; the walls bearing the street signs daubed with artless graffiti. There were few cars on the roads and those he *had* seen looked barely roadworthy. But probably by virtue of the weather, the streets were fairly deserted. There was hardly anyone in evidence to notice him. And what few people there were seemed to pay him little heed.

He sat up sharply as, in his rear-view mirror, he caught sight of the woman, appearing from around the block.

The woman with badly bleached blonde hair, pushing an old-fashioned, coach-built pram.

She was swaying slightly, a cigarette burning between the fingers that gripped the handle of the baby carriage. The man rolled his eyes. Sitting up, he observed her short skirt and teetering movements once more with distaste. He'd watched her earlier, meandering down the street.

He thought she was heading this way. It was obvious she'd been drinking. Hopefully it would have slowed her reflexes.

The woman drew nearer. His pulse quickened as she came to a halt outside the shop just a few feet from the car, slapping on the brake of the pram with her foot. She paused to take a final puff of her roll-up, then ground it out with the toe of her platform shoe on the pavement, just below the shop window. He heard the jangle of the entrance bell as the door closed behind her.

This was even better than he'd anticipated. But time was of the essence.

Quickly, he got out of the car and strode across towards the shop, his heart thudding. The pram was battered, the hood worn with age; a cigarette burn on the cover. His eyes narrowed as he scanned around anxiously, ensuring no one had seen him, then leaned in to inspect the sleeping infant, unhooking the lip of the brown canvas apron. The blanket stretched beneath was blue. He caught his breath. Reaching in with trembling hands, he peeled it back carefully. A *blue* jacket. He smiled inwardly.

Glancing to left and right once again, he seized his chance. The baby snuffled, drawing up its legs a little, but mercifully didn't wake as he lifted it with both hands to his chest. Within seconds, the infant was lying on the back seat of the Daimler.

And like a bat out of hell, he was on his way home.

CHAPTER 1

Stretmore, October 1972

'*Our Father, Who art in Heaven . . .*'

Every time, he would make her recite the only prayer she'd been taught, the one they chanted each morning in assembly. Whenever they said it in school now, it made her want to be sick.

Flora kept her eyes squeezed shut, knees drawn to her chest. She huddled, barefoot, against the grimy wall, palms pressed together, clamping her father's moth-eaten teddy bear beneath her arm. She tried hard to think of something nice, something to take her mind off what was happening. Whenever she woke from a bad dream, Daddy always used to come and tuck her in tightly, sit beside her bed. He would stroke her hair; tell her to think happy thoughts, remember something good. A trip to the seaside; a visit to Granny Jean's in the countryside. She'd loved Granny Jean, with her wispy white hair and twinkling blue eyes. She used to make blackcurrant jam and delicious, crusty soda bread; produce fairy cakes with pink icing and little silver balls, especially for Flora. Daddy was her only son and Flora her only grandchild, and she doted on them. Her little house was neat and tidy, filled with black and white family photos and the sweet, comforting smell of baking.

But now she was gone forever. And so was Daddy. It was just Flora and her mum against the world. But more to the point, against Uncle Roger.

The thudding of Flora's own heart rang out in her ears, her breaths coming in rapid, short gulps. The panic was getting progressively worse. The cloying smell of mothballs and old shoe leather made her gag; the spiders that grazed her bare arms, cobwebs sticking like candyfloss to her unruly hair, feeling like props from an all too real ghost train. Shoved in the corner, the huge plastic bucket that Daddy always used to make his home brew in still bore vague traces of hops and yeast. The scent that was once comforting now had only negative associations. Since he had gone, the last two of her seven years had been reduced to varying degrees of daily misery.

The bare bulb dangling above Flora's head had long blown; the thin sliver of light that bled through the cracks around the door served as a reminder of what lay beyond and what, yet again, she was being excluded from. Once, this spot under the stairs had been a favourite hiding place, but that was before. That was in another life.

A charmed life; a life where someone like *him* existed only between the pages of one of her darkest fairy tales.

Now, every morning as she reached the foot of the stairs, she'd glance, hollow-eyed, in the hallway mirror, then fly past on her way to the kitchen. If she didn't look at the hellhole, she might convince herself it didn't exist; that it was all in her head. The very sight of the yellowing paint peeling from the triangular wooden panel, the loose Bakelite handle, turned her legs to jelly and made her stomach lurch.

But worse was its incongruously shiny recent addition.

The lock on the outside.

In spite of Uncle Roger's total disinterest in helping around the house, he'd been quick to produce his toolkit for this purpose.

'*Hallowed be Thy name.*'

Flora could feel the quaver in her throat, her voice barely more than a whisper.

'Speak up, girl!'

Gruff sniggering came from the other side of the door. She knew he'd been there the whole time; could almost taste the coarse fibres of the filthy donkey jacket with its leatherette elbow patches; smell the Brylcreem on his slicked-back hair, his putrid beer breath. She squeezed the teddy tighter.

'*Please*. I need a wee.'

A throaty guffaw now. 'You haven't finished yet.'

'*Thy kingdom come . . .*'

The tears she'd fought hard to suppress began to flow. It was almost impossible to speak between the sobs. She didn't know how long she'd been in there, only that she had barely finished her bedtime hot milk before he'd rolled in, fresh from an afternoon in the pub and keen for some sport. There was always a ready excuse, some minor misdemeanour on her part, and a spell under the stairs was supposed to help her see the error of her ways.

That evening, it had been the pool of liquid she'd slopped onto the table as she put down her mug.

Flora was clumsy, she knew it, but she really couldn't help it. Too often she would smash cups or plates accidentally, and Uncle Roger seemed to relish the opportunity to treat it as a felony for which she needed punishment.

She prayed he'd grow bored of this 'game' soon.

'*Thy will* . . . Please . . .'

'Get on with it.'

She could hear the glee in his voice, picture the sadistic glint in the cold, dark eyes she'd come to loathe. The sudden warm puddle forming on the lino beneath her thin pyjamas told her she'd lost control of her bladder for the third time that week. She cowered in the knowledge that further humiliation and chastisement would follow.

The sudden rattle of the bolt made her sit up sharply, pushing herself as far back as the limited space would allow. Shielding her eyes with a trembling hand against the harsh electric light, she looked up into the roughly unshaven face leering down at her in disgust.

'*Get up*.' He almost spat the words.

Thick, callused fingers gripped her by the wrist and yanked her to her feet. 'Shei-*la*!'

His bark brought her mother scuttling, red-faced and flustered, from the kitchen.

'What's up?'

'Your brat's pissed herself again. She should be bloody toilet-trained at her age.'

Flora felt herself shoved hard towards Mum, who pulled her against the warmth of her cotton apron, wrapping an arm around her shivering shoulders. Her mother stared at Roger in cowed silence.

His attention was caught suddenly by the sound of the TV coming from the living room. A lobotomised grin spread across his face, revealing tobacco-brown teeth and folding his leathery cheeks into deep grooves. Muttering under his breath, he staggered from the hallway, leaving stale alcohol fumes in his wake as he closed the door clumsily on the opening strains of the *Dad's Army* theme tune. Within seconds, a burst of raucous, drunken laughter could be heard from the other side.

Mum sighed, tucking a stray curl behind Flora's ear. She pulled a cotton hankie from her pocket and crouched down, wiping her daughter's tear-streaked cheeks.

'Come on, Flo. Let's get you cleaned up.'

Still whimpering, Flora allowed herself to be led up to the bathroom, where she stripped off and climbed unsteadily into the tub. She plonked down into the few inches of lukewarm water Mum ran for her. After a few moments' silence she spoke, her voice still wobbly.

'I hate him, Mummy.'

Mum was standing at the sink, rinsing out the sodden pyjama bottoms. She stiffened, pausing for a moment.

'He's not so bad most of the time. You just . . .'

Flora watched as Mum gripped the edge of the basin, staring at the pinched reflection in the mirror. Narrowing her eyes, she stared reproachfully at the back of Mum's head. Mum looked away in guilty discomfort, busying herself once more with squeezing water from the pink brushed nylon as Flora, teeth chattering, rubbed at her legs with the flannel. She thought resentfully about why she was here, when she should have been in her warm bed with the hot water bottle Mum always pushed beneath the sheets, falling asleep to a chapter of *Anne of Green Gables* or the next instalment of *Little Women,* which she was so looking forward to. How comforting the cosseted, safe world of the March sisters seemed compared with her own wretched existence. How she wished she had an older sister like Jo to turn to, who would protect her.

She said the words aloud, as much to confirm her feelings to herself as to her mother.

'I *hate* him. I wish he was dead.'

CHAPTER 2

Little Hambley, November 2001

Flora wondered if the ancient bus would ever make it to the top as it rattled and twisted its way up the hill. Herself aside, she'd counted eleven other passengers, all swaying rhythmically with the movement. Most sat in silence, although a fortyish oily-haired man and a woman wearing an acid-yellow cagoule towards the front were having a heated debate about something in low, angry voices, the volume increasing on the occasional expletive. Flora had made her way to the back and was perching awkwardly on the long seat facing inwards, knees clamped around her suitcase, gripping the metal pole to her left with one hand, and attempting to steady the ancient wicker cat basket on her lap containing poor Rufus with the other. She shushed him from time to time, offering soothing reassurances. The journey had felt interminable; her train had been delayed by more than an hour and the local bus service was sporadic to say the least. She was trying hard to remain focused on what lay ahead, not to dissolve into tears and make a public show of herself.

The purple-haired girl sprawled across the seat opposite was watching her with mild curiosity. She blew a huge pink bubble from her lips. As it burst, a stud-tipped tongue flicked out and hooked it expertly back into her mouth. She began to chew again.

'How old's the cat?' she enquired.

'Almost ten.' Flora mustered a smile. 'First time he's been on a journey like this.'

The girl nodded, staring sympathetically at Rufus, whose anxious face was squashed against the plastic-coated grille. 'Can't be much fun being cooped up in that. You got much further to go?'

'No, nearly there now.'

The girl leaned forwards and reached out, allowing Rufus a tentative sniff at her hand through the gap in the bars. Her eyes widened.

'He looks pretty big.'

'He is. He's part Maine Coon, the vet says.'

Flora watched the girl, vaguely amused. She looked about fifteen but was heavily made-up and aspiring to something like sophistication. The crimson smudge on her two front teeth was almost endearing. *Not quite there yet.* Flora thought how much she reminded her of Iola. Not physically, but the ballsy attitude was all there. The spikiness hiding a marshmallow centre. Her throat tightened as she thought of her friend. Absently peeling back her cuff, she gazed wistfully at the tiny leaping hare and remembered the day she'd finally given in to Iola's nagging so they would each have a mirror image of the other's tattoo: she on her right wrist, Iola on her left.

The girl's oversized leather jacket crackled as she righted herself. 'Ooh – is that a tat?'

Flora gave her a brief flash of the hare before lowering her arm self-consciously. 'Yes. From when I was much younger.'

'I'm getting one – I want a sleeve – you know, where it covers your whole arm?'

'Ouch.' Flora winced. The pain of her own small one had been more than enough, let alone one of these elaborate pieces of art that so many seemed to be opting for these days. But it had been worth it.

'*We'll be just like sisters, then. Bonded for life.*'

Iola's words echoed in her ears. Flora's eyes shifted to the window behind her travel companion. It was dark outside now, and all she could see was her own wild-haired reflection, haggard and pale, staring back.

The bus began to slow. Flora squinted up at the list of stops displayed behind the Perspex panel on the wall, preparing herself to get up. She read the next port of call aloud and sat back in her seat.

'Ah, not this one. One more to go.'

The girl sat forward, suddenly interested. 'What, Homity's Mill?'

'That's right. D'you know it?'

'Can't really miss it. Easily the biggest house in Little Hambley. Creepy old place.' She paused. 'They reckon it's haunted. Me and my mates used to dare each other to go up there after dark when I was a kid. Never saw anything, though.'

When she was a kid. As if she was much more, even now, Flora thought. She wasn't too keen on the idea of a resident ghost, but tried not to dwell on the suggestion.

'I suppose every old house has its stories. Do you know them at all – the Homitys?'

'Oh yeh – everyone round here does. *Of* them, any rate.' She studied Flora for a moment. 'I'm Yaz, by the way. Short for Yasmine.'

Flora smiled. 'Hi, Yaz. I'm Flora.'

The girl nodded. 'My nan's neighbour cleans for them up at the mill. 'Nuff said.' She raised a thickly pencilled-on eyebrow. 'You staying there, then?'

'I'm starting a new job. I'll be Mrs Homity's live-in carer.'

Yaz pulled a face. 'Rather you than me.'

'Oh.' Something contracted in Flora's chest. 'Is there . . . I mean, why d'you say that?'

'It's that son of theirs – Hannibal, or Hadrian, or whatever he's called. I forget. *Proper* friggin' weirdo. He was in my auntie's year at school – creeped everybody out, so she reckoned.'

Flora gripped the pole tighter.

'In what way?'

The girl's eyes lit up. She wriggled forward a little more, as though about to impart some salacious nugget of information. Flora raised a palm.

'Actually, I don't think I want to know, thanks all the same. I'll draw my own conclusions.'

Yaz shrugged. 'Suit yourself. You'll find out soon enough.' She blew another bubble. 'The old fella's a miserable-looking sod. I've seen him in the village a few times – never cracks a smile. Maybe the wife's okay –

never laid eyes on her, though. Don't think she's left that house in years. She ill or something?'

'Mrs Homity is bedridden, from what I've been told. Her husband isn't getting any younger and he needs a helping hand.'

The girl sniggered. 'I bet he does.'

Flora felt her cheeks flare. She dropped her eyes, suddenly uncomfortable.

Someone pressed the bell at the front, alerting her to the stop she needed. Shakily, she got to her feet.

'This is me, then. Nice talking to you.' This wasn't entirely true but Flora was grateful that someone had actually made the effort to speak to her.

Yaz grimaced apologetically. 'Soz, didn't mean to put the wind up you. I'm sure it'll be fine.'

Flora managed a reticent smile. 'Yes, I'm sure it will.'

The bus drew to a juddering halt. A rush of heat and diesel fumes hit her as the door swished open. Lowering her case onto the tarmac, Flora stood for a moment and took in a few breaths. Still on the bus, Yaz cleared a patch of condensation away from the window with her sleeve, raising a thumb. Flora returned the gesture. Hesitantly, she turned to look at the road behind her. When she looked back, the bus had begun to pull away.

Flora gazed up at the old mill house, tightening her scarf as a shiver passed through her. Autumn had brought an unpleasant chill to the evening air, which was damp and heavy with fog. The craggy building itself, set high above the single winding track and a good mile outside the nearest village, had an air of hostility, as though prepared to challenge anyone daring to darken its door. Partially shrouded by the rising mist, it appeared almost to be hovering in mid-air. The outline of another, slightly smaller construction was visible behind it, like the ghostly shadow of the main house. She could hear the gurgle of flowing water somewhere ahead but the light levels were too dim to discern the source.

For a moment she stood rooted to the spot, clutching the mewing Rufus in his carrier, the bulging suitcase at her feet. She felt a sudden, inexplicable flash of foreboding and wondered if she'd made a terrible mistake. Turning anxiously, she could see the red glow of the bus's rear lights disappearing round the bend of the hill. She thought of the girl's words. *Proper friggin' weirdo*. Her heart quickened. She had little option now. Steeling herself, she heaved the bag up the wide stone steps cut into the hillside towards the forbidding edifice.

Here began the next chapter in her life. She prayed it would be better than the last.

CHAPTER 3

Stretmore, October 1972

Monday mornings were met with almost as much dread as Uncle Roger's ale-fuelled Saturday evenings. School was a daily ordeal for Flora and one she built up in her mind each night as she lay in bed. But Mondays were the worst. Butterflies would rise in her stomach as she anticipated the next endless, miserable week ahead. The feeling that she would never fit in; the crippling, self-conscious shyness that prevented her from interacting with the other children. Infants' school had been bad enough. But on the very first day of juniors', she wet herself on the way to the toilet block and had to borrow a pair of knickers from the teacher's emergency selection. Flora's cheeks still burned at the humiliating memory of her classmates pointing across the playground and laughing as she tearfully carried her own damp knickers home in a paper bag. It seemed she was destined to be haunted by the incident forevermore.

The taunts and whispered giggles behind small hands as she sat alone at the back of the classroom continued even now. She was an object of ridicule. Or at least, that was how it felt to Flora. In desperation, she would feign illness: stomach pains, the beginnings of a cold, a terrible headache. The thought of staying at home, with Uncle Roger out at work, tucked up in bed with hot soup and a book, was so much more appealing than struggling through maths and spellings, or worse still, the lonely lunch and break times, kicking her heels with her back to the wall, excluded from her peers' games. But Mum had grown wise to these invented ailments, and despite the daily battle, she would eventually coax Flora out of the house with the promise of something nice for tea, or a trip to the library, if she complied.

Books were Flora's salvation: somewhere to retreat to when the world in which she existed felt too much to bear. For her last Christmas present, Mum had saved up to buy two huge volumes of fairy tales from *Reader's Digest*. Flora would sneak her small torch under the blankets at night and read until her eyes could no longer hold themselves open. The chapters that really caught her imagination were dark, disturbing morality tales, such as *The Goose Girl* and *The Robber Bridegroom*, from the aptly named Brothers Grimm; the unsweetened, and to many unpalatable, versions of stories like Hans Christian Andersen's *The Little Mermaid* and *Thumbelina*. Increasingly, these seemed to resonate with her far more than those of the 'happy-ever-after' ilk. The thought of Uncle Roger being rolled down a hill in a barrel full of spikes like the wicked servant in *The Goose Girl* filled her with immense satisfaction.

It was late October; the nights were drawing in and there was a bite in the air. Half term was only a week away, but five days still felt like an eternity to endure. Flora grumbled as Mum helped her into the stiff, scratchy duffle coat which, despite Flora's protests, Mum had bought from the Oxfam shop. It swamped her and still had that weird musty smell that seemed to linger on everything from nearly new shops and Flora hated it. Mum led her gently but firmly by the hand down Ostleton Road to the school gates. The sky was a bleak grey-white and their breath hung in clouds as they walked.

A girl of Flora's own age passed by, dragging a reluctant, much smaller and loudly complaining boy behind her. Her tawny hair was unevenly cropped and gold hoops swung from her ears. The sleeves of her cardigan and hem of her skirt were too short, as though they had shrunk in the wash. The school's regulation knee-length white socks, grey with wear, gathered at her ankles, their elastic long perished. Her little brother's clothes were equally shabby, but in contrast hung from him like a scarecrow's. Flora recognised the girl as Iola Chappell. She was in the same school year but from a different class – the one which contained the 'problem children', as they were labelled. She could often be seen sitting outside the classroom or the headmaster's office for some offence or other. Iola stopped suddenly and turned to face her brother, jerking the hood of his torn anorak impatiently and ripping it even more. Flora noticed how thin and pale they both looked and, aside from its scruffy appearance, how wrong their clothing was for the time of year. She loathed her own coat, but at least it was warm.

'Stevie, I'm gonna boot your arse in a minute if you don't pack it in.'

Her voice was quiet but menacing. Stevie's shoulders slumped. Begrudgingly, he slipped a hand into his sister's outstretched palm and dropped his head so that his shaggy, dirty blond hair covered his huge, sooty-lashed eyes. He continued sulkily across the tarmac, where he was finally deposited outside the door to the infant classes in the main building. Released from her role as carer, Iola seemed to pull herself upright immediately. There was attitude in the way she walked, a swagger; a 'cross me if you dare' expression etched into her fine features. She disappeared through the door of the prefab classroom on the opposite side of the playground.

'Stay away from that one, Flo,' Mum warned in a low voice, tightening the grip on her daughter's hand. 'That whole family is bad news.'

Everyone on their estate knew the Chappells – by reputation, if not personally. There were three unruly and unkempt children under the age of eight, all allegedly with different fathers, who were conspicuous by their absence. Iola was the eldest of the siblings; Carly, as different from her sister as she could be with her chubby, freckled cheeks and shock of frizzy red hair, the youngest and still in the nursery class. She was nowhere in evidence this morning. Stevie was just five and had already been suspended twice, on one occasion for climbing a tree outside school and refusing to come down, on another for kicking a teacher in the shins. Their mother, Doreen, was a belligerent, loud woman who favoured short skirts and platform heels, even on trips to the corner shop, where she could often be found replenishing her supply of Bulmers and Park Drive. Having seen her once, sashaying along across the street from the school, painted-on eyebrows, a smouldering cigarette suspended from scarlet lips, Flora had stared. She knew she shouldn't: Mum had always told her it was rude to. But she couldn't help it. In a whisper, she'd asked why 'that lady' had a dark stripe along the parting of her white-blonde, back-combed hair.

'That's what colour her hair *should* be,' Mum had replied, rolling her eyes. 'The rest of it comes straight out of a bottle.'

Flora wasn't sure what she meant, but found the woman at once fascinating and slightly terrifying. Her own mother dressed in sensible flat shoes, a modest beige mac that buttoned to her chin; kept her wavy brown hair short and manageable and covered in a plastic rain hat at the first sign of drizzle. She owned an old make-up purse that contained one lipstick and a powder compact, but Flora could never remember seeing her use either of them. In her seven-year-old mind, Doreen Chappell seemed to have come from another planet.

She had observed her from a safe distance on several occasions, and crossed the road to avoid her if she was ever out alone. Flora wasn't sure what she thought might happen if they ever met: but everything Mum had said aside, she had a deep-rooted dread of coming face to face with Doreen Chappell. She exuded hostility and aggression, much like her eldest child.

Ironic, really, that Iola and Flora should become such good friends. But that was much later, of course.

After Flora's life changed forever.

CHAPTER 4

Little Hambley, November 2001

The main entrance to Mill House was reached via a small slatted footbridge, crossing the wide, ink-black pond which encircled the property. The sound of Flora's footfall rang out as her flat shoes slapped across the planks, cutting through the unsettling silence. Flora looked about her uneasily, trying to dismiss any notions of restless spirits. As she reached the end of the bridge, a security light from somewhere above flashed on, illuminating her path but making her squint against its glare. Before her hand could reach the knocker, the huge door began to creak open.

As her eyes adjusted to the brightness, the dark silhouette before her was revealed as the slight, hunched figure of an elderly man. He wore a shirt and tie beneath a dark V-neck sweater, receding grey hair combed back from an unsmiling angular face. Standing in the aperture, he peered out suspiciously over the square black frames of his glasses.

'Ye-es?'

'Mr Homity?' He was not what Flora had been expecting at all. She wondered initially if she had mistakenly come to the wrong building. Perhaps this was the neighbours' property.

But the old man was quick to set her straight.

'I am he.' He gestured irritably to the ivy-clad brass wall plaque to the side of the door, etched with the words *MILL HOUSE*.

'Abraham Homity the fourth. This mill has been in my family for three hundred years.'

Flora wondered if he always felt the need to introduce himself in such a formal manner. His voice sounded clipped and condescending. He nodded towards the basket, from where Rufus had begun to complain vociferously.

'Ahh – I presume you are Miss Lanyon, then? Hector's been looking forward to seeing the cat.'

He smiled drily, as if she ought to know by the process of osmosis who Hector was. Before she had a chance to respond, he pulled the door wide and began to retreat into the hallway, calling over his shoulder, 'This way.' There was neither a word of welcome nor offer of help with the suitcase; no inquiry as to how her journey had been. Flora felt a little deflated.

Her jaw dropped as she entered, setting down the case for a moment on the buffed flagstone floor. Lit by a huge brass lantern in the centre of the ceiling, the hallway's oak-panelled walls were hung with portraits of what she assumed were generations of the Homity clan males, all severe and thin-lipped. She felt numerous pairs of long-dead eyes scrutinising her; judging this wretched, shabby creature invading their ancestral home.

'*We'll be watching you*,' they seemed to say.

Flora shuddered.

'Miss Lanyon?' Mr Homity was out of sight now, but his tone was impatient. 'Step lively.'

'Sorry. I'm just coming.'

Abandoning the case for the time being in favour of Rufus's basket, which she hugged to her, she continued falteringly along the corridor, glancing left and right. She passed by a grand staircase, its banister polished to a high shine, which swept upwards from the centre of the hallway. The passageway began to grow darker and narrower, the floor slippery beneath Flora's feet. Aside from two further closed doors to her right, the space felt empty and strangely deserted. She felt increasingly ill at ease.

'Mr Homity?'

His head appeared suddenly from behind a door on the left, at the end of the corridor.

'In here.' He sounded imperious.

She found herself in a spacious, dimly lit room. The air was cool but the embers of a dying fire still glowed in the grate. Two winged armchairs stood either side of the fireplace with their backs to her, a low table between them.

Beneath the one small window, Mr Homity was lowering himself onto a chair behind a wide, heavy oak desk. Light from a traditional brass banker's lamp spilled over its contents. An old-fashioned French blue telephone with a rotary dial. Pens and pencils, upright in a carved wooden stand; a clear crystal paperweight, dancing swirls of green trapped within. Papers stacked in a dark leather tray. A brass paper-knife. Everything was laid out neatly and precisely, evidence of fastidiousness. She noticed a silver-framed photograph, set at an angle, of an angelic-looking little girl with blonde curls, smiling out from the corner of the desk. Not related to Mr Homity, surely?

'Please. Sit.' He indicated a high-backed, buttoned leather wing chair, positioned strategically directly opposite the desk. Flora pictured her host swivelling the lamp's green glass shade towards her and wondered if an interrogation was about to ensue. She sat anxiously at the edge of the seat, placing Rufus on the floor beside her. She had been hoping at least for some sort of hospitality; the offer of a cup of tea, perhaps. A small demonstration of humanity; of warmth. But warm was the last word to spring to mind as she studied the downturn of her new employer's mouth, harsh lines etched by a permanently sour expression. Mr Homity seemed oblivious to her discomfort.

'This is our library.' He gestured towards the walls, covered from floor to ceiling with shelf upon shelf of books. A tall wooden stepladder on wheels stood behind him to the left.

'No shortage of literature, if you're a bibliophile. Are you?' Mr Homity peered at her as if he thought it unlikely.

'Sorry?'

'A reader. Do you enjoy books?'

Flora brightened a little. 'Oh yes. I . . .'

'Good, good. You will have this room at your disposal. Whenever you aren't working, of course.' He offered her a tight smile.

She shifted awkwardly in her seat, hands twisting in her lap. Normally she would have liked nothing better than the prospect of being surrounded by books. But despite the book-lined walls, the library felt less than inviting. She wondered, too, what sort of reading matter such a man would choose to occupy his mind.

'Now then, there is the small business of the contract.'

Straight down to the nitty-gritty, then. Flora felt even more deflated – but, she reasoned, she was here in the capacity of employee, not guest. She had accepted the position, having little alternative, and ought to be grateful for this opportunity; she realised that.

Shuffling forward, she reached out to relieve him of two thick sheets of paper, stapled together at one corner.

'Just confirming what we discussed over the telephone. If you'd like to sign and date the document – you can peruse the minutiae at your leisure later.' He looked up at her from above his thick-lensed glasses with small, deep-set eyes, their gaze piercing. His tongue darted back and forth over his thin lower lip. The movement was almost reptilian. Flora felt a shudder of repulsion. She prayed it didn't show in her face.

Glancing over the bullet-pointed typescript, Flora recalled the stilted conversation she'd had with Mr Homity just two days earlier. Yes, there were to be no visitors brought to the house – no argument on her part, since there was no one on earth to call on her. One day off – arranged at mutual convenience – for her to do as she pleased. Meals (prepared generally by her) and accommodation for as long as the post required (reading into this, she assumed until anything should happen to the unfortunate Mrs Homity). It all looked, as Mr Homity had stated, above board. But still her heart felt heavy.

'Where should I sign?'

Mr Homity produced a fountain pen. Removing the lid, he passed it across the desk, still watching her closely.

'Anywhere at the bottom will do. Just to say that you've understood the terms and are in agreement.'

He looked on, a smile fixed on his face, as she scrawled her name across the blank space, smudging the wet ink slightly.

'Oops – sorry – I'm not used to these pens.'

'No matter.' He waved a hand airily, leaning back in his chair. Flora noticed his shoulders drop a little. He let out an audible exhalation of breath.

'Now then, I imagine you would like to meet Mrs Homity. She may be a little . . . confused. It's often the case in the evenings, I'm afraid. The dementia, you know. It fluctuates. We can talk more in depth about your responsibilities later.'

'Yes, that would be lovely.' Flora wondered just how badly the condition impaired the old woman's mental capacity. She realised that, in her haste to take the job, she hadn't fully considered the implications of the illness. It was a worrying thought.

'Erm – would it be possible to use the bathroom first, please?' She felt like a schoolgirl, asking permission to leave the lesson. 'And I ought to let Rufus out – he's been in that basket for ages now.'

'Of course, of course. Do follow me.'

Retrieving the cat carrier, Flora followed Mr Homity's shuffling form back out into the corridor. Rufus, quiet for a time, had now begun to make his presence felt once more, scratching and mewing plaintively.

'You have a litter tray, I assume?' Mr Homity looked round at her sharply and then down at the basket.

'Yes, it's in my suitcase.'

He arched an eyebrow in apparent disbelief, then nodded, stopping at the foot of the winding staircase.

'Hec-tor!'

A door opened abruptly somewhere above them and the chiselled face of a young man, dark-haired and wild-eyed, peered over the banister of the galleried landing.

'What do you want?' The tone was irritable, as though he had been interrupted in the middle of something important.

'Miss Lanyon has arrived. Can you assist with carrying her suitcase up the stairs? Right away.'

Muttering under his breath, Hector came galloping down the stairs. It sounded like a herd of elephants descending. Upon seeing Rufus, his face lit up.

'The *cat*!' He hopped about like an excitable child. Seizing the basket from the bemused Flora, he held it aloft, peering through the grille at Rufus, who began to growl softly.

'You said he'd be friendly, Daddy.' He looked over at Mr Homity accusingly.

'I'm sure he is, Hector. The animal probably needs time to adjust to his new environment, that's all.'

Flora looked on in dismay at this bizarre exchange. Hector didn't appear to have even registered her presence. Rufus began to hiss and yowl as the carrier was swung carelessly from side to side like a lantern on a pole, right in front of Hector's leering face.

'Meow, Mr Pussycat. Are you hungry? Shall we find you a nice mouse?'

Mr Homity cast Flora an odd look. He gave an almost imperceptible shake of his head.

'Hector, I think you should put the cat down now.' Relieving the young man of the basket, he handed Rufus back to Flora, whose hands clamped around the handle fiercely. She glared at Hector, a bubble of anger rising inside her. What the hell was he playing at? Poor Rufie.

'Mr Homity, could you show me to the bathroom, please? I can let Rufus out to use his tray once I can empty my case – I think he's becoming distressed.'

'Grumpy cat. I don't like grumpy cats.' Hector scowled, rocking from one foot onto the other, a hand rubbing the back of his head agitatedly.

'I'm sure the cat will be much better once he gets to know you.' Mr Homity's voice was high-pitched, the cords in his neck standing proud. Flora wondered how often it was necessary to placate Hector in order to defuse a situation.

'Now, will you carry the suitcase upstairs, there's a good boy.'

There's a good boy? He must have been at least twenty-five. But clearly all was not right with the Homitys' only son. Still clutching the carrier, Flora followed the grumbling Hector up the stairs diffidently. They reached the centre of a long landing, an equal number of doors to left and right.

'Bath. Room.' Hector's staccato announcement was loud; arrogant, even. He deposited the case with a thud, pointing sullenly to the second door on the left. Leaning forward, he peered into the basket once more, jabbing a finger towards poor Rufus. 'Nasty little bastard.'

Flora bristled. She withdrew the basket from Hector's reach.

'He's very nice really. You're scaring him.' She tried

to sound calm but bit her tongue just short of adding, 'you idiot'.

Hector shot her a look of utter contempt. He was making her uncomfortable. Maybe she should try to mollify him.

'I'm sure you'll be great friends eventually.'

Even as Flora said the words, she knew with conviction she'd have to ensure the danger of Hector and Rufus becoming acquainted without supervision never arose. The thought made her shudder.

Hector harrumphed and stomped off across the landing. He disappeared into one of the rooms, slamming the door shut behind him. Flora could hear voices from the other side, Hector's angry tones and pacing footfall; a softer, wheedling female voice. She assumed it must belong to Mrs Homity.

Flora looked up and down the dark, empty landing and debated if one of these rooms was to become her living quarters. Tonight would be her first night away from home since she was a child. She felt tears threaten and tried to push thoughts of Mum, of everything that had happened, to the back of her mind.

That chapter had closed. Life as she had always known it had imploded; there was to be no going back. Ever.

This was a new start and she must make the best of it. She had to look to the future, not wallow in the past. And, the job aside, she had to focus on her main reason for coming to Little Hambley.

CHAPTER 5

Stretmore, November 1972

With no one she felt she could confide in, Flora began to whisper her dreams and, more often, her despair into the beautiful, thick notebook that Mum had bought her. Clothbound, and with the tantalising image of a pagan hare leaping across a moonlit harvest field, it had become like a friend to her.

Earlier that year, on the morning of her seventh birthday back in April, after Uncle Roger had left for work, Mum had knelt beside her on the living room floor in front of the fireplace, watching with a rare smile as Flora carefully peeled off the flowery wrapping paper, trying not to tear it.

'*That* is Ostara,' she had told her, her dark eyes shining. Flora studied her face. Mum looked beautiful when she smiled. Apart from their colouring and wavy hair, their appearances were poles apart. Mum was petite and fine-boned, with a heart-shaped face and pointy chin. Flora's jaw was squarer. She hated her thin lips; the fact that her nose was a touch too wide. She was tall and gangly for her age, long-limbed like Daddy had been. Maybe she'd look more like Mum when she grew up. But right now, she couldn't ever imagine herself being remotely attractive.

'My nan used to tell me about her when I was little,' Mum went on. 'She was a goddess who could turn herself into a hare and run like the wind.'

The idea of being able to transform herself, to escape from danger or discomfort, ignited Flora's imagination at once. She secreted the journal beneath her mattress and, along with her books of fairy tales, brought it out after dark, when she would painstakingly spill the contents of her miserable day onto its gilt-edged pages with her awful spidery handwriting. Each entry would begin with the same two words: *Dear Ostara*. She fancied she was sharing her innermost thoughts with the magical, shapeshifting deity who had inspired her. As Flora finally laid her head on the pillow, she would close her eyes and picture her own soul rising from her in animal form, running free through fields of swaying corn lit by a huge silver moon in a navy-blue sky. Free from the misery of her reality.

The only person Flora really connected with at school was a girl in her class called Sita. She was tiny for her age and had thick, glossy black hair, which she wore in a fat plait that she could almost sit on. Flora loved the colourful dresses that Sita's mother made for her with fabric from the market, the bangles that encircled her minute wrists. Sita's mum didn't say much, but she was pretty and always seemed smiley. She would greet her and Mum at the school gates with her hands clasped together as though she was going to say a prayer. She dressed in clothes that looked like long pyjamas to Flora; she wore lots of bangles too, and even had a sparkly red jewel in her nose.

But Sita had moved away with her family after only six months to the heart of a largely Asian community in Birmingham, when racist taunts and repeated spray-painting of their front door had finally driven them from their home.

They hadn't had much in common if the truth be told; Sita was always top in every subject, first with an eager hand in the air, while Flora sat quiet as a mouse and prayed the teacher wouldn't notice her, shrinking down into her desk and keeping her eyes to the ground, terrified of making a fool of herself. But they had both been misfits in their own way: Sita, resented because of her intelligence and, moreover, the colour of her skin; Flora because of her awkward, clumsy gait, and hideous pink NHS glasses, one lens patched with sticking plaster to correct a convergent squint. With Sita gone, Flora felt suddenly exposed; if anything, their brief friendship seemed to have further alienated her from many of the other children.

Flora retreated into her own imaginary world at home, scribbling fervently into the book that had become her refuge, sometimes embellishing daily events to make life sound more exciting than it really was. But most of the time, she had to be honest about what was going on. Home had ceased to be a haven after Daddy died. She and Mum were beholden to Uncle Roger and his contribution to the household. Flora had soon realised that Mum was every bit as scared of him as she was. Maybe even more so. She remembered more than one occasion when he had flung his plate across the room because the dinner wasn't to his liking, leaving the walls and floor splattered with broken crockery and food. Once she had walked into the kitchen to find him twisting Mum's arm behind her back and growling something in a low, threatening voice right into her face, his eyes dark and menacing. She had hurried out again, frightened that he might turn on her next. She wondered how many other things had happened that she wasn't aware of.

Mum was never assertive, but had never really needed to be in the past; Flora had been too young to know exactly how things were between her mother and father, but from her perspective, everything had seemed perfect. There were never any fights to her knowledge; both she and Mum would await his return from work eagerly, always bringing laughter and hugs and horseplay. Friday nights were board game nights: Monopoly, Cluedo, snakes and ladders. And a huge bag of pick-n-mix to share. Saturdays were for trips to see Granny Jean or to the park; sometimes the pictures if the weather was wet. His week off during the summer meant a few days in Skegness, always the same caravan park; ice-creams and sandcastles, paddling and being lifted high over the waves as they rolled in, squealing with laughter. The cocoon of Flora's early home life hadn't prepared her for the misfortune to come.

It all seemed to start when Flora brought home her new shoes. *Pride always comes before a fall*: that was something she remembered hearing. Probably from

Granny Jean. Despite Daddy showing her endless times, Flora still struggled to tie her shoelaces, and Mrs Baker, her class teacher, seemed to be getting a bit annoyed that she had to re-tie them for her every time they'd had PE. So, before the new school term, Mum had taken her into town and to Woolworths, to buy shoes with an elasticated strap which she could easily slip on and off. They were navy blue, with a small plastic daisy on the side, and Flora loved them. She had carried the bag containing the shoes in their shiny box all the way home on the bus. When they got back into the house, Flora had proudly pulled out the box and placed it on the kitchen table, ready to show her father when he arrived home.

'Look, Daddy! Look what I got.'

Daddy peered at the contents. 'Well, aren't they pretty,' he'd said with a smile. 'Fit for a princess.'

He'd lifted the box and placed it carefully on the floor.

'But we mustn't put new shoes on the table, you know. Your Granny Jean always swears it'll bring bad luck.' He'd looked at Mum and given her a slow wink, one side of his mouth lifting into a grin. She had prodded him playfully.

'You should show a bit of respect for your mum, you know, David. She talks a lot of sense. Most of the time.'

But even though they'd often laughed good-naturedly about things that Granny Jean said, there must have been something in it. Because that day, Daddy was there, larger than life, and the next he was gone. It was a Friday, that much Flora remembered. Instead of her father breezing in at the end of the working day, two uniformed police officers had knocked at the front door. Puzzled, she'd waited in the hall while, caps removed, they took Mum into the living room. Flora remembered feeling frightened and covering her ears as she heard Mum let out the most terrible, high-pitched sound, like a wounded animal. A driver had lost control of his van and mounted the pavement, the police had told her. There was nothing anyone could have done. He had been in the wrong place at the wrong time.

Just a case of very bad luck.

From that moment on, their whole world was turned upside down. For weeks, Mum seemed to be in a fog, as though she wasn't quite sure what had happened herself. Flora would pull the pillow over her head at night to drown out the sound of her sobs. Mum's brown eyes were permanently red and swollen, her clothes and hair unwashed. Throughout those early days, she just kept hugging Flora, shaking her head, her chin trembling. Flora was hurled into confusion. All she knew was that her beloved daddy wouldn't be coming home ever again. Within six weeks, poor Granny Jean was taken into hospital and never came home. Mum said that losing her only son had destroyed her and she'd died of a broken heart.

And it was all the fault of those stupid, stupid shoes.

Nowadays, the slam of the front door at quarter past six sent Flora's stomach plummeting to the floor. By then, she had eaten a hurried tea and shut herself away in her room, hoping that if she stayed quiet, Uncle Roger might forget she even existed and leave her alone. Being ignored was infinitely preferable to the kind of attention he gave her.

Mum never seemed to laugh any more. Sometimes she'd smile sadly and pat Flora's curls, whisper that she was a good girl, but any spark she'd once had seemed to have been extinguished. Her elder brother spoke to her as though she was something he'd picked up on his hobnail boot, barking instructions and derision. He was the archetypal bully. Years later, Mum told Flora that their dad, her grandfather whom she'd never met, considered him a failure, and had told him so in no uncertain terms. Apparently, Roger had squandered his grammar school education and every opportunity he'd been given since. He was bright; could have been a white-collar worker, an accountant or architect. But he had been a lazy scholar: in his youth the draw of the pub and the bookmaker was far greater than the promise of a better, more prosperous existence further down the line if he knuckled down. Whether this realisation too late had made him the embittered, angry individual that he'd become, Flora wasn't sure. Or maybe it was just inherent in him.

Either way, she and Mum were the ones who bore the brunt of his foul temper. The fact that he'd spent the last twenty-odd years sweating over machinery and damaging his back in the process clearly rankled with him, and the mood in their home was now dictated by whether he had endured a mediocre or particularly arduous day. He had been married in his early twenties, but his wife, Mavis, had been made of sterner stuff than Flora's mother and had walked out on him after only eighteen months, declaring him a selfish bastard. Flora prayed nightly that he'd find someone else and move on, but it seemed that God wasn't listening.

It seemed they were stuck with him.

CHAPTER 6

Little Hambley, November 2001

Flora stood looking round apprehensively as she waited on the landing. The light was dim, flickering slightly as if the bulb was about to expire. She was startled by one of the doors ahead creaking open. Mr Homity appeared from what she now realised was a narrow lift. She wondered why he hadn't suggested they use it for bringing up her luggage.

'The lift is reserved for mine and Mrs Homity's personal use.' He offered an unsolicited, tight-lipped explanation. 'Maybe you would prefer to use the facilities within your allocated room. Please, follow me.'

With no offer of assistance, Flora hefted the suitcase and Rufus alternately, counting the doorways until they arrived outside the eighth, at the far end and to the left of the landing. Mr Homity twisted the heavy oak door's brass handle, flicking on the light just inside the doorway.

The bedroom was vast: high-ceilinged and cold. The stone-mullioned window beyond the plain, dark-framed four-poster bed had been left ajar and faded brocade curtains were flapping in the breeze. From outside, the rush of water could be heard, carried in on the damp evening air. An owl hooted somewhere close by. A small, old-fashioned cast-iron fireplace on the wall to one side of the bed now housed an uninviting single-barred electric heater where logs would once have burned. One small brass lamp with a plain fabric shade stood on a bamboo table at the side of the bed. All purely functional, no adornments or homely touches. She had a brief flashback to her cosy little room at home, the sturdy shelf across the width of one wall crammed with well-thumbed novels, the dressing table covered in nick-nacks. Laughing teenage photo-booth snaps taken with Iola on Saturday outings into town Blu-Tacked to the mirror, the small rocking chair her father had made with such pride when she was born, from which his battered old teddy stared out. The patchwork quilt handed down from Granny Jean. Mostly tat – but things that shaped a home. Omnipresent and comforting – something she realised only now that they were gone. Part of her and who she was.

Who she *had* been.

The hollow feeling in the pit of her stomach deepened.

Flora put down first the basket, then the suitcase, on the large, threadbare rug which covered much of the floor, surrounded by darkly stained boards. She shivered. The space felt unloved and impersonal; reserved, she suspected, for occasional visitors only – and ones that weren't expected to return, at that.

Mr Homity, one arm extended towards an open doorway near the window, had been giving her a running commentary, most of which had been going in one ear and out of the other. She suddenly tuned back in to what he was saying.

'. . . and the hot water system is somewhat antiquated, I'm afraid, so the shower can be a little temperamental.'

She crossed the room and peered into the dingy, windowless bathroom. It smelled musty and dank; the hint of stale pine disinfectant lingering as a bass note. The suite looked ancient: the toilet with its cistern high on the wall and long, rusting chain; a crack zig-zagging through the shattered cream glaze of the basin. The bath was pitifully small; a mildewed curtain, pushed to one side and hanging from a tarnished chrome rail above it, revealed a shower head attached to the mixer tap: not vintage, just genuinely decrepit. She hoped the disappointment wasn't evident in her face.

'I trust you have everything you need.' Mr Homity glanced down at Rufus, now scrabbling frantically at the door to escape the basket. 'You'll keep the animal in here, I assume? It may not be wise to let him roam freely outside – we do have foxes in the area.'

'Yes, definitely.'

From the encounter with Hector, Flora suspected the foxes were the least of Rufus's worries. Hurriedly, she fumbled with the buckles on the suitcase and lifted out the cat's litter tray, well wrapped in two heavy-duty bin liners, then proceeded to unfasten the old shoelaces she'd used to tie the basket shut.

'I'll let him out in the bathroom for now. He's completely house-trained – I did say . . .'

'You did. Anyway, I'll leave you to let him out and use the –' Mr Homity tipped his head towards the en suite. 'I'll be waiting on the landing. As soon as you're ready, I will introduce you to my dear wife.'

The door clicked shut behind him. Flora felt bone-weary; it had been eight days now and she'd barely slept. She was tempted to flop down on the bed, as uninviting as it looked. Her eyes felt heavy and gritty, and she ached to close them. Rubbing at the sockets with the heels of her hands, she let out a long breath. She crossed the room and closed the window. An old oak ottoman was pushed against the wall to her right and Flora sat down on its padded lid for a moment, staring absently at her reflection in the glass. There was little to see below; no street lighting to reveal either the waterwheel or the grounds surrounding the house. She would have to wait until morning to familiarise herself with the layout. An animal nearby – a fox, perhaps even a badger – gave a sudden haunting yelp, making her heart pound. Aside from the chill, the air gusting through, clearly intended to freshen the space, had left an unpleasant marshy odour. After using the toilet herself and releasing a wide-eyed and cautious Rufus into the bathroom to do the same, Flora splashed cold water on her face and stared in despair at her reflection in the mottled mirror above the sink. This was not how she had envisaged spending the rest of her thirties.

But needs must.

She filled Rufus's metal bowl from the tap and put down a handful of kibble on one of the old saucers she had brought with her. He rubbed around her legs, purring, then sniffed warily at the food as if it might be poison.

'Back soon, Rufie.'

Mr Homity was leaning against the door of the room she'd watched Hector enter, his fingers tapping out a rhythm against the frame. Seeing Flora emerge, he straightened, the merest suggestion of an upwards curve on his thin lips. She painted on a smile and, taking a deep breath, followed him into the room.

The curtains were drawn. Compared with the chilly suite Flora had been given, the bedroom felt stiflingly warm. The air smelled synthetically sweet and floral from a recent mist of air-freshener. Propped up in the midst of a cloud of pillows, thick, silver hair fanned out behind her, a frail, elderly woman stared out at her vacantly. A soft halo of light surrounded her from the wall sconce above the polished mahogany headboard. A crocheted white shawl was wrapped around her skeletal shoulders. The unwelcome image of Dickens' Miss Havisham sprang at once to Flora's mind.

'Agnes, darling. This is Miss Lanyon. She will be helping to take care of you from now on.'

From the way in which the bedroom was set out and the old woman's position in the bed, it was quite apparent that the room was for Mrs Homity's use alone. Flora wondered how long it had been since she and her husband had shared a room. It was rather sad. She peered through the door which had been left ajar on the wall to her left, wondering if he had adjoining quarters, but realised at once that it was in fact a bathroom.

Mr Homity gestured to Flora with a subtle twitch of his eyebrows. She stepped forward tentatively.

'Hello, Mrs Homity.'

A brief flicker of awareness crossed the woman's face.

She mumbled something unintelligible, raising a delicate hand limply from the bed. Her pale skin was paper-thin, almost transparent, a network of blue veins snaking beneath the surface.

'What was that, my dear?' Mr Homity leaned in to place an ear close to her gaping mouth. Flora noticed a trail of saliva slithering down the woman's chin. Quickly she plucked a tissue from the box on the bedside table and mopped at it gently. Mr Homity nodded in approval.

'She says she is pleased to meet you,' he asserted.

Flora looked dubiously at poor Mrs Homity but placed her own cool hand lightly on the older woman's slightly clammy one. 'And I'm very pleased to meet you, too.'

Mrs Homity raised her grey, almond-shaped eyes to meet Flora's. She had clearly once been quite beautiful. There was a moment of clarity, a definite connection. But her gaze shifted almost immediately onto something behind Flora and a look of anguish crossed her face. Flora turned to see what might have distressed her and saw Hector looming in the doorway, transferring his weight angrily from one foot to the other.

'Why are you even here? We don't need you. I can help look after Mummy.' His slightly bulging eyes were wide, his voice sounding almost desperate. He turned to his father reprovingly. 'Why did you have to get another one?'

Mr Homity's small eyes narrowed behind his glasses. 'Hector, we've already discussed this at length. You know your mother needs a little more attention these days. I am simply employing Miss Lanyon to help lighten the load.' He shot Flora a condescending glance.

'Flora. Please, call me Flora.' Her pulse quickened.

She hadn't realised negotiation skills were part of the job requirement. 'I – I only want to . . .' She looked back at Mr Homity helplessly.

'There may be things that Mummy would prefer a woman to assist her with . . .'

'What *things*?' Hector waved his arms wildly above his head. 'Oh, this is all total *crap*!'

He flounced out of the room. The atmosphere was charged; Flora watched the door fearfully, as though he might burst back in at any moment wielding an axe.

Mr Homity puffed out his cheeks. He stood beside the bed, his hands clasped in front of him, the thumbs circling each other in agitation. His hands were small for a man's, she noticed; manicured and almost dainty. They looked barely any larger than Mrs Homity's.

'I must apologise for my son's reaction, Miss . . . Flora. As you've probably gathered, Hector's a little highly strung. But he'll settle once he's used to you. He just takes time to adjust to change. It's one of his . . . idiosyncrasies.' He gave a hollow laugh. 'Now, where were we?'

Flora looked back at Mrs Homity but, clearly drained from witnessing this outburst, the old woman's eyes had begun to close. Mr Homity stared at her, his face unreadable.

'My poor sweetheart. We'll leave you to rest.' The coldness of his tone belied the expression of endearment. He leaned forward and planted a kiss rigidly on her forehead, his eyes slanting in Flora's direction, then made his way towards the door.

Before leaving the room, Flora took a last look round and felt a stab of familiarity. The dressing table was covered with bottles and blister packs of various medications, a large bottle of Chanel No. 5 and a jar of Elizabeth Arden moisturiser just visible behind them. A wheelchair had been left underneath the bay window, an ivory silk dressing gown draped across one armrest; a pair of fluffy cream bedroom slippers were placed neatly beside the aluminium walking frame tucked into one corner. Atop the mahogany tallboy opposite the foot of the bed stood a vase of pink roses next to a framed photograph, larger than the one in Mr Homity's library but containing an identical image of the smiling little girl.

Mr Homity glanced over his shoulder and followed her gaze. He smiled sadly.

'Ah. That is Xanthe, our beautiful daughter. She is . . . no longer with us. Sadly, we lost her when she was only five.' He cleared his throat.

'I'm so sorry.' A wave of sorrow washed over Flora. She studied the sweet face; the huge, laughing eyes staring out from the picture. Her throat tightened. The little girl looked so full of joy and mischief. It was unthinkable that she should have been snatched away so young. She wondered what tragedy had befallen her, but didn't dare ask.

'It was a very long time ago.' He stared at the picture a moment longer, his eyes glazing over. 'Sometimes it feels as if she was just a lovely dream.'

CHAPTER 7

Stretmore, October 1975

Two significant things happened that week. Both would stick in Flora's mind forever.

It was a couple of hours after school had finished on Halloween; tea time on a wet, cold Friday. The sort of cold that seeps into your bones, that no amount of clothing can drive out. The rain had finally stopped, but the sky was still bruised black with cloud. Flora was sitting, huddled against the radiator in her bedroom, when the knock came at the door. Tentatively, she got up to peer down the stairs and saw the grave-faced policeman on the doorstep. She wanted to hide; the sheer terror of what such a visit might mean. The last time police had come to their door was the day Daddy had died.

But this was nothing to do with Flora or her family. The police officer had some shocking news. The most recent addition to Doreen Chappell's brood, six-week-old baby Warren, had been snatched from his pram, right outside the shop on the corner. The police were going door to door all over Stretmore, appealing for witnesses. Flora was glad Uncle Roger wasn't at home: he was usually rude to anyone who came to the door. It wouldn't have been nice if he'd been rude to the policeman, who was just doing his job.

Flora looked out of the window after he had gone. She felt suddenly sick, a tide of panic rising inside her. She wanted to crawl under her bedclothes; to block it all out. People from all over the neighbourhood were coming out in force, helping to look for the lost baby. It was terrifying to think that such an awful thing had happened right on their doorstep, she'd heard Mum saying to the policeman. What was the world coming to?

And then, the very next day, Uncle Roger walked out.

As she always did on the first day of a new month, Flora had chanted '*White rabbits, white rabbits*' when she woke up. Granny Jean said it was supposed to bring good luck. Flora needed all the luck she could get.

Mum was waiting outside the school gates after Saturday maths club, her polka dot plastic rain hat tied beneath her chin, clutching an unopened brolly which she appeared to have forgotten about. Flora spotted her mushroom-coloured mac from across the playground. From Mum's demeanour, Flora knew at once that something must have happened. She was chatting to one of the other mothers, which in itself was unusual; animated and smiling, her eyes slightly wild. Seeing Flora, she waved madly, enveloping her in a damp hug as she reached her, shaking icy droplets of rain onto her cheeks and her glasses, before opening the umbrella and taking her by the hand. She could feel that Mum was shivering and her hands were freezing. Mum needed a warmer coat; but coats were expensive. As they began to walk, Mum asked her about her day; what would she like for tea.

'By the way, Flo, I have some news,' she'd said. She proceeded to tell her, at first in an oddly casual way, that Uncle Roger had left and they wouldn't be seeing him any more. No explanation, no goodbye. But from now on, it would just be the two of them again. Flora could tell from the slightly manic edge creeping into Mum's voice, her wide, shining eyes, that she was every bit as delighted about it as she was.

Flora hardly dared believe he was really gone for good. She knew that her uncle had recently lost his job. He had been spending a lot of time moping around the house, grouchier and nastier than ever, with no money to spend in the pub. Maybe he'd found work elsewhere and moved on. But wherever he'd gone, whatever fate had befallen him, she didn't care. Only that she and Mum were finally free of him. It was as though they'd been living in the dark for the last five years and someone had suddenly turned on the light.

That afternoon, Flora helped Mum to bag up the few worthless belongings he'd left behind and they took them to the local charity shop. Together, they scrubbed the room he had claimed as his own from top to bottom, opening the window despite the sleet and cold, to let clean air blow away any last trace of stale sweat and tobacco. Mum had thrown out the filthy brown rug that had covered the centre of the floor, saying it wasn't worth salvaging. She took down and washed the curtains, declaring she would paint the room shocking pink as soon as she had money for a can of emulsion. Removing all evidence of his oppressive presence almost helped to eradicate the bad memories and the pain he had caused.

Almost.

By this time, Flora was approaching her eleventh birthday and would be moving up to the local comprehensive the following September. She hoped it would mean a fresh start all round.

She had finally said goodbye to her eyepatch, although the glasses were still annoyingly necessary. She realised she was probably stuck with them for life. But vision aside, she still seemed to struggle with everyday activities. She had recently had a growth spurt and was now one of the tallest in her class, which made her feel even more awkward and conspicuous. No matter how many times she was shown, she still couldn't get to grips with tying shoelaces, nor could she tell the time. Producing legible handwriting was such an effort that her hand would begin to ache from steering the pen. Her clumsiness and lack of co-ordination had been noticed by her wonderful fourth year Junior class teacher, Miss Carter, who told Mum at the parents' evening she believed that Flora might actually have some kind of disorder called dyspraxia. She'd never heard the word before, but after listening to Miss Carter, Mum seemed hopeful that something could be done to improve things for her, and she had been given a referral to a specialist. In the meantime, she was feeling buoyant and actually beginning to believe there might be light at the end of the tunnel.

Flora still kept her head down at school, but thanks to Miss Carter, PE lessons were no longer the nightmare that they had previously been. She made every effort to see that Flora felt included. Flora was given responsibility for keeping score and handing out the bibs, instead of being expected to catch or throw a netball; for ensuring all equipment was brought out and then packed away in the correct place, rather than having to pass on the baton in the relay race or leap over the vaulting horse. The other kids seemed accepting of this, and Flora no longer had to dread being the butt of everyone's jokes or the loser who had cost them the match. At break times, she had been given the role of librarian's assistant. She even had a smart badge with the word *LIBRARIAN* edged in gilt. Flora was slowly beginning to feel more confident and, frankly, useful.

For the first time since Daddy died, things seemed to be looking up.

CHAPTER 8

Little Hambley, November 2001

Mr Homity's face hardened. The mention of his lost daughter had loosened something within him, but for the briefest moment. He clapped his hands together, drew himself up a little, shaking his shoulders. Flora imagined he would consider any display of emotion a sign of weakness.

'Come now, I would like to show you the kitchen. You'll want to know all about Agnes's dietary requirements, I'm sure.'

More than anything, Flora would have liked a huge mug of tea and maybe a sandwich but didn't dare ask. Hopefully it might occur to Mr Homity at some point that she would need something after her journey. She felt wrung out, physically and emotionally.

She took the stairs and waited at the bottom, listening to the hum of the lift descending. Mr Homity emerged from the door immediately to her right. His face was lined with concern and Flora noticed him patting his trouser pockets as though looking for something. Seeing her, he stopped at once. He gave her a tight-lipped smile.

'We don't have many visitors, you understand, mainly on account of Hector's . . . condition,' he began to explain as they made their way down the passage. 'We . . . I try my best to accommodate him. Your predecessor found his behaviour – challenging, shall we say. But she was rather young, I suppose. I have every faith you'll cope very well – I believe you said you cared for your own mother for many years?'

Flora thought of Mum, of her final cruel, miserable months. Her stomach clenched. 'Yes. My mum was bed-bound for the last part of her life. It was . . . tough.'

'I'm sure, I'm sure. Never easy seeing someone you love suffer, is it.'

There was a beat of silence, a strange sort of concord.

Mr Homity stopped abruptly. 'Right. Well, here we are . . .'

He opened the door onto a large, old-fashioned scullery. It felt unpleasantly cold, not helped by the expanse of ancient stone floor. For the size of the room, it was sparsely furnished. A small table, covered with a wipe-clean gingham cloth, was pushed against one wall. Two wooden chairs were tucked beneath it. Flora was alarmed to see a range stove, something she had no experience of cooking with. A hefty wooden worktop ran the full length of one wall, with numerous cupboards beneath. There was a huge, American-style fridge-freezer with stainless-steel doors and, at the far end of the room, three steps leading upwards into an alcove with a door set back into it.

'The pantry.' Mr Homity waved a hand towards the recess. 'You'll find it well stocked. We do try to give Agnes as varied a diet as possible, even if much of it has to be liquidised.'

He proceeded to list the various meals they would generally have during the course of the week and the necessity for thickener in his wife's drinks – 'to reduce the risk of choking. She had an episode . . .' The list of prescribed drugs that needed to be administered at regular intervals. The length of time after which she would tire and need to rest. The fact that she was often confused and resistant to taking her medication and would need to be coaxed.

Flora was exhausted. It was all too much to take in and, eventually, she raised a hand, interrupting him mid-flow.

'I'm really sorry, Mr Homity, but I think I'll need to write this all down. Hopefully I'll be thinking more clearly after a night's sleep.'

He stared at her for a moment, clearly taken aback. She stood rigidly, biting her lip. Mr Homity managed a thin smile.

'Of course. You must be tired after your journey. Silly of me.' He pointed to an old electric kettle sitting on the work surface, flanked by stone jars of tea, coffee and sugar. Further along stood a toaster and microwave oven.

'Please, help yourself to a hot drink. Or there's cordial, I believe.' He paused. 'Have you eaten?'

Flora shook her head. Her cheeks flushed.

'Well then, I'm sure you will find something to your liking in the fridge or the store cupboard. There are fresh eggs – the milkman brought some only this morning. I'll leave you to it – I'd better pop to Hector's, just to check on him. He should have calmed down by now.'

'Oh – doesn't he live with you, then?' Flora's heart gave a tiny, hopeful skip.

'Well, yes and no. In a manner of speaking. He lives in the annexe next to the waterwheel – we had it converted for him a few years ago. Gives him a bit of independence, you know.' His hands patted his pockets, his head wobbling slightly. 'Carry on. I'll be back shortly.'

Flora stood alone, looking round the kitchen despairingly. It was painted white and spotlessly clean but felt sterile, with no evidence of any homely touch. She hadn't the energy to start cooking anyway. She would settle for tea and toast. Filling the kettle from the tap, she flicked the switch, then opened the fridge to look for butter.

She opened cupboards and drawers until she found plates and cutlery, an earthenware mug. There was no evidence of a bread bin, nor a loaf in the pantry, which looked as though it was stocked for a siege with cans and jars, boxes of cereals, packets of pasta and rice.

She opened the freezer, in the hope of finding a sliced loaf to toast. It was crammed to the brim in each section. She slid out one drawer after another. Finally, she discovered a squashed wholemeal loaf, its slices almost welded together.

Having prised off three pieces, she popped them into the toaster to defrost, and returned the loaf to the drawer at the top of the freezer, inadvertently pulling it too far out, and bringing the smaller section containing the ice tray above with it.

She let out a scream and sprang back, dropping the loaf. The drawer and its contents clattered to the floor.

There on the partially opened tray before her, as though tucked up in bed, lay the corpses of two large white rats, flattened and stretched out side by side in cling-wrap shrouds, mouths gaping to reveal pointed yellow teeth, their straggly pink tails stiff and rimed with ice.

A wave of revulsion swept over Flora. Her heart hammering, she shoved the tray back in, then slammed the freezer shut with shaking hands. She leaned against the door for a moment as though the animals might attempt to escape.

Taking deep breaths, she tried to collect her thoughts. Okay, so there were dead rats in the freezer.

In the freezer.

However she tried to rationalise it, this appalling discovery had left her sickened and perplexed, her mind racing. Who would do such a thing?

What on earth had she let herself in for?

CHAPTER 9

Stretmore, January 1977

Secondary school didn't turn out to be the new improved incarnation Flora had hoped for – not initially, anyway. Despite the fact that her co-ordination, and hence the way she carried herself, was much improved by the physiotherapy she'd been receiving, she still struggled with the curriculum. Without the support and kindness of Miss Carter, she felt like a fish out of water.

Flora hated the building itself. Stretmore High was dauntingly large, and finding her way through the maze of corridors and up and down flights of stairs, hauling a satchel heavy with text and exercise books, was an ordeal. The changeover of lessons felt like a free-for-all; Flora found herself pushed and shoved as she tried to weave her way through the sea of bodies, barged aside by elbows and bags. She frequently arrived late for classes and even though she'd apologise profusely, the teachers, with so many other pupils to contend with, were unsympathetic. Everyone, the staff included, seemed to find her irritating. Flora would generally find herself an empty desk at the back of the classroom and try, as she'd always done, to make herself invisible.

There were plenty of students who were new to her, but with the school falling in the same catchment area as her primary, inevitably she had known many others for years. People gravitated naturally to those they had come up with from junior school, and the same little cliques could be seen huddled together at break times. Once again, Flora felt isolated and out on a limb.

There was the odd snipe about her walk or her awful glasses; she'd come to expect that. But she wasn't bullied exactly; just ignored, for the most part. She'd resigned herself to five more years of misery. Mum no longer walked her to and from school and it was a temptation to not turn up at all. At least she no longer had Uncle Roger to contend with at home. At break times, she would head for the library and find a book to lose herself in.

Just over a year after Uncle Roger left, and only a matter of months after Flora had started high school, a man knocked at 29 Ostleton Road late one Friday afternoon. Flora had gone upstairs to get changed after school. She heard Mum's voice, slightly hesitant as she answered the door. Whoever the man was, it was clear she wasn't going to ask him in. Flora opened her bedroom door and crouched down on the landing, listening to their conversation. It always worried her when anyone she didn't know came to the house. What it might mean for her – and for Mum.

The man sounded gruff and impatient. And he was

asking about Uncle Roger. They'd worked together for a few years and used to drink in the same pub, he said. He'd managed to get Roger an interview for another position when he lost his job in the foundry, but he'd been annoyed when Roger hadn't turned up. Made him look a fool, he said. But after he'd calmed down, he'd been a bit concerned when he hadn't heard from him – and nor, from what he could gather, had anyone else. From the way he was talking, this wasn't the first time the man had been to the house looking for him, but no one ever answered. He made it sound as though he thought they were actually in, but ignoring the door. Mum sounded jumpy. Flora noticed she was getting her words mixed up. She told him that Roger had moved on, somewhere up north she thought, but she was sorry, she didn't have a forwarding address. That if he wanted to leave his number, she'd tell Roger to contact him if he should get in touch. But she didn't think it was very likely.

Flora peered out of her bedroom window as the man walked away, looking back up at the house, an irritated and slightly baffled expression on his face. He was probably about the same age as Uncle Roger, short and swarthy with a beer belly, and wearing workman's overalls. She didn't think Uncle Roger had even had any mates. Maybe he owed the man money. That seemed far nearer the truth. She couldn't see why anyone would want to have him for a friend, unless they were equally horrible. Admittedly, the man hadn't sounded very nice.

Flora thought no more about it at the time, but she did notice that Mum seemed a bit distracted after he'd gone. Not herself at all; as though his visit had upset her. She burned the casserole and smashed two of the plates when she was drying up after dinner. But it may just have been that she was sickening for something, because only the following week, Mum complained of feeling unwell one day. It was unusual for her to complain about anything: she would usually soldier on, even with a streaming cold or the monthly cramps which left her face grey and pinched.

But this was different.

Flora would remember that dreary January afternoon until the day she died: that fateful day when her whole life was turned on its head. More than anything, she would remember the terrible feeling of panic, that Mum might not get better. Flora came home from school to find the house in silent darkness, the breakfast dishes unwashed in the sink. Puzzled, she called out for Mum, going from room to room. She finally found her curled up in bed, something which was unheard of during the daytime.

Mum opened her eyes and smiled weakly.

'Sorry, love. Felt a bit under the weather so I came for a lie-down.'

She tried to sit up but slumped back down, flinching. Flora stepped forwards to offer her a hand but was waved back.

Mum grimaced. 'Give me a minute or two and I'll come down.'

'Stay there. I'll bring you a cup of tea.'

Flora watched anxiously as the cup and saucer rattled in her mother's hands, as though she was struggling to keep a grip on them. She helped Mum guide the warm liquid to her mouth and waited until she had finished.

'Shall I ring the doctor's?'

'No!' Mum's voice was sharp, eyes wide with alarm.

She took a deep breath and sat back. 'No, I'll be fine. Just need a bit of a rest, that's all.' She reached out and patted Flora's cheek. 'There are fishfingers in the icebox, a tin of beans in the cupboard. Can you manage to see to yourself, just for this evening? I'm sorry Flo, I really haven't the energy to do anything at the moment.'

Flora nodded, glancing back as she left the room. Mum had closed her eyes once more. Flora cooked enough fishfingers and beans for both of them, and buttered some bread. But Mum's portion, carried carefully up to the bedroom on a tray, remained untouched.

That night Flora lay awake, worried sick that Mum was really ill; worse still, that she might die and leave her all alone in the world. She wasn't sure what was wrong with her, but even at her young age sensed that this was something potentially serious.

Her instincts proved to be right.

The following day, Mum tried to get out of bed and collapsed. Ignoring her pleas, Flora tearfully called for an ambulance.

After several days of tests, the doctors diagnosed Guillain-Barré Syndrome, a virus which attacks the nervous system. After her initial admission to hospital, Mum's symptoms got progressively worse: she complained of pains in her stomach and back, and was unable to stand or even pick up a spoon. It was frightening.

She was hospitalised for two months. With no one else to care for Flora, Social Services stepped in and she was found an emergency placement with foster parents.

Mr and Mrs Oakley were a kindly couple in their fifties, without children of their own. Flora was waited on hand and foot, taken to and from school in their warm car, since they lived a few miles from her estate. There was always a hug, and hot chocolate and biscuits ready when Flora walked into the cosy kitchen in their neat semi-detached house. They took her to visit Mum daily. Mr Oakley even took her to the optician's and bought her a trendy new pair of gold-rimmed glasses, so that the hated National Health ones could finally be put away for good.

Flora felt torn when Mum was eventually discharged from hospital; she desperately wanted to have her back, but knew she would miss the Oakleys terribly, just as they would her.

'You can come back any time, darling.' Teary-eyed, Mrs Oakley had cupped Flora's chin in her plump hands the day she was due to return home. 'If we'd had a little girl, we'd have wanted her to be just like you. You'll always be welcome here. You know that, don't you?'

Flora had nodded, but no words would come. She'd cried all the way to school that morning, knowing that by the end of the day she would be home with Mum once more, and unlikely to see the Oakleys again. It felt bittersweet.

But even though she was deemed fit to go home, Mum still wasn't well. She no longer had any stamina, seemed exhausted after the smallest exertion and would spend all day either in bed or lying on the sofa. Her mobility had deteriorated and she moved awkwardly, lifting and lowering her legs like a puppet on strings. Her hands had developed a tremor and she often rubbed at her eyes, saying her vision was blurred.

The once sweet, patient disposition that Flora knew and loved was frequently overtaken by a snappy, irritable persona. Although Mum tried her best, she had no one else to lean on and the responsibility inevitably fell on Flora much of the time. In that first couple of weeks after she'd come out of hospital, there were occasional good days when Mum would find a burst of energy from somewhere, but over the next month or so these seemed to get fewer and further between. Flora withdrew into herself, spending more and more time writing her thoughts in her diary. For an eleven-year-old with no friends, she felt she had nowhere else to turn.

A couple of months after her discharge from hospital, Mum received a follow-up visit from their elderly GP, Dr MacLean. Concerned by what he saw, he sent Mum for further tests. Things seemed to have got worse rather than better and she was struggling to do the most basic tasks. Something wasn't right.

Flora came home one afternoon to find Mum crying in the living room, a letter from the hospital crumpled beside her on the settee. She patted the seat cushion and beckoned to Flora to come and join her.

'I'm so sorry, Flo.' She sniffed, blotting her eyes with the cotton hankie balled up in her hand. 'I know I can't be easy to live with and things aren't much fun for you. The doctors tell me I have something . . . something quite unusual, wrong with my brain. That explains why I can't do the things I used to, and why I'm so bloody tired and crabby all the time.'

Flora stared at her, wondering about the implications of what she was being told.

'So – will you get better now? Are they going to give you pills or – or an operation, or something?' Flora felt a flutter of panic in her chest. One particularly bad day, when Mum had shouted at her, she had actually wished for her to become ill again; to have to return to hospital. She had poured her anger and frustration into her notebook. It was all there in black and white. And now, it felt as though she, and ultimately poor Mum, were being punished for her selfishness.

Mum shook her head, her bottom lip quivering, all the while looking down at the letter which she had picked up and was now trying to smooth out absently on her lap.

'Nothing will make it better. They can give me tablets to help with the symptoms, but they're a bit hit and miss, apparently. The doctors say sometimes it goes away on its own, but that's rare.' She looked into Flora's face helplessly, her dark eyes scanning her daughter's. 'I've just got to get on with things and hope for the best. But we'll be all right, won't we Flo? We'll manage, just like we always have.'

She pressed Flora's hand gently and forced a smile, which she returned. But inside, Flora had aged ten years in an instant. The future, which had felt so much brighter only months before, now seemed bleaker than ever.

That night, Flora flicked through her diary and reread the entries from when she had been staying with the Oakleys. It felt like a lifetime ago, those happy weeks she'd spent being spoiled and treated like a princess. And now it felt as though she'd become the Goose Girl from her book of fairy tales; Cinderella, Gretel. Every poor unfortunate she could think of rolled into one, but without the prospect of a happy ending. She remembered crying herself to sleep then, wondering what else life could possibly throw at her and Mum.

Sometimes, it's better not to know.

CHAPTER 10

Little Hambley, November 2001

Returning to her room after her grim discovery in the kitchen, Flora's heart rate gradually began to slow. She'd lain on the bed, taken deep, calming breaths; just as Mum had taught her to when she was a child. In; out. Focused her thoughts on the peaceful image of blue skies over a wildflower meadow. Eventually, the picture of the rats began to recede from her mind. It was almost unheard of, but she'd been too tired to write in her diary. Even though the bedroom was so cold she could see her breath and had kept Mum's old dressing gown wrapped round her beneath the covers, she'd fallen asleep almost instantly. She slept soundly, more as a result of sheer exhaustion than anything else. And this despite the heavy classical music which had begun to blare from the annexe shortly after she had fallen wearily into bed. She'd assumed it was Hector's way of venting his spleen and buried her head beneath the pillow. If anything, it had been a further distraction from the disturbing thought of what lay in the freezer.

Mr Homity had already compiled an extensive list of the tasks required of her, saying he would talk her through his wife's medication schedule and clarify anything she wasn't sure of in the morning. All she could think of as he talked in his peculiar stilted way was the rats. It made her shudder. She had watched him closely; his quick, lizard-like mannerisms, his piercing coal-dark eyes, wondering what other unpleasant discoveries might be lurking somewhere in the back of the store cupboard. It didn't bear thinking about.

She opened one bleary eye to find Rufus next to her head, purring loudly. She scratched him gently under the chin and he gave an appreciative chirrup, licking her hand gently with his rough tongue.

Thank God for Rufus. He was the only thing that had kept her sane these last weeks. She had rescued him as a tiny, scrawny stray, all matted fur and gungy eyes. He had been crouching behind their front hedge one November morning, mewing pitifully, shivering and wet. Flora had put up a notice in the corner shop window in case someone was missing him, but no one came forward. And now here he was, ten years on, a huge, fluffy beast of a cat: so distinctive with his striped face, as though someone had drawn a line down the centre – one side ginger, the other white with a black splodge around his eye.

Rufus was a one-off. His solid, gentle presence was her last link with home. She relived the moment she had closed the door on her old life forever and shuddered.

The persistent and increasingly angry-looking letters from the gas board weren't going to stop, and sooner or later, she would have had to answer the door. She felt cowardly now, that she hadn't stayed to face the music. But she had chosen this path and there was to be no going back.

She pulled herself upright in the bed now and reached for her copy of the contract, which she had left folded on the bedside table. It would have been pointless trying to read through it last night, when the words had danced and blurred illegibly before her on the page. Silly of her, really, though. Mum had always impressed upon her that she should never put her name to *anything* without reading the small print. The *minutiae*, as Mr Homity had put it.

Line by line, and with an increasing sense of alarm, Flora began to go through the clauses crammed together in tiny print on the back. No property of the Homity family was to be removed from the premises under any circumstances. Her employer's word on all matters was final and should never be questioned. Entrance was permitted solely to the rooms within the house specified (i.e. the kitchen, library, bathroom, her own quarters and those of Mrs Homity). Entrance to the annexe building was by prior agreement with Mr Homity or Hector only. Everything witnessed or discussed within Mill House was to be treated with the strictest confidentiality and must never be divulged to ANYONE (this word in bold capitals) outside.

Failure to comply with any of these requirements would result in instant dismissal and eviction from Mill House.

Flora sat back for a moment, her mind darting. Just

what had she agreed to, exactly? What if she needed to speak to someone about something in the house? It all seemed a bit extreme; draconian, even. She instinctively reached beneath the bed and lifted the open lid of the suitcase, feeling for the canvas tote bag she had left at the top. The weight of the diary in her hands was strangely comforting. She ran her fingers over the cover. Here was a brand-new volume for her new life, a life which held increasing uncertainty.

The book was adorned with a different picture now: a butterfly with iridescent peacock-blue wings. She'd looked out for a notebook depicting a hare, though it had proved sadly impossible to find. But in her mind, she was still writing to the same pagan spirit that had captured her imagination as a child. Who would have thought that one book given to her on her seventh birthday would have sparked a lifelong obsession? Keeping a record of her thoughts and events, even the trivial ones, had been part of her daily routine ever since she'd received that first magical notebook. It had left her feeling slightly panicked that she'd had to leave all those pages behind, all those memories and reflections, crammed into the diaries that Mum had bought, year in, year out, until she was no longer able to leave the house. But there was no way Flora could have brought them all with her. So they had stayed, an archive of her past thirty years, filed in date order into old shoe boxes in the top of her wardrobe.

She wondered fleetingly if they might be discovered one day, sometime in the future when she was no more than a distant memory to anyone. Initially, a puzzle to the finder as to who the mysterious Ostara may have been; then the identity of the pitiable, anonymous diarist. Not that there was anyone to remember her, even now. Not anyone important. The neighbours probably wouldn't even realise she was no longer at home. Apart from old Mrs Malone, they'd always looked at her as if she was some kind of weirdo, anyway. Maybe she was. The thought made her throat constrict, and she swallowed down a painful lump. She unclipped the biro from the front cover and turned to the first brief, almost hysterical entry she had made. The day before she'd left Stretmore for good. Her eyes scanned the page and a wave of nausea passed through her. She flicked over, smoothing down the new empty sheet, and filled her lungs with resolution. It was time to start living in the here and now.

Dear Ostara, she began.

She shrugged the covers higher around her shoulders against the draught wafting through the leaded window panes and considered for a moment. Desolately surveying her surroundings, she chewed over the previous evening's bizarre encounter with the apparently unhinged Hector; the frozen rats. Mr Homity's cold, unnerving manner. The contract.

I think I may have just made the worst mistake of my life.

CHAPTER 11

Stretmore, November 2001

The arrival of two police cars late that morning outside number 29 Ostleton Road had set the net curtains twitching. Two burly men from the gas board had barged their way into the house only an hour or so earlier; when she was opening her living room curtains, Molly Baxter at number 39 had seen them strolling up the path, calm as you like, and coming out just minutes later, faces taut and ashen, in such a rush you'd have thought the hounds of hell were at their heels.

She tweaked the blind and watched from the corner of her bedroom window – easier to see what was going on from upstairs – as a dark blue Transit van with blacked-out windows rolled up, and yet more officers, dressed in white hooded suits and carrying some sort of equipment, made their way up the garden path and disappeared into the house.

She stood there patiently for a good twenty minutes, but nothing much seemed to be happening. Spotting a small gathering of some of the neighbours on the opposite side of the street, she decided to go down to see whether anyone else knew anything. As she passed through her gate, she glanced back at the house and saw that the police had stretched a blue and white cordon across the threshold of number 29. Looking up, she could see movement in the front bedroom; people moving back and forth, the intermittent flash of a camera bulb.

In slippered feet, she crossed the road hurriedly to where the others were standing in a huddle. There were five of them in all now: herself, George and Elsa from next door but one, elderly Mrs Malone from the house opposite, who rarely came outside these days; the slender young Somalian woman who'd recently moved in next door. They were joined by the good-looking gay guy from round the corner she often saw in the park, with his little shih-tzu in tow. Another door further down the street opened and old Joe Santoro, fag in hand and still in his pyjamas, shuffled out onto the pavement, peering down the road with screwed-up, sleep-heavy eyes as though he'd just woken up.

'What the hell's gone on there, d'you think? Something happened to Mrs Lanyon?'

They all turned to look at her. Mrs Malone looked vaguely disgusted. Molly realised she might have sounded a little too eager. She felt heat rise in her cheeks and gave a small cough, putting a hand to her mouth.

'I mean – is the old dear okay? I know her health hasn't been good for a long time. Haven't seen her Flora in a while, either.'

'You mean, has the poor woman finally kicked the bucket?' Mrs Malone narrowed her eyes. 'Sheila passed away. Over a fortnight ago, now – the funeral's already been and gone. I'm surprised you didn't know – you don't usually seem to miss much.'

Molly folded her arms, her cheeks glowing with discomfort. 'Oh. I – I hadn't realised. I was in bed with a bug all last week . . .' She tailed off as Mrs Malone fixed her with a look of contempt. 'Well, something else is obviously up, then. Must be pretty serious. I mean, you wouldn't get all *that* lot turning out for nothing.' She gestured towards the vehicles parked along the pavement.

A tall, uniformed policeman emerged suddenly from the house and walked towards the garden gate. He clocked the little clutch of onlookers. Glancing from left to right, he crossed the street. His expression was grim.

'Nothing to see here, folks. If you'd like to move along, please.'

No one budged. George bristled, drawing himself up to his full five feet six inches. Elsa gripped him by the crook of his arm, possibly worried he might say something inappropriate. What George lacked in height, he more than made up for in words. The young Somalian woman looked uncomfortable and the shih-tzu began to yap and strain at his lead as his red-faced owner yanked him back.

'Can't you tell us what's happened, officer?' Molly leaned in towards him, flashing what she hoped was her most appealing smile, her eyes bright. 'Is Flora . . . all right?'

Mrs Malone tutted and rolled her eyes.

The officer responded with a tight-lipped grimace. 'Not for me to say, I'm afraid. Please, if you could all just be on your way. We'll be finished up here soon enough.'

He stood firm, hands behind his back, and watched pointedly as they all gradually dispersed reluctantly and returned to their respective homes.

It was several hours before Molly saw the black zipped-up bag being carried on a stretcher from number 29 into the waiting van. She very nearly missed it, having left her post briefly to make a cup of tea and some toast. She looked across the road and saw that Mrs Malone was also watching from her living room window. Seeing Molly, she glared and pulled her curtains across, disappearing from view. So, it looked as though Flora *was* dead, then. She'd thought as much. The coppers wouldn't have been there for something trivial.

But what could have happened to her? Her mind went to the letter that had been sitting in her kitchen drawer for all those months. A letter that wasn't hers to open.

Might there have been a clue in it?

CHAPTER 12

Stretmore, September 1977

When Flora moved up to the second year at Stretmore High, life took an unexpected turn for the better.

It was the third week of the autumn term. The new English teacher seemed to have it in for Flora from the start, but perhaps to her the girl seemed remote and disinterested. So far, she'd spent most of Mrs Owers' uninspiring lessons gazing out at the playing field, imagining herself as Ostara in the guise of the hare, leaping away to freedom through the spinney that bordered the school playing fields.

Mrs Owers was forty-something, and intimidatingly large in both height and breadth. She wore her long, greasy hair scraped back into a thin ponytail, and swept around the classroom in a paisley print kaftan, wafting body odour unsuccessfully masked by a spritz of Tweed. Flora recognised the perfume as it was the only one Mum ever wore; she had always quite liked it before.

'Flora Lanyon. I'm talking to you.'

Flora realised with horror that she had been singled out to answer a question about the dull class book, which, being distracted as ever, she hadn't been following properly. Frantically, she pored over the page in front of her but had no idea what she'd even been asked, let alone how to respond.

'Well?' Mrs Owers' voice had raised an octave. 'Do you have an opinion?'

She marched across to Flora's desk and grabbed the dog-eared textbook, which was opened on the wrong page. Glaring, she flicked through and slammed it down again in front of her, jabbing with a stubby finger at the relevant passage.

'I'm sorry, am I boring you?'

Flora opened her mouth but nothing came out. She dropped her eyes as her cheeks burned.

'Get up.'

Her response was a croak. 'Pardon?'

'Get up. I'm going to sit here – *you* can go to the front and take the lesson. You obviously know all about the plot already, so you can tell the rest of us what we should be thinking.'

Flora was horrified. She realised suddenly that every pair of eyes in the room was on her, some throwing sympathetic glances, most looking gleeful.

'I'm *waiting*!'

She began to rise slowly from her seat when a voice from the other side of the room piped up.

'*I* have an opinion, Miss.'

Every head swivelled sharply to see a petite girl, her short, spiky hair dyed jet black, sporting a ring through one nostril, who had hoisted herself up onto her desk, feet crossed at the ankle on the seat. The tip of her tongue probed the corner of her open mouth as she fixed the teacher with a challenging stare. She wasn't pretty exactly, but small-featured and striking, exuding confidence and a maturity beyond her years.

Mrs Owers glowered. 'Iola Chappell, sit back on your chair properly.'

'You never ask *me*. Don't you want to hear *my* opinion?'

Thankfully for Flora, this disruption had deflected the attention from her. She sank back down, praying to be forgotten as the teacher, red-faced and simmering, moved towards the girl.

'I said, sit down.'

'And *I* said, don't you want to hear what *I* think for a change?'

Mrs Owers looked agitated. Her eyes flicked from the girl to the door, as though looking for an escape route. She cleared her throat loudly. 'Well, do share your thoughts with us, if you really must.'

Iola smirked. She slid down from the desk and drew herself to her full height, which was no more than five feet; a good seven or eight inches shorter than the teacher, who was standing less than a desk's width away from her.

She stuck out her chin defiantly. 'I think you're a smelly old bag who likes to pick on anyone smaller than you. And your lessons are shite.'

A collective intake of breath could be heard, followed by one or two smothered sniggers. The atmosphere in the room felt charged with anticipation.

Mrs Owers' face was crimson. Her blubbery throat moved up and down like a bullfrog swallowing a worm.

'Get out – *now*! Straight to Mr Poole's office. He can deal with you.' She turned to Flora, eyes blazing. 'That goes for you, too.'

And so Flora found herself outside the headmaster's office, sitting opposite the girl she'd always been warned to stay away from. Iola sat, one monkey-boot-clad foot tucked beneath her on the plastic chair, the other swinging. She leaned back, looking Flora up and down, and gave a brief tip of her head, arching her eyebrows slightly.

'You went to Clutchley Primary, didn't you? I remember seeing you in assembly – didn't you always get put on the end of the row?'

Flora was amazed that Iola had even noticed her. Her cheeks grew warm. She wondered if the girl was aware of the cruel names her classmates taunted her with; whether she had laughed behind her back as the others had.

'I used to have trouble with my legs. Miss Carter thought it was best for me to be able to get in and out first as it took me a while to get moving. They're much better now, though.'

Iola considered this for a moment then nodded slowly, her bottom lip jutting. 'So what d'you think of this shithole?'

'Not much. But I've never liked school anyway.'

'Me neither. Can't wait till I'm sixteen – I'll be out of here like a rat up a drainpipe!'

Flora managed a grin but could think of no response. She couldn't quite get over the fact that here she was, in conversation with the most infamous girl in her year. And that Iola, the girl she'd felt so wary of with the even scarier mother, had actually recognised her and wasn't making fun of her in any way. It all felt quite surreal.

'Ever been sent to see Poole before?'

Flora shook her head, remembering why they were there. She gripped the sides of her chair, feeling suddenly queasy.

Iola stretched her arms lazily above her head and blew out her cheeks. 'Pfft. He's a drip. Makes all these threats and tries to look like he's in charge, but he's frigging useless. Might as well send you to see one of the cleaners.'

Flora smiled weakly. She wasn't entirely reassured, but felt glad she wasn't sitting there alone. She wished she possessed even a pinch of Iola's hutzpah. It must be nice not to give a damn about authority.

Mr Poole did indeed turn out to be a pushover. They heard him mutter something to his secretary about Mrs Owers clearing up her own messes, and he was quick to send them back to the classroom with a half-soaked reprimand. It felt like an anticlimax.

They'd just reached the end of the corridor in the English block when Iola turned to Flora.

'D'you fancy wagging it? Owers will just be glad we're not in her poxy lesson and it's Maths after break. I hate Maths.'

Flora felt a shiver, both of fear and excitement.

'I'm not sure . . .'

Iola shrugged. 'Suit yourself. I'm off anyway.'

She began to walk casually towards the exit and Flora felt her stomach drop. This was the only time anyone had actually invited her to do anything, and could be an opportunity to make a friend. Whether Mum would approve was another matter entirely.

But Mum didn't need to know.

'Wait! I'll come with you.'

CHAPTER 13

Little Hambley, November 2001

Mr Homity, having ensured that Flora had been supplied with the necessary instructions regarding his wife's care requirements for the day, seemed to be itching to get away. He'd called a taxi to take him into Cheltenham – he needed to attend a meeting with a Kenneth Ogilvy, his solicitor, he'd said, and would then be going for lunch, so might not be back for several hours.

In the cold light of day, Flora felt panic begin to set in. This was to be her first experience of looking after a helpless stranger, whose welfare was entirely her responsibility. She had been used to Mum, who, being fully compos mentis despite her physical ailments, was able to talk her through things and remind her if she had overlooked something, or tell her if there was anything she needed. But Mrs Homity was a different kettle of fish altogether. The accountability for her client's welfare weighed heavy on Flora and she was petrified of administering the wrong dose of medication or of the woman choking on something. In desperation, she had ended up in this job with no formal training and had now begun to doubt her own capability.

Mrs Homity, however, seemed considerably more lucid than she had done the previous evening. Sitting up in bed and wrapped in a pale pink bedjacket, she was staring through the opened curtains pensively. She turned and broke into a smile as Flora entered the room carrying a tray of porridge and tea containing the requisite thickener in a toddler's beaker.

'Ah, you must be my new lady.' She eased herself up further so that her head was against the headboard, her back arched over the pillows. 'I'm sorry – have we already met? My memory's not so good these days.'

'We met last night, actually. I'm Flora.'

'Flora. A pretty name. And you must call me Agnes. No point being formal when we're going to be so intimately acquainted, is it.' She gave a wry grin.

Flora cringed inwardly. She had been briefed about the open-bottomed chair she would have to wheel into the wet room adjoining Mrs Homity's bedroom and the old woman's toileting requirements. Having to bathe a total stranger was something she was going to have to get used to. It was all part of the deal, and she needed to focus on the fact.

She mustered a weak smile. "I'm sure we'll get along very well."

The old woman tilted her head, lifting an eyebrow as though waiting for something.

"Agnes," Flora added.

Mrs Homity nodded her approval. 'Well Flora, what delights have you got for me this morning?'

Placing the tray carefully across the old woman's lap, Flora almost winced. She could feel Mrs Homity's legs through the covers, the bones so sharp that she wondered how much flesh was actually covering them. Mrs Homity arched her eyebrows as she peered down at the porridge.

'More slop. What I wouldn't give for a proper fry-up.' She looked up at Flora and grimaced. 'Abey won't hear of it. I began to choke – just *once* – on a piece of fried bread. That was it. Never allowed anything I can get my teeth into any more. It feels like a penance.' She rolled her eyes.

'Shall I – would you like me to . . .?'

'Feed me? If you must.'

Mrs Homity obligingly opened her mouth like a baby bird as Flora began to spoon in the unappetising grey goo. Within minutes, the bowl was scraped clean. There seemed to be nothing wrong with the old woman's appetite, at least. She managed to pick up the beaker with both hands and slurped the liquid noisily through the spout.

'Decent cup of tea, anyway. Even if it is a bit slimy.' She laughed, slightly bitterly. 'So, Flora. Tell me about yourself. Why would an attractive young woman like yourself want to move into the middle of nowhere to care for an invalid like me?'

Flora felt anything *but* attractive. And she didn't really want to discuss her reasons for needing to get away from Stretmore. She stiffened and remained silent, busying herself by removing the empty bowl from the tray and placing it on the bedside table. She leaned across to plump the pillows that Mrs Homity was propped against. There was a strangely sweet odour emanating from the old woman. Mrs Homity tilted her head, watching her. She looked suddenly anxious.

'I'm sorry. It's none of my business really. I just wondered where you came from – what you were doing before.'

Flora felt bad then. It must have seemed rude, not responding. She let out a long breath.

'My mum passed away recently. I'd been looking after her for a long time. It's all I've ever known, really.' The words tasted as bitter as a lie in her mouth. But it was the pitiful truth. She swallowed hard.

'I wanted to move away – make a new start. And of course, I needed a job. Can't live on fresh air.' Flora tried to smile but felt her throat tighten. She looked away and brushed a hand across her eyes.

'I'm so sorry for your loss.' Mrs Homity put down the beaker and gently placed a hand on Flora's arm. 'I hope that you'll be happy here. We're not so bad when you get to know us.'

'Thank you.' Flora's lips twitched uncertainly as she remembered Hector's outburst from the night before and Mr Homity's brusque, unfriendly manner. And above all else, those rats. Maybe there was a rational explanation – although she couldn't think of a single reason why any sane person would freeze dead rodents, let alone next to food. Every time she thought of them, and of what might have made someone do such a thing, it made her stomach turn over.

Mrs Homity studied Flora, clearly homing in on her anxiety. She flopped back against her pillows. 'Oh, don't worry about Hector. He's a little . . . different, I admit. But he's always been nervous around people he hasn't met before. I'm sure you'll get on well, once you get to know one another.'

'Yes, I'm sure we will.' Flora smiled tightly, picking up the empty beaker. 'I'll just get your medication.'

The old woman's eyes widened earnestly. 'Not just yet. *Please.*'

Flora was taken aback by her pleading tone.

'Do you find it hard to take the tablets? I know my mum struggled with swallowing stuff sometimes.'

'The swallowing isn't the problem. It's how they make me feel – not like myself at all. I'd rather wait a while, if you don't mind. Abey is such a stickler – he's so insistent I take them all the time. *But he doesn't need to know.*' She said these last words in a hushed tone, her hands pressed together imploringly.

Flora looked dubiously at the pill dispenser containing the various medications that Mrs Homity took daily. The plastic tray was marked with the days of the week, with four separate boxes marked with the times for each day. Mr Homity had already inserted the tablets for the coming week into the dispenser. He had been most specific about when they should be administered, and the fact that his wife could be awkward.

Flora recognised some of the labels on the bottles and packets lined up on the dressing table, but not others. Lansoprazole. Fentanyl. Naproxen. Simvastatin. *Amiodarone*. She remembered that one from somewhere, but wasn't sure why or when. No wonder the poor woman felt peculiar with all that swimming around her system.

'I have a spot of heart trouble and a . . . what d'you call it? – a *syndrome*. Something called CMT, I think. It affects my nerves, the doctor said. That's why I have trouble walking now.'

Flora nodded sympathetically. Something similar to Mum, then. She knew that fentanyl was a strong analgesic and an opiate. Mum had been given it in slow-release patch form, as her pain was chronic. It had often made her confused and drowsy.

'Is it a painful condition?'

'Sometimes. But I can usually cope with it. More than anything, it just leaves me so weak all the time. I feel pretty helpless. And when my brain is full of fog because of the pills on top of everything else, I feel I've lost control completely. Some days I can hardly remember who I am.'

Flora felt torn. Mrs Homity looked almost desperate. She knew that people with dementia could have periods of clarity, and the old woman certainly seemed to know her own mind – in this moment, if not always. It seemed cruel to rob her of that. Who knew how much longer she'd be able to express her wishes – or have any say in how she was treated?

She drew in a deep breath. 'Okay – we'll wait a while, then. But if anything starts hurting, you must *promise* to let me know straight away. I don't want to be in your husband's bad books when I've only just started.'

Mrs Homity's face lit up. She clapped her hands together like a delighted child. 'In that case, I'd like to go for a walk. Not literally, you understand,' she added quickly. 'But if you could take me outside, that would be a real treat. It's chilly but quite dry this morning. I can wrap up. Abey won't let me go out, especially if it's cold – I'm sure he's convinced I'll contract pneumonia and die.' She gave a shrill laugh. 'As if that could be any worse than *this*.'

She looked down in disgust at her wasted outline in the bed, shaking her head. 'I am not living, Flora. I'm existing. You do understand, don't you?'

Flora could find no words. She dropped her eyes. It was all too close to home; to what Mum had been through. An echo of the conversation that had played out so many times in those final weeks. The constant wrestling with her own conscience.

'I'm sorry to burden you with my feelings,' Mrs Homity went on. 'But it's best to be frank, I think. Anyway, Abey won't be back for hours. I can be tucked back into this coffin well before he returns and he'll be none the wiser.' She sighed. 'God knows what he finds to talk to Kenneth about. I suspect they just set the world to rights, rather than discussing anything important. Drink too much and reminisce. They were at school together, you know.' She gave a strange little laugh. 'I think he prefers his company to mine.'

'What about Hector?'

'Hector? He probably won't even notice. He spends most of his time in his little house. I expect he's still in bed, anyway. He's often up during the night, doing whatever it is that he does.' She turned to Flora, something like distaste crossing her face for a second. 'No, we don't need to worry about Hector. He has plenty to keep him occupied.'

CHAPTER 14

Stretmore, October 1978

Mum had always impressed upon Flora that, however bad anyone might think things were, there was always someone much worse off than themselves. And getting to know Iola, Flora realised how very true that was.

As Flora's friendship with Iola blossomed, it was as though the invisible wall around her new friend began to crumble, little by little. Flora had begun to realise that Iola operated on a 'quid pro quo' basis: that whenever Flora shared something about herself and her home life, even stuff about Uncle Roger, however reluctant she may have been to say it aloud, the shared misery seemed to bring them closer, and Iola began to reciprocate.

'My mum's an alcoholic,' she told Flora casually one lunchtime. They were sitting on the cold wall outside the chippy, sharing the steaming bag of chips placed between them. A cloud of hot breath escaped Iola's mouth as she chewed. She stared straight ahead of her at the queue of chattering fifth-formers snaking out of the chip shop's door and onto the pavement. 'She's pissed from dawn till dusk these days. She's always done it though – drank, I mean; even when the kids were really small.'

It seemed ironic to Flora that her friend didn't appear to class herself as one of the 'kids' – as though she and her mother were peers, rather than parent and child.

Iola's mother's drink problem dominated her family's existence. Too often, the girl was left trying to control her two wayward younger siblings and manage the running of their household. With everything she had going on at home, it was small wonder that she treated school so flippantly. It must have felt overwhelming for a twelve-year-old. Over the years, Doreen had had a series of male friends, none of whom had stuck around long enough for her to even remember their names. Iola herself had been conceived as a result of one drunken encounter when Doreen was only seventeen, and didn't know any more than her mother did who her real father was. Iola professed not to care, saying all men were a waste of space, anyway. But Flora suspected that she actually cared a great deal. And Flora knew that, even though Uncle Roger might have been worse than a waste of space, her own dad had been wonderful, and she missed him every single day.

Doreen swore that Iola's younger brother, Stevie, and the baby, Warren, had shared the same father, a devastatingly handsome man with thick, dark hair and numerous colourful tattoos, passing through with the annual visiting fair. It appeared, however, that he'd only stuck around long enough to impregnate her on both occasions before disappearing into the ether. Young Carly, on the other hand, looked like a miniature version of one of the local refuse collectors, with his equally bright auburn hair and freckled face. She would hover on the pavement and follow the bin lorry like a lost puppy whenever he came to empty their dustbin, although Doreen denied ever having any connection with the man. Either way, he would sometimes hand Carly a chocolate bar with a wink and a smile if he thought no one was looking. Whether he just felt sorry for the child or it was a sign of a guilty conscience, no one knew. Iola was convinced it was the latter.

'I mean, what's that all about?' she had commented angrily once. 'If a kid's yours, you should be prepared to pay towards their upbringing. Tight bastard.'

'Do you get on with your mum?' Flora ventured, helping herself to another chip. Iola considered for a moment.

'Most of the time. She drives me nuts, but her heart's in the right place. Oh, she's bloody useless as a parent, but she loves us all to bits really. Soft as shite, she is. That's part of her trouble, I reckon. Things get to her, you know?'

Iola shook her head, her mouth setting into an angry line. 'My nan always reckoned she was just a good-time girl. Not cut out to be a parent. But after our Warren . . .' She tailed off, idly tossing a squashed chip to a pigeon that had been pottering hopefully nearby. 'Things went completely tits up. He was such a good baby; proper little sweetheart. Happy as Larry just staring up at the sky from his pram for hours.' Her face clouded. 'She's never got over it. Don't suppose she ever will.'

She slid from the wall, licking her fingers then wiping her hands on her blazer pockets.

'It'll finish her off one day. I'm expecting to find her drowned in a puddle of her own puke every time I go home.' She frowned, chewing her lip. 'I'm never having kids, me. All they give you is grief. Break your arms, then they break your heart; that's what my nan used to say. Never really understood what she meant at the time, but now I reckon she had a point.'

Iola drew in a deep breath. Flora studied her friend and was alarmed to see her eyes brimming with tears. She thought of Doreen Chappell; of the brash, hard-faced woman who had put the fear of God into her; the woman she'd crossed roads to avoid. She remembered watching her from afar, with a mixture of fascination and disgust, weaving drunkenly down the road one afternoon a few weeks after the baby had been snatched, rambling incoherently, hair dishevelled, cheeks tear-streaked with mascara. She remembered her own mother's comments: that the poor mite was probably better off, whoever had taken him. Suddenly Flora felt desperately sorry for Doreen and slightly ashamed.

It had been almost three years now since tiny Warren Chappell had been taken from his pram outside the corner shop. There had been so much activity on the estate in the aftermath: police combing the whole area, knocking on doors, searching houses; pulling in likely suspects for questioning. But not a trace of poor baby Warren. A single blue bootee dropped at the kerb was the only clue to the direction in which he'd travelled, so it seemed increasingly likely he had been bundled into a car and driven to God knows where. He might even have been taken out of the country. Whatever had happened to him, the trail had gone cold and the Chappell family, and moreover Iola, had been left to pick up the pieces.

Some weeks after Warren had been kidnapped, Flora remembered watching Iola in the primary school playground from a safe distance, her brittle exterior spikier than ever. She seemed to be getting into scraps with other children, boys and girls alike, at the drop of a hat.

Now Flora understood why, and it made her feel worse than she could ever have imagined.

CHAPTER 15

Little Hambley, November 2001

Once they were outside, Flora was better able to inspect her new surroundings. She guided the wheelchair carefully across the slippery footbridge and looked back at the main house. It stood, wide and proud against the azure backdrop of the sky, the honey-coloured, weathered frontage in shadow. Water bubbled from a weir at its back, deepening as it collected and forming a sort of moat around the property. The morning air was cold and crisp, a light frost glittering on the neat lawn which was laid out to three sides of the building. A dense border of tall trees loomed to the right. Peering down straight ahead of them, she could see the steps she had climbed the previous evening plunging towards the road below, before disappearing from view.

Hector's annexe, set back from Mill House high on a slope and to its left, had once been the housing for the millstone, used for centuries to grind the wheat which supplied the local community with flour. Although smaller and less grand, the building was still a sizeable, tall structure, rendered in the same mellow stone and rising from the watercourse which tumbled to one side. The huge vertical wheel, partially submerged in the stream, was wedged between the side of the annexe and a steep, grassy embankment bordered by a sturdy wall.

The sound of water rushing was somehow invigorating. Flora wanted to get a better look, but Mrs Homity was intent on pressing on towards the trees in the opposite direction. She sat forward eagerly and Flora had to pause to tuck the blanket round her legs more tightly and swaddle her in the fleecy shawl so that all extremities were completely covered. The poor woman looked like a mummy.

Flora glanced back anxiously at the annexe, but it remained silent, the curtains closed, and there was no sign of Hector. It was half past nine now; she prayed that he wouldn't surface until after they were safely back indoors.

The grass crunched slightly beneath Flora's feet and the weight of the unwieldy wheelchair, which was wayward as a shopping trolley. Flora found it an effort to steer in a straight line.

'This way.' Mrs Homity pulled a hand from beneath the blanket as they reached the perimeter of the lawn and pointed. She was taking her through a gap in the trees, a well-worn dirt path. Flora felt a shiver of apprehension as the canopy above enclosed them, all but obliterating the daylight. The occasional twitter from a bird aside, it was unnervingly quiet. Something scurried across the path ahead, making her catch her breath. As they continued for a couple of hundred yards, she looked continually from left to right, gripping the handles of the wheelchair tightly. Her hands were frozen, already chapped and sore after the previous day's journey, and she wished she'd worn gloves.

Eventually, they reached a clearing. Flora felt a sense of relief as they passed from the corridor of trees and back into cold sunlight. She could see a diminutive grey-stone building ahead, enclosed by a low wall, with a wrought-iron gate at the centre of the side facing them. As they drew nearer, Flora realised that the building was a chapel. They had come to a small graveyard.

'As you will see, this is where the Homitys are laid to rest,' explained the old woman.

Flora manoeuvred the wheelchair through the gate and stopped abruptly, letting out an involuntary gasp. There must have been around thirty headstones, many mottled with age, the limestone covered in moss; others with clearer inscriptions etched into the surface. Parents, grandparents. People who had enjoyed long and full lives. But it was the poignant sight of the gravestone with white-winged marble cherubs looking down from their plinth that brought her to a halt.

'And here lies my darling Xanthe,' murmured Mrs Homity, her eyes glistening. 'My beautiful little girl.'

CHAPTER 16

Stretmore, October 1978

It was first thing on Thursday morning and the daunting prospect of double Maths loomed large. Flora was leaning against the wall of the Humanities building, trying to look casual and inconspicuous as she waited for Iola. Although she'd arrived ten minutes early, Iola was running late, true to form, and therefore she would be now, too. But it was a small price to pay for having a friend who stuck up for her and had actually given her some sort of credibility in the eyes of the other kids. Someone who seemed to truly like her for who she was.

Seeing Flora, Iola waved frantically from across the quad and began to run. Flora knew immediately that something had happened. Iola would never break a sweat unless there was a very good reason. She was like a cat on hot bricks, breathless; her eyes wide with excitement.

'You been waiting long? Just had to walk the kids up to school.'

Flora shook her head, forcing a smile. She glanced anxiously at her watch. They were already fifteen minutes late for the lesson. One more late mark and she knew a detention was on the cards. She was more worried about Mum's reaction than anything else.

Grabbing Flora's hand suddenly, Iola dragged her round the back of the English block where the smokers all gathered at break time. Judging by the carpet of scattered dog ends, the caretaker either wasn't aware of this habit or not prepared to add to his workload.

Iola reached into her blazer pocket and pulled out an envelope, waving it at Flora as though it were one of Willy Wonka's Golden Tickets.

'What's that?'

'Ah, *this* arrived this morning. Addressed to Mum, but I opened it – half her mail finishes up binned anyway – she ignores the bills. But this looked, like, *important*.'

Flora's gaze shifted from the envelope back to her friend.

'O-*kay*. And . . .?' she asked slowly.

'It's one of them anonymous things – y'know, when someone's cut out letters from a newspaper and stuck them on a piece of paper? Like you see on telly sometimes.'

Flora felt a flutter of anticipation. 'Well, what does it say, then?'

'It's about our Warren. Someone's tipping her off about a blue car. And a number plate.'

'What about the blue car?'

Iola blew out her cheeks, rolling her eyes.

'It was the car that some bloke put the baby in, you

divvy. I'm taking it to the cop shop – right now. Wanna come?'

Flora was torn. She didn't want to get into trouble again. Her recent association with Iola had brought negative attention from several of the teachers and a phone call home was the last thing she wanted. But she was desperate to find out what the police would say. And above all, hopeful that it might lead them to Warren.

'Go on, then.'

The bus into town was late and heaving with people on their way to work. Flora and Iola had to stand all the way, jostled between a sea of bodies, clinging to the metal poles near the front and teetering every time the bus turned a corner. It seemed to take an eternity to wade through the heavy morning traffic. It was a ten-minute walk from the terminus. Flora was struggling to keep up with Iola, who was walking at full pelt and talking non-stop, fuelled with adrenaline, her battered hessian rucksack swinging from her arm.

Finally arriving at the station, Flora's heart began pounding, both with nerves and excitement as to what the police might say. She had never been to a police station before. She followed her friend through the double doors into the building and looked around anxiously. The floor lino was still wet from a recent swab of disinfectant and a scruffy-looking middle-aged man sat slumped in a plastic chair against the wall, looking decidedly peaky. The world-weary cleaner passed by with her mop and bucket, casting him a withering look. She pointed to the door marked *Toilets*.

'Try to make it into the loo next time, if you think you're going to throw up again,' she warned him. The man mumbled something and closed his eyes. The cleaner tutted and disappeared through a door to the right of the reception desk.

Iola sauntered up to the counter, as though she'd done it a thousand times before. Flora wondered how often she had been there in the past, and whether it was because she or her mother had been in some kind of trouble.

'Is DS Baines here?'

The bored-looking man seated behind the desk looked up at her, a slight smirk on his lips. 'And what might you want with Detective Sergeant Baines, young lady?'

'He's been our main contact. Since my baby brother went missing.'

The man looked at her for a moment. Recognition appeared to have dawned. Flora thought his eyes flickered with something like irritation. 'Oh yes. I know. Miss Chappell, isn't it? I'm afraid DS Baines is on annual leave at the moment, in Majorca for a fortnight. Is there anything I can help with?' He tapped his pen against the counter, glancing at his wristwatch.

'*This*. My mum got this today. In the post.' From her pocket Iola produced the envelope, now slightly crumpled, and with it a shower of ragged fragments of a used tissue. She prised out the letter and thrust it towards the officer. 'It's like – a clue. Someone saw the car that took our Warren. You need to investigate it right away.'

The man scowled at her. He held out his hand and took the letter, then began to read, his lips mumbling silently as he did so.

'This looks like someone having a little joke to me,' he said, stifling a yawn. 'I wouldn't get your hopes up. But I'll pass it on. You'd better get yourselves back to school, the pair of you, or you'll have the wag man on your case.'

Iola stepped back, incredulous. 'But aren't you going to look into it *now*? It's been nearly three years since my brother went missing. This is the first proper, like, *evidence*. Someone *saw* something.'

The man gave an impatient sigh. 'They may or may not have. We will look into it – but all in good time. Now off you go – unless you want to arrive at school in the back of a panda car.'

'Twat.' Iola said it loudly enough over her shoulder for the desk sergeant to hear as they went back out of the main doors. 'What a total *twat*.'

Flora trotted anxiously after Iola, who had begun marching back down the road, her expression murderous.

'I can't go back to school now. I'm wired.' She aimed a furious kick from one of her scuffed monkey boots at the tyre of a parked car. 'I mean – why would anyone send something like that for a laugh? They'd fucking well *better* look into it.' She shook her head, stopping for a moment to face Flora, who was watching her with trepidation, wondering what her friend might be capable of in this irate state. But rather than angry, Iola looked almost desperate suddenly, her eyes swimming with tears of frustration.

'You think I'm right, don't you, Flo? This might be an actual, *real* chance of leading us to Warren but most of those bastards in there never take us seriously. They probably think the bab's better off with someone else.'

Flora's eyes dropped. She felt her cheeks burn and tried to focus her attention on the cracks in the pavement. She wondered if Iola realised that virtually everyone who knew Doreen was of the opinion that, for baby Warren, it was probably the best thing that could have happened.

Iola appeared not to have noticed. 'See what happens when your mum's a single pisshead parent with a hotch-potch of kids?' she ranted on, rubbing her sleeve across her nose. 'They don't give a shit. Nobody does.'

Flora gently placed a hand on her arm. 'I do,' she said in a small voice. 'And I don't think it's a joke. I don't think it's funny at all.'

Iola dropped her rucksack suddenly and wrapped her arms around Flora, burying her face in her shoulder. Flora could smell fried food and stale cigarette smoke coming from her friend's hair and clothes. Iola seemed suddenly so small and vulnerable that it made Flora want to cry. She returned the embrace, patting Iola on the back as though comforting a baby.

'You're the best mate I've ever had, do you know that, Flo? The *only* one, really. Thanks.'

They stood like that for a moment and then Iola stepped back abruptly, looking as though she had dropped her guard. She straightened, ran a hand through her fringe and picked up her bag.

'Fancy coming back to mine? I haven't had any breakfast. We can get tea and toast if you like.'

Flora felt a warm glow, like an invisible hug. Despite being friends now for over a year, this was the first time Iola had actually invited her back to her home. It seemed they had turned a corner.

'Thanks. If you're sure it's okay?'

''Course. C'mon then.'

But when they arrived, the Chappells' house stank. There was no polite way of putting it. A thick waft of tobacco fug and sour milk was the first assault on Flora's senses as they entered through the back door and into the kitchen. The work surface was littered with crumbs and piled high with dirty crockery and saucepans; the plastic swing bin was overflowing, its lid encrusted with a dollop of something mustard-coloured and unidentifiable. Iola casually stepped over the mound of dirty washing dumped in front of the washing machine, evidence of an unemptied load within.

Flora could see now why Iola had always made excuses in the past not to take anyone home. Hovering awkwardly in the doorway, she picked at the dry skin on her lips as she watched Iola filling the old electric kettle and plugging it in.

'Takes a while,' Iola grimaced, as the thing began to grumble into life. Her eyes flicked over the detritus covering every inch of the room. Hastily, she swept a hand across the work surface, gathering a pile of crumbs which she brushed off into the open bin, nudging aside the mountain of washing with her foot as she did so.

'Erm – tea or coffee?'

Flora wasn't sure she wanted either, but, not wishing to seem rude, chose tea. Iola lifted the lid of a rusting rectangular metal box marked 'Bread' and replaced it, shaking her head. She opened the fridge, releasing yet another pungent odour, and wrinkled her nose.

'Eugh. These beans have got fur growing on them.' Removing a half-empty can, she stuffed it into the bin.

Its corners curling, a large piece of card bearing the faded charcoal sketch of an elephant was taped to the fridge door with grubby strips of masking tape. Flora stared. It was actually really good.

'Whose is the picture?' she asked.

'Hmm? Oh, that was one I did in Art in the first year.' Iola rolled her eyes. 'Mum wanted to keep it. Dunno why.'

'Wow. I wish I could draw like that,' Flora said, thinking of her own sorry attempts that she would never have even bothered taking home. She was surprised, too, that Doreen seemed to have shown such pride in something her daughter had produced. It suddenly dawned on her that there was so much about Iola and her mother that she didn't know.

The tea was as unappealing as Flora had anticipated. Curdled white bits danced across the surface. She sipped tentatively, almost retching at the thought of what she was consuming. Iola spluttered, spitting a mouthful back into her own mug.

'Eugh, this is rank,' she declared, relieving Flora of hers. She tipped the contents of both into the washing-up bowl, which was full of dirty water, globules of fat floating on its surface. 'Come on, I'll get some money from Mum and we can go to the café up the road instead. I'll clean this lot up later.'

'Should I – shall I wait here?' Flora was fearful of the kind of reception she might get.

Iola shrugged. ''S up to you.' She studied Flora's worried expression and laughed. 'She doesn't bite, you know.'

Flora followed Iola out of the kitchen, then skulked behind the living room door as her friend went through the dingy hallway to speak to Doreen. A pair of scuffed red platform slingbacks had been discarded, skewwhiff, behind the front door, next to a filthy-white, belted plastic mac. The worn carpet felt tacky beneath her feet and the paper was peeling from the nicotine-yellow walls. She could hear Doreen mumbling. Iola's tone grew louder and more impatient.

'I'm taking two quid out of your purse. I'll go to the shop after and pick up a loaf, and some milk and stuff.'

More mumbling.

'*Okay*? Try to get yourself dressed for when I get back.'

As Iola came back out into the hall, through the doorway, Flora could see a puffy-eyed Doreen sprawled across the sofa, hair like a bird's nest, the filthy pink dressing gown she wore falling open to reveal a torn red petticoat which had ridden up above lacy black knickers. The floor around her was populated with crushed beer cans, a half-empty bottle of whisky and an ashtray piled high with cigarette butts. The smell of alcohol emanating from the room was overpowering.

The woman lifted her head blearily and offered Flora a watery smile.

'Zis your li'l mate y'always on 'bout, Yol?' she slurred.

Doreen raised a hand but instantly let it drop like a stone and flopped back, closing her eyes as if the effort had completely exhausted her. Flora didn't know where to look but Iola simply rolled her eyes.

'So now you've met my mum,' she told Flora, as they made their way out of the front door. 'See what I mean? She's more of a danger to herself than anyone else. She always gets really bad around Halloween. You know, when Warren . . .' A flicker of despair crossed her face briefly, but she shook it off quickly with a grin.

'Come on, they do great Chelsea buns in the café

round the corner. Dunno about you, but I'm bloody starving.'

Flora glanced back at the house. She felt slightly queasy. Suddenly, more than anything, she wanted to go home; to have a hug from her own mum, to forget about Doreen and the squalor Iola and the other children were living in.

But then she thought of baby Warren and how everything that had happened three years earlier had helped to bring them to this.

And suddenly their problems became hers.

CHAPTER 17

Little Hambley, November 2001

Mrs Homity seemed distressed by the state of little Xanthe's grave.

'Abey hasn't brought her any fresh flowers! I should have got something for her. Roses. She always loved to smell the roses.'

Flora wheeled the chair as close to the plot as possible so that Mrs Homity could lay her hands on the stone. The old woman stroked the sparkling white granite, gazing wistfully at the frozen ground which held her daughter's bones. Flora's throat contracted as she read the inscription.

In loving memory of Xanthe Kezia Homity
17th February 1959 – 29th November 1964
Our cherished daughter
Loved with a love beyond telling,
Missed with a grief beyond all tears.

Flora had no wish, no *need* for any reminder of death or loss. It was still so raw, so painful. She thought of Mum lying there, eyes closed, cheeks waxy and sunken. An incongruous slick of pink lipstick applied by the well-meaning mortician. The single yellow gerbera between the motionless fingers interlaced across her chest. They had always been her favourites. '*Like little rays of sunshine.*' That was how she'd described them. Flora had begged for a few more precious minutes at Mum's side before they'd finally screwed down the lid. She remembered the feeling of rising panic, the loss of her only real purpose in life. Of the only other human being who cared if she lived or died. She felt totally, utterly alone.

Lost in her memories and oblivious to Flora's own grief, Mrs Homity continued to speak to her dead child, in a voice so soft Flora couldn't make out the words. She scanned around desperately for a distraction. The graveyard was well tended; the turf, still spangled with frost, low, with not a weed in sight. The pristine gravel path from the gate led between the plots and directly to the door of the chapel. This would have been a lovely place to lay Mum to rest, surrounded by trees and gentle birdsong. Rabbits roaming freely. Bluebells in spring, snowdrops in winter. No traffic, no unsightly gasworks looming over the horizon; no rowdy drunks weaving their way through the cemetery after hours, seeking a tree to piss against with neither an iota of respect for the sleeping dead or compassion for their grieving families.

Mum had always loved nature. Flora's chest ached as she thought of the green plastic container handed over by the kindly funeral director at the crematorium, the pity in his eyes as he watched her vacantly scatter the last grainy remnants in the Garden of Remembrance to be carried away forever by the harsh east wind. She had been beyond tears at the time, just hollowed out and desolate. How she'd hated the impersonal service, the handful of mourners who barely knew Mum but had dutifully turned out to pay their last respects. She had stood alone in the front row in the cold chapel, wanting to scream as she watched the curtains finally close around the coffin, signalling the imminent committal. The body soon reduced to a pile of meaningless dust, to be swept up and disposed of as though its occupant had never existed at all. She'd wanted a proper burial for Mum, a place where her bones could gradually return to the soil; a neat, lovingly tended plot with a marker to show that she had lived – that she had *mattered*. But cremation, the cheaper option, was the only choice available to her, and she had reluctantly agreed to scattering instead of interring the ashes to avoid incurring further cost. The local council were picking up the tab and Flora had little say in the matter. After a miserable final few years, her mother's departure from the world had been equally wretched. It was not what she deserved.

'Shall we go inside?'

Flora turned to the old lady, startled from her reverie. She pulled a scrunched-up tissue from her pocket and dabbed at her cheeks.

'Sorry?'

'Into the chapel. It's very pretty – and so peaceful. I haven't been here in a long time. Abey thought it too unsettling for me and stopped bringing me a couple of years ago. He means well I'm sure, but I find it a comfort now, knowing I'll be joining my little angel soon.'

It occurred to Flora that perhaps this was anything *but* a comfort to Mr Homity. He had already lost his beloved daughter, and Hector's welfare must be a source of real concern to him. She could see why he wouldn't want to dwell on the thought of losing his wife. He'd seemed so devoted.

Flora twisted the weighty iron ring hanging from the oak door and heaved it open. She wheeled the old woman into the chapel. The building was tiny, with only three rows of pews in blackened wood, pitted with age, either side of the narrow aisle. Flora noticed deep grooves in the back of one bench, where several sets of initials had been carved. Flanked by two votive candles, a polished gold cross stood on the simple white cloth covering the altar, bathed in a prism of colours cast by the stained-glass window at its back. The dank, frigid air was suffused with incense.

Mrs Homity gazed around in wonder as if seeing it all for the first time. 'Our children were baptised in here, you know.' Her cheeks lifted. 'Xanthe screamed the place down when the vicar anointed her. I remember him saying what a fine pair of lungs she had. Oh, it seems a lifetime ago now.' She gazed up at the vaulted ceiling, her face clouding suddenly, then swivelled round to face Flora. 'Please, take me nearer the window, will you.'

Flora obliged, then perched awkwardly on the front bench beside the wheelchair, as Mrs Homity lowered her head to pray. They sat in quiet contemplation for a few minutes until Flora felt compelled to break the silence.

'Mrs Homity . . .'

'*Agnes*, please.'

'Agnes, I don't want to upset you, but d'you mind me asking what happened – to Xanthe?'

A shadow fell across the old woman's face. It took her a few moments before she finally spoke.

'It was an accident. A horrible, needless accident. I should never have left her . . .' Her voice trailed off as she stared straight ahead. She lifted a frail hand to her throat. 'The memory's still so clear in my mind. I – I went shopping. For a new dress.'

She dropped her head to her chest at the shame of the thought. 'Can you imagine? A bloody dress! Not that I even needed one, but Abey said I had to look my best, for the dinner dance we were due to attend with some acquaintance or other of his. He's always been *most* insistent that I'm well presented. His trophy bride. Ha!' She gave a hollow laugh.

'I would normally have taken Xanthe along to the shops, but she'd had an awful cold and I thought it best she stayed in the house.' Her knuckles blanched as she gripped the arms of the wheelchair. 'I knew – as soon as I got out of the taxi, that something was wrong. The house was in total darkness. It was only five o'clock, but it was dusk. At the very least, the porch light should have been on.'

She turned her attention back to the altar, a distant look on her face. 'I can't blame anyone else. I was her mother. I shouldn't have left her.'

This sounded quite alarming. Flora sat up sharply. 'But what actually – I mean, you didn't leave her on her own, did you?'

'No! No, of course not. I would never have done

that – *never*. She was with Abey. But he was busy; easily distracted, as usual. It's as though his mind is always elsewhere.' A muscle in the old woman's jaw twitched. 'Xanthe could be a little minx. Abey said she must have slipped out of the house when he wasn't looking.' She paused. 'Little children and water are not a good combination, Flora. It holds a fascination for them. I'm sure you can guess what happened.'

The sudden image of a small child, face down, golden hair spread out on the water, filled Flora's mind. An unpleasant chill crept upwards from her feet. There was something deeply unsettling about the thought of a tiny, helpless girl being robbed of life by the cold, dark waters that worked the mill; that had provided her family with a generous living. The place she had known as home. Flora remembered the sweet photos in the library and Mrs Homity's room; she had never known Xanthe, but the cruel twist of it all made her stomach lurch.

'I'm so sorry,' she said quietly, reaching out to take Mrs Homity's hand in her own.

The old woman squeezed feebly in response. 'It was Abey that found her. He was completely broken. She was the apple of his eye.' Her face contorted, the pain tangible. 'We just drifted through life for months afterwards. We – I – couldn't function. It was several years until I felt ready to try for another baby. And then it took me three years more to actually fall pregnant.' She sighed. 'I love Hector dearly. But he could never replace the child we'd lost. Xanthe was a very special little girl, bright as a button. And so loving; so thoughtful. Maybe that's why our son . . .' She stopped, biting down on her lip. 'Well, I'm sure you understand me. Every child is different. But God forgive me, sometimes even as a parent, it's hard not to draw comparisons. To judge. However wrong that may be.'

Flora felt a sudden twinge of sympathy for Hector. It couldn't have been easy, trying to live up to the memory of a perfect dead sibling. Constantly seeking approval. He may have been a little strange anyway, but his upbringing probably hadn't helped. Nobody wanted to feel like a consolation prize.

Oh God. Hector.

She glanced at her watch and grimaced. Almost half past ten. *Shit.* Flora's pulse quickened. She prayed she hadn't blown it – despite Mrs Homity's assurances, she felt sure Hector would take great pleasure in reporting her to his father if he spotted them. She couldn't risk losing this job – not when she had a mission to fulfil first. And for the time being at least, she had nowhere else to go.

'Mrs . . . erm . . . Agnes, I think maybe we should get you back home. Before anyone notices you're not there.'

'I suppose we should.' Mrs Homity smiled resignedly. 'Come on. Wheel me back to my cell, then.' She leaned forwards, lowering her voice. 'But can this be our little secret?'

Flora nodded. Maybe this was a good opportunity to share a secret of her own. She took a deep breath.

'Agnes – can I just ask you – apart from your last carer, has another girl – well, a woman – about my age, ever called to the house? In the past year or so?'

'A girl?' Mrs Homity's brow knitted. She pushed out her lower lip, looking up at Flora questioningly. 'Can you be a bit more specific?'

'I'm sorry, I'm not being very clear. It's just – I've been trying to find my friend. She's quite small, spiky black hair. At least, it was when I last saw her. But she stands out – dresses like a punk, lots of piercings and tattoos . . .'

Mrs Homity shook her head vehemently. 'I've never seen anyone like that round here. Not that I recall, anyway.' She scratched her head, her eyes absently exploring the walls for a moment. 'At least . . . But no. No, I'm pretty sure I'd have remembered someone so distinctive.'

'Oh.' Flora's heart sank. 'Never mind. I just wondered, that's all.'

Even if Iola *had* been to Mill House, with the way Mrs Homity's cognition fluctuated, she would probably never remember anyway. And Flora definitely wasn't going to ask Mr Homity or Hector.

'Is she a close friend?' Mrs Homity placed a hand on Flora's arm.

Flora thought about Iola; about their last meeting. Her stomach turned over.

'She was once; yes. We . . . we sort of lost touch.'

'A shame when that happens. I hope you manage to find her. Life's too short.'

Flora felt tears threaten once more. She gave a brief nod of her head. This was no good: she needed to remain positive. It was the one thing that was keeping her going. She had only just arrived in Little Hambley: someone here *must* be able to point her in the right direction. She couldn't give up hope – not yet.

Flora drew herself up and without another word, grappled the wheelchair out of the chapel and across the graveyard, back towards the trees, moving with as much urgency as the uncooperative wheels would allow. Her gut churned now at the thought of what Mr Homity would say if he knew she'd disregarded his instructions. But surely there was no harm in it? She thought of Mum, confined to the house; day in, day out. She should have made more of an effort, taken her out while she was still able. Before things got as bad as they did. Before she had begun to beg Flora constantly to release her from her misery.

Before . . .

'My cell.' That's what Mrs Homity had called her room.

Was that how it must have felt for Mum, too? And Flora, however unintentionally, had been her jailer.

CHAPTER 18

Stretmore, November 1978

Three weeks had passed. Desperate for news of any light the anonymous letter might have shed, Iola had called the police station daily from the phone box on the corner of her street. DS Baines was now back from his holiday and more amenable than the majority of the officers she spoke to, but the search for the car registration number quoted in the letter had amounted to nothing. He had told her gently but firmly that it may have been a prank, as his colleague had first suggested. Iola was convinced that the police hadn't actually bothered following it up, but had no proof.

Iola was waiting for Flora outside the school gates at the end of the afternoon. She looked tired and pale, her hair unwashed and tousled. She stood with her back to the wall, bouncing her heel against it angrily as if it was the cause of all her troubles. It was Friday: she had been absent all week and Flora was worried in case something had happened to Doreen. She pictured the woman lying in that living room, had considered going round to the house to check on Iola, but felt too scared after her previous visit.

'Our Stevie's had chickenpox,' Iola told her. 'And Mum's been in such a bad way since that bloody letter turned up, she's in no fit state to look after him. Even more than usual.'

Flora thought of the stupor in which they'd found Doreen that first time she had set foot in Iola's home, and the indescribable mess surrounding her. She thought of her own house; shabby maybe, but always clean and tidy. A hot meal on the table every evening, even when Mum wasn't really up to it. Her clothes always freshly washed and ironed. Routines and clear ground rules set out; even though Flora might grumble, she understood, albeit begrudgingly, that they were imposed for a reason. There seemed to be no such thing in Iola's world. No set bedtimes, nor mealtimes. Cleaning teeth and bathing appeared to be optional. No wonder the Chappell children were bordering on feral.

'It's like I told you, Flo. We're not important. *My mum's* not important. Losing our Warren like that has ruined her life, even if it was already crap to begin with.'

Flora was at a loss. If the police had been unable to find the blue car, assuming they'd actually looked properly, maybe the car's owner had put on a false number plate. Or resprayed the car a different colour. Or both. She'd seen that on TV a few times, so it must happen. After three years of having almost resigned themselves to Warren's loss, it was as though the family's hopes had been cruelly raised only to drop them back into the depths of misery once more.

It would have been better – *kinder* – if the letter had never reached them.

CHAPTER 19

Little Hambley, November 2001

Exhausted by their outing, Mrs Homity asked to return to her room. Thankfully there had been no sign of Hector, although the curtains to the annexe had been opened. To Flora's relief, she had no trouble persuading the old woman to take her medication now. Hopefully the extra couple of hours' delay would have no detrimental effects. The awkwardness, mostly on Flora's part, of changing her incontinence pad over with, Mrs Homity, now tucked back into the bed, fell asleep quickly. Her expression was serene and contented, the only clue to her excursion a hint of colour painting her pale cheeks. Flora gazed at her for a moment before leaving the room, quietly closing the door behind her. She may have been going against Mr Homity's instructions, but the change of scenery appeared to have done the old woman a power of good. Flora felt her actions had been justified; once she was better established in her post, she might voice her thoughts to Mr Homity. But it was too soon: she was still in her probationary period and daren't do anything to jeopardise her position. She would have to bide her time.

Poking her head round her own bedroom door, she spotted Rufus curled up asleep atop the eiderdown. She smiled to herself. At least he seemed to have made himself at home. She had wondered if he might be nervous and try to hide, but he'd quickly settled beside her during the night. She would have to invest in a harness and lead at some point, so she could take him outside. It seemed unfair to keep him cooped up when he'd been used to roaming freely in Ostleton Road.

It was almost midday and the walk in the brisk air had given Flora an appetite. She decided to take her lunch break in the next hour, before waking Mrs Homity for hers. But the sudden thought of the freezer made her stomach roil as she headed downstairs and along the dingy passageway to the kitchen, averting her eyes from the sinister scrutiny of those in the family portraits.

As she approached, the tinny jangle of a radio and someone moving around on the other side of the door made her heart sink. She froze, fully expecting another confrontation with Hector, and was about to turn back when the sound of a female voice singing made her reconsider. She opened the door tentatively to see what Mum would have referred to as a 'matronly' woman of around fifty wiping down the work surfaces energetically. Turning to see Flora, she paused, dishcloth in mid-air, her ruddy face breaking into a smile which revealed a large gap between her front teeth.

'Ah, hello. You'll be the new carer, then?'

Flora nodded uncertainly.

'How's it going so far? I'm Rita, by the way. *Mrs Mop* – that's how they think of me.' Rita put down her cloth and came forward, extending a thick hand. Flora took it in her own, feeling the strength behind the gesture. It was somehow reassuring.

'I'm Flora. Nice to meet you.' She studied the woman with interest. Her hair was cropped short and dyed an unnaturally bright shade of red, her full cheeks flushed almost the same colour. She was wearing a kind of boiler suit in a camouflage print and tan fake Ugg-style boots.

'It's – erm – it's okay. Still finding my feet at the moment.'

Rita grinned. 'Met the menace yet, have you?'

'Sorry – which . . .?'

Rita roared with laughter. 'Ha – yes, I s'pose it could apply to the pair of 'em. But I meant the younger one. Him *up there*.' She tipped her head in the direction of the annexe.

Flora grimaced. 'We were introduced briefly last night. I don't think he was that pleased to see me.'

'Oh, he'll settle down soon enough. Don't let him scare you off. All bark and no bite. I take no bloody notice.'

'What, is he funny with you, too?'

'He's funny with every bugger. Well, he's just funny; full stop. Mrs H has had a string of people in to look after her these last few months, since things started to get too much for the old boy. None of 'em have stuck it out. I think the last girl would've had a breakdown if she'd stayed much longer, and she was barely here a fortnight. But she was far too young. A *sensitive soul.*' She rolled her eyes scathingly.

'Hector can make things . . . uncomfortable. But he's definitely a few sandwiches short of a picnic . . .' She spiralled a finger towards her head. 'So I make allowances. I've been cleaning here since just after we moved to Little Hambley. Nearly four years now. I wouldn't say he likes me, but I'm tolerated. About as much as anyone can expect, I reckon.'

Flora felt relieved that the animosity displayed by Hector wasn't reserved for her alone. She wondered, not for the first time, about her predecessor and exactly what had unsettled the girl so much.

'What about Mr Homity? How d'you find him?'

'He's all right. Bit anal, but he pays pretty well and just lets me get on with things. I don't see much of him really. It's not like I'm expected to go to the pub with him or anything. Thank God.' She laughed throatily.

Flora smiled but made no comment. The woman seemed nice enough, but it was perhaps a bit soon to confide her true opinion of her new employer. Especially after reading the contract properly. She needed to get to know Rita better first. But there was one subject she wasn't afraid of broaching.

'You don't happen to know if a young woman has called here at all in the last few months, do you? Small; tattooed, lots of piercings?' She watched Rita's face hopefully, but was disheartened immediately by the woman's blank expression.

'Not to my knowledge. Hardly anyone ever comes here, so I'd definitely remember if I'd seen someone like that. S'pose she could've shown up on one of my days off, though. Why d'you ask?'

'I'm trying to track down an old friend. Dunno why, I had a hunch she might have come here, to Little Hambley.' Flora pasted on a smile. 'I s'pose the Cotswolds covers quite a big area.'

Rita laughed. 'Yeah – and lots of the place names are very similar – all gets a bit confusing sometimes.'

Flora nodded. She had a point. 'Erm – I was just going to grab a bite to eat, but I don't want to get under your feet if you're trying to clean—'

Rita waved her hand casually. 'Carry on. Plenty of room in here.'

Flora glanced at the range warily. 'I wonder – d'you know how to work the cooker?'

'That thing?' Rita studied Flora's face and chuckled. 'Don't look so worried. It's not rocket science.'

She crossed the kitchen and lifted one of the huge polished chrome lids covering the hot plates. 'As long as the oven's on, these are permanently hot; ready to use. You'll find all the pans in that cupboard –' she indicated the one to the right of the stove. Opening the left-hand door of the double oven beneath the hob, she showed Flora a dial. 'This turns it on if it's been left off, which isn't often. Takes about twenty minutes to warm up, then you're away. See? No different from any other cooker, really. Easy-peasy.'

Flora nodded. 'Thanks. I've never used a range before. Looks much more straightforward than I'd thought.'

'Not that I ever need to use it, mind. But yes, nothing tricky about it at all.'

'I can't tell you what a relief that is. Threw me into a flat spin when I first saw it.'

Rita laughed. 'Like a lot of other things around here, I shouldn't wonder.'

Her jovial manner put Flora at ease and she managed a grin. It felt good to have someone a bit more normal to talk to. 'How often do you come – to clean?'

'Once a week for the main house; once a fortnight up at the annexe. Should probably be the other way round.' Rita pulled a face.

An image of wading knee-deep through Hector's dirty laundry flashed through Flora's mind. She grimaced. 'Is Hector . . . untidy, then?'

'That's one way of putting it. Bloody chaotic, I'd call it.' She puffed out her cheeks. 'And as for the stuffed menagerie . . . *well.*' She screwed up her nose. 'I think that's one reason his dad moved him into a separate building. He doesn't have to go in and see them, or the mess – unless the lad's had one of his hissy fits.'

'Oh dear.' Flora felt a shiver of disgust. Her thoughts turned once more to the freezer. 'Um – you don't know anything about some rats, do you?'

Rita raised an eyebrow. 'What, Hector's "babies"? That's what he calls them. Eugh – they make me feel all funny, the way they dart about. And those tails . . .' She shuddered. 'I draw the line at cleaning them out. That's one thing he can do himself.'

'It's just – well, I opened the freezer yesterday just after I got here and . . .'

'Christ, has he put stuff in there again?' Rita looked aghast. She strode across to the freezer and opened the door, her eyes scanning the various drawers.

'Top shelf.' Flora felt suddenly queasy as she watched the woman pull open the shelf containing the furry little corpses.

Rita groaned. 'Oh, good God. I'll have to have another word with Mr H. We've had all sorts in there – a dead jay he found in the woods, couple of starlings. A squirrel. He stuffs them, you see. Gives me the bloody heebie-jeebies.'

Bile rose in Flora's throat. She looked away squeamishly as Rita tentatively removed the offending creatures and, tearing a bin liner from a roll on the worktop, deposited them inside.

'I'll tell him, he has to get 'em done pronto or they're out with the rubbish tomorrow. Can't have that; it's just not hygienic, apart from anything else. Mind you, I blame his parents. All began when Hector was a lad and his pet dog died. Apparently, he was in such a state, they had the animal stuffed and mounted for him. And look what it's started.' She shook her head. 'Shouldn't pander to people when they've got unnatural tendencies, if you ask me. It just feeds it.'

Flora stood rigidly, glancing queasily from the dustbin bag suspended from Rita's sizeable hand back to the fridge.

'Anyway, don't mind me. You just carry on and get yourself a bite to eat.'

Flora's hunger was diminishing by the second. 'Erm – I think I'll just have a tin of soup from the pantry.'

Rita laughed. 'Don't worry, I'll check the other shelves in the freezer just in case, and give it all a thorough clean. Have your lunch, love. I'll just take Pinky and Perky here over to his lordship. Next time you see them, they'll probably be sitting in a glass case in his sitting room.'

'Will I actually need to go over there? To the annexe?' Flora felt a jolt of panic at the thought.

'Almost certainly, at some point. Mrs H asks for him sometimes. But don't go worrying about it – like I said, his bark's worse than his bite. I don't think there's any real harm in him, whatever the rumours are flying round the village.'

'Rumours?'

But Flora's anxious voice was drowned out by the haunting minor key hook from Blue Oyster Cult's 'Don't Fear the Reaper' pulsing from the radio. Humming tunelessly, Rita was already making her way out of the kitchen, holding the bag in front of her at arm's length.

Flora opened a tin of bland-looking vegetable soup and heated it on the hob. She sat down at the small table to eat, but the room was so cold that the soup cooled quickly and was even less appetising than she'd anticipated. Thankfully, she wasn't particularly hungry any more. She swilled the remainder down the sink, then washed the bowl and utensils. From the kitchen window, she had a clear view of Hector's annexe. Flora considered what Rita had told her about his penchant for dead animals and wondered what horrors lay beyond the entrance. It gave her an unpleasant feeling, like worms crawling in her gut, and she tried to shake off the thought. She turned and glanced up at the clock. Almost ten past one. Time for Mrs Homity's lunch. She placed a plate on top of the hotplate cover to warm, then took two eggs, along with a block of butter from the fridge, and diced a handful of mushrooms finely. Within minutes, she had whipped up an omelette. It looked golden and runny in the centre; just how Mum had liked them. She flipped it over and slid it onto the plate, covering it with a saucepan lid. Flora felt pleased that she'd got the hang of the range so quickly. One small success, at least. She poured a small beaker of apple juice, stirred in some thickener and popped on the spout, then found a pot of raspberry yogurt. Placing everything on a tray, she carried it carefully from the kitchen, down the passageway and up the stairs.

There was no sign of Rita, or of Hector. She wondered how he might have reacted when presented with his frozen pets. All the time Rita's words were turning over in her mind – *whatever the rumours are*. Exactly like that girl Yaz had told her. It made her feel peculiar. She thought again of Mrs Homity's last carer.

Maybe Hector had done something to scare her off. She didn't dare imagine what it might have been.

CHAPTER 20

Stretmore, April 1980

A visiting fair came to the local park every Easter. Flora would see the lorries arriving and the various rides being erected. She remembered wistfully the time Daddy had taken her when she was small. He had won her a funny-looking toy monkey with googly eyes and long arms, from the 'hook-a-duck' stall, and carried her round on his shoulders. She'd finished up with her hair in a sticky mess from the toffee apple he'd bought her and Mum had scolded him when they got back, but he'd just laughed and said it would wash out easily enough and where was her sense of fun? Mum had never been a fan of fairgrounds. She had told Flora since that the attractions always made her queasy and even the smell of the place was enough to set her off.

After Uncle Roger left, Flora had asked a few times if they could go to the fair, and the answer had always been no. But for the first time ever, this year Mum had given in, saying Flora was old enough and she supposed she could go along with some friends. It might have been a different story if Mum had known that the only friend she'd be going with was Iola, but Flora thought a white lie wouldn't hurt. Just to stop her worrying. Over the last two years, she and Iola had become virtually inseparable. She only wished Mum could get to know her as she did. But knowing Mum's opinion of the Chappells, that was never likely to happen.

So, as far as Mum was concerned, Flora was meeting up with a group of girls she'd got to know at the after-school club. After all, Flora reasoned, she rarely got out and the fair only came round once a year. The weather was warm for April and she felt a rush of excitement as she waited for Iola at the end of Ostleton Road. The park was a ten-minute walk away, and as they approached, they could hear the squeals of people on the rides and the thud of music.

The air was filled with the smell of diesel fumes and frying onions. They crossed the field, which teemed with people, some families with young children, but mainly teenagers. The noise was almost deafening. Flora felt suddenly like a fish out of water, apprehensive as she gazed up at the big wheel, her stomach roiling at the height of the car at the very top, which had paused in mid-air. The two girls inside swung their legs back and forth, leaning forwards and screaming in mock horror as the wheel was set in motion once more.

Iola rolled her eyes. 'Silly sods. Come on, Flo, let's go on that first. We'll be nearly touching the clouds!'

Iola dragged the reluctant Flora by the arm towards the

queue for the enormous Ferris wheel, where soon a car had stopped at the bottom and a girl and boy of about their age alighted and fell onto the grass, helpless with laughter.

Flora stood back, hesitant at first.

'Don't be such a wuss! You'll love it once we're up there, promise.' Iola was eagerly impatient.

Shakily, Flora climbed into the car next to Iola and shuffled back as far as she could into the seat, as the muscly lad taking the money roughly closed the bar in front of them with a clunk, setting the car in motion with one almighty heave.

'Hold tight, ladies,' he said with a grin.

Flora gripped the safety bar for all she was worth, with no intention of letting go. She closed her eyes for a moment, her heart pounding. Soon they were rising. She felt a light breeze on her face and opened one eye. The fairground below was beginning to look small and distant, the noise abating. She shut both eyes again, telling herself they would soon be safely back on the ground. Suddenly, the car swung slightly and then all movement ceased. They must have reached the top.

Iola sounded elated. 'Woo-hoo! Look, Flo. I told you we'd be in the clouds.'

Flora opened her eyes and looked down. It was a big mistake. She felt suddenly terror-stricken. All she could think was, what would happen if the wires holding the car snapped? What if the mechanism failed and they were stuck up there for hours? Or worst of all, what if the bar failed and they were hurled into mid-air when the car began to move again?

She had begun to hyperventilate, her head swimming now. She felt faint.

'I want to get down.'

'What? What are you on about – this is brill!'

'Iola, I've got to get down. *Now.*'

Flora had begun to shake uncontrollably. She closed her eyes once more, trying to focus on her breathing, but it was no good. She was having a full-blown panic attack.

Realising something was very wrong, Iola shouted down to the lad below.

'Oi Mister? Can you get us down? My mate's not feeling too good.'

The lad looked up, raising both palms into the air. 'You'll be down soon enough. 'Fraid she'll have to wait.'

By the time they had reached the bottom, Flora was distraught. Iola helped her off, as the people in the queue stared. Some sniggered, and two girls Flora recognised from their year nudged each another, the one whispering something to her friend.

'Yeah? Got a problem?' Iola glared at them, slipping an arm around Flora's shoulders, which rose and fell with each hiccupping sob. The girls fell silent, dropping their eyes. Iola helped Flora over to the edge of the field where they sat down on the grass, while Flora gradually began to calm down.

'I'm sorry,' she said quietly, staring straight ahead. 'You must think me a right wimp. It's just . . . I can't . . .'

'You don't have to explain yourself, Flo. Lots of people are scared of heights. It's no biggie. Don't sweat it.'

'But I've ruined the afternoon. I was really looking forward to it, too.'

Iola was sitting beside her, hugging her knees. She

jumped to her feet suddenly, brushing the grass from her backside.

'You've ruined nothing. Look, tell you what: we'll just go on the slow rides. Or we can go somewhere else altogether, if you want. I'm sorry. I didn't realise you were kind of phobic about it. You should've said.' She lowered her voice. 'Me – I don't like the dark much. Always have to keep a light on, all night.'

'Really?' Flora widened her eyes. She couldn't imagine Iola being afraid of anything.

'See? – everyone's scared of something. Nothing to be embarrassed about.' Leaning forward, she extended a hand and hauled Flora to her feet. 'Come on. I'll buy you some of that disgusting candy floss. Tastes great but it's probably full of plastic.'

Flora grinned. She felt better instantly. Linking arms with Iola, she allowed her to lead the way to the candy floss stall. Iola chattered incessantly, but Flora barely heard a word. Just the comforting tone of her voice was enough to erase the harrowing memory of the Ferris wheel incident.

She knew she couldn't tell Mum she'd been to the fair with Iola. But how she wished she could make her understand what a wonderful friend she had found. The kind of friend that only comes around once in a lifetime.

Stretmore, May 1980

Iola had long seen it coming, of course, but when Doreen finally succumbed to her alcoholism it didn't make it any easier to bear. Arriving home having just broken up for the Whitsun week to find Doreen's lifeless body in the bathtub had been only the start of the trauma. To lose your mother and the lynchpin, albeit a wobbly one, of your whole family at the age of fifteen was a cruel blow. For the two younger children, it was even more devastating. If Iola had only been a couple of years older, she might have been deemed mature enough to care for her siblings. As it was, Social Services swooped and rounded them all up immediately. Stevie and Carly were found placements with different foster families, and Iola was dispatched to a local care home with a reputation for turning out hard nuts and those who fell on the wrong side of the law. It was tragic.

Flora was heartbroken for her friend. Iola was skilled at putting up a brave front, but Flora knew what it must have done to her, finding her mum like that. It was worse, somehow, that she couldn't let her feelings show; let it all out. She also knew how protective Iola was of her brother and sister, and how it would be tearing her apart to be separated from them. Flora wished there was something she could do, some way she might help. With Iola's lack of regard for rules and regulations, she worried too that her friend might go off the rails completely if she was surrounded by like-minded individuals.

Almost three weeks had passed since Iola had been moved into the children's home. Flora had been biding her time, waiting for a good day; one when Mum was in a brighter mood and less tired. Often, a half-decent day would be followed by a particularly bad one, but Mum had been doing well all week. She'd managed the housework and even to cook dinner every night so far without feeling completely drained. Maybe it was the warmer weather that was helping her symptoms. It was these small victories that gave both of them a boost; gave them hope that there was a chance of recovery.

Flora had cooked their evening meal in her Home Economics lesson, carried home from school in a wicker basket with a plastic cover over the top. She had chosen to make toad-in-the-hole, knowing it was one of Mum's favourites.

Mum cleared her plate appreciatively as Flora watched hopefully across the kitchen table.

'Well, that was lovely, Flo. Well done. You're becoming a dab hand with these recipes.'

Mum rose to fill the washing-up bowl and rolled up her sleeves as Flora cleared the table. 'Right, pop the kettle on, will you, love. I'll just do this lot and then we'll have a nice cuppa.'

Flora steered her gently away from the sink. 'You go and watch telly – I'll finish up in here and bring the tea through when it's ready.'

'Well, I'm being properly spoiled this evening.' Mum glanced at the crockery piled next to the draining board. 'Do be careful though, won't you?' Pausing at the door, she cocked her head, turning to give Flora a wry smile. 'You're not trying to butter me up for some reason, are you?'

Flora's cheeks flushed. She chewed her lip.

'The thing is, Mum, it's just that . . . d'you think . . . I mean, would Iola be able to come and stay with us at all?' she blurted out.

Mum's face fell. 'Iola? Chappell?'

'Yes.' Flora twisted her hands together, watching her

mother anxiously. 'She's having such a rough time since her mum died, and I thought . . .'

Mum raised a palm towards her, shaking her head. 'Just hold on a minute. For one thing, it's costing more than enough just to keep the two of us. My money doesn't go far, you know that. And for another, if we *were* to have a house guest, as sorry as I am for her predicament, it wouldn't be someone like *that* I'd want under my roof.'

'But Mum, she's really nice when you get to know her, and—'

'*No*. Just no. Please don't ask me again or I'll get cross. I've got enough on my plate without adding that . . . that bloody *delinquent* into the mix. She's not my concern – nor yours.' She fixed her with a hard stare for a moment, then stormed off into the living room.

Flora's heart sank. She knew arguing was pointless. These days, once Mum had made up her mind about something, there was no reasoning with her. She would have to come up with something else.

Remembering her own predicament when Mum was taken into hospital, she thought suddenly about the Oakleys. They were such kind, decent people. She'd kept in touch, birthdays and Christmas; the odd letter to let them know how she was getting on. True, they weren't getting any younger, but if they were still fostering, maybe they'd be prepared to take Iola on. It was worth a try.

Mum had fallen asleep in front of the TV. Seizing the opportunity, Flora crept from the living room, closing the door behind her as quietly as she could. Gingerly, she picked up the receiver and dialled from the phone in the hallway, willing someone to answer. Mrs Oakley sounded delighted to hear Flora's voice as she picked up.

There was no point beating about the bush, so Flora plunged right in and told her about Iola's situation; how worried she was about her friend being in such a horrible place when she'd just lost her mum, how she'd been separated from her brother and sister. About baby Warren, and the shadow the whole affair had cast over the family. She had to be honest, too, about Iola: no one could ever describe her as an angel. But she had a good heart, and Flora was sure that, given a chance, she'd behave herself and wouldn't let the Oakleys down if they could offer her a home.

'Well, I'm not sure how these things work, love.' Mrs Oakley sounded hesitant. 'We haven't had any placements for almost a year now. The last girl was a bit of a nightmare as well and it put us off, to be honest. Shoplifting and stuff. She even pinched money from my purse. Social Services seem to be making it harder to foster, too – we've had to go on a couple of courses already and they keep introducing all these new rules and regulations. It's all feeling a bit much like hard work at our age, especially if we get someone a bit wayward.'

'But I'll talk to Iola, make sure she's not a nuisance,' Flora pleaded. 'I feel sort of responsible for her – she's helped me a lot and I'd like to help her out now she needs it, too.'

There was a lengthy pause and a deep exhalation of breath from the other end of the line.

'Let me have a word with Frank. I'll ring you again in a few minutes.'

Within half an hour, Mrs Oakley called back. 'Right,

we've had a bit of a chat. I need to contact our social worker, who'll need to speak to your friend Iola's social worker, so you'll need to find out who that is.'

There was a pause. Flora held her breath, crossing her fingers.

'*But* if she agrees to behave herself – which I hope she will – and she wants to come to us – and everyone's in agreement of course – we're prepared to give her a chance. She'd be better off with us than in that dump. I've heard plenty about it myself. It does sound like she's had a bit of a raw deal, poor girl. And I'm sure if she's a friend of yours, she can't be all bad.'

Flora's heart soared. She thought of her own time with the Oakleys and knew what a wonderful home they could give Iola if everything worked out.

'That's so kind – thank you. I knew you'd be the best people to ask.' Flora neglected to mention Mum's stance on the situation. 'I'll see her in the morning, so I can tell her then. I know she'll be really grateful.'

But the following day, Iola was nowhere to be seen. Flora always waited for her, and she hovered outside the school as usual, until she was almost half an hour late for registration. When she finally entered the classroom, the other pupils were whispering excitedly amongst themselves and a policeman in uniform was standing just inside the door, speaking in a low voice to her form tutor, Mrs Kwofie. They turned to look at her.

'Ah, here she is. Flora – this gentleman would like a word with you, please.'

Flora looked from the teacher to the police officer, prickling with dread. Without a word, she followed him out of the room, closing the door behind her. The other children began to chatter, all eyes swivelled hungrily towards the glass panel, eager to see what was happening. She heard Mrs Kwofie reprimanding them and a hush descended. The unappetising smell of cabbage was already drifting from the dining hall further down the corridor and it made Flora feel even sicker than she already did.

The policeman offered her a reassuring smile. 'Flora, isn't it? I understand you're a close friend of Iola Chappell. Have you had any contact with her today – or yesterday evening, maybe?'

Flora shook her head mutely.

'You're quite sure?' He tilted his head, looking as if he didn't really believe her.

'I saw her yesterday, straight after school. We walked to the end of the road together, chatted a bit, then she crossed the road and I went home. She's just been moved into the children's home on Smithfield Avenue.'

'Was she walking with anyone else?'

'No. The other kids from the home were walking together in a group, but she always walks on her own after she leaves me. She doesn't like them much. She says . . .' Flora hesitated.

'Go on.'

'She says they're all saps and she'd rather stick pins in her eyes than join them.'

'Ah, I see.' The trace of a smile twitched on his lips. 'Has she said anything to you about the home itself? Did she – is she happy there? Apart from the other saps?'

'No. She hates it. Her mum died just a few weeks ago and they've split her up from her brother and her little sister.'

He nodded, tapping his foot slowly on the green linoleum. 'Yes, we've spoken to Steven and Carly. They say they haven't heard from her, either. Do you have any idea of anyone else she might confide in about things? *Anyone* she might go to if she was in trouble?'

'Is she in trouble then?' Flora suddenly pictured Iola having some sort of blow-up and attacking one of the other residents, or even a member of staff. She dropped her eyes, and began to pick nervously at a hangnail on the side of her thumb.

'Not exactly. But we're anxious to trace her. She wasn't in her bed this morning and no one seems to know where she might be.' He narrowed his eyes, studying Flora's anxious face. 'And you're absolutely certain you haven't seen or spoken to her today?'

Flora shook her head vigorously. 'Honestly. I'd tell you if I had. And no, I can't think of anybody she might go to. She hasn't really got any other close mates.'

He stepped back, regarded her questioningly for a moment, but eventually seemed satisfied that she was telling the truth.

'Well, if you do hear from her, you be sure to let us know. Or Mrs Kwofie.' He pulled a small card from his jacket. 'Here's the number for the station. You'd better get back to your lesson, then.'

'You don't think something really bad's happened to her, do you?' Flora called after him, as he turned to walk away. All sorts of horrible scenarios ran through her mind. Iola could have been dragged from her bed in the middle of the night and kidnapped. Fallen into the river and drowned. Killed by one of the other kids, her body dumped somewhere. There were some really scary-looking older boys in the home: anything was possible. She wondered whether to voice these suggestions to the policeman.

'I think, given what you and the staff at Smithfield House have told us, she's probably run away. Don't worry, I'm sure she'll turn up. It's not uncommon for children in care to abscond. We've got people out looking for her. And you be sure to do the same.'

'I will. Of course I will. She's my best friend.'

Flora watched for a moment as he walked away down the corridor, his shoes squeaking, then disappeared through the double doors. She let out a deep breath, picked up her bag and made her way back into the classroom.

CHAPTER 21

Little Hambley, November 2001

Mrs Homity seemed quite different from how she'd been earlier that morning. Although awake, she wore a stupefied expression and was uncommunicative. Flora assumed it must be a combination of the medication and the fact that her outing had exhausted her. She propped the old woman up in the bed and managed, eventually, to get her to co-operate with eating most of the omelette, although it seemed to take forever. She took a few sips of juice but refused the yogurt. Flora cleaned round her mouth with a wet wipe, then helped her to recline once more as her eyes began to close. The whole operation had taken over an hour. It was wearying.

She closed the door behind her and, leaving the tray on the landing for a moment, went back to her room to check on Rufus. He was nowhere in evidence and Flora's pulse quickened with anxiety. She hurried into the bathroom but he wasn't there. Frantically, she scanned around the bedroom. Then, lifting the valance to look under the bed, she found him, wide-eyed and cowering beneath the sagging springs of the ancient mattress. He growled softly. Dropping to her knees, she leaned forwards, extending her fingers towards him gently. At once he licked her hand and she tickled gently beneath his chin.

'Hey, Rufie, what are you doing under here?'

Flora stood up sharply, suddenly detecting a familiar scent in the air. It was there: faint but distinct. The smell of aftershave. She recognised it from when Hector had pushed past her: heavy, dated. The sort of thing an older man might have worn. A chill passed through her. Her eyes darted around the room, but were drawn at once to the bed. She had tidied it that morning, but now the sheets were rumpled. Flora caught her breath, her hand reaching for her throat. Right in the centre of the cover stretched over the pillow was an unmistakable head-shaped dent.

Hector must have been in here.

The thought made her skin prickle. It was just too weird. What had he been doing? She would have to ask for a key to lock the door. Almost frenziedly, she stripped off all the bedclothes and balled them up on the floor. She had seen clean linen and blankets in the ottoman. She would re-dress the bed once it had aired. Her nose was attuned now to the lingering smell of the aftershave and the thought of its wearer being anywhere near her sleeping quarters repulsed her. Who in their right mind would lie down on someone else's bed without invitation?

Despite Rita's assurances that he was harmless, all

Flora could think about was the disturbing animal mausoleum that existed just yards from her; the whispers about Hector in the village. His outrageous reaction to her arrival.

This served only as confirmation of everything she suspected about him. Everything she knew deep down.

From her bedroom window, Flora had a prime view of the steps leading from the main road. She paced up and down as she waited. Anticipating Mr Homity's return, anger began to build within her. She rehearsed over and over in her mind what she wanted to say. She must choose her words carefully, not raise her voice. But she was the wronged party here, and something needed to be done. Whoever Hector was, it was completely unacceptable for him to enter her room without permission, much less to lie in her bed. Seeing the old man weaving unsteadily up the steps and then across the footbridge about an hour later, Flora waited a respectful few minutes, then, mustering courage from she knew not where, marched downstairs to complain as politely as possible about this intolerable violation of her privacy.

She found her employer in the library, reclining in one of the high-backed chairs in front of a crackling fire, a large brandy swirling in his hand. The room felt much more welcoming than it had when she first arrived, with the wall sconces either side of the fireplace providing a warm glow.

Mr Homity was in a buoyant mood. Clearly an hour or two spent in the company of an old friend, plus, judging by the fumes, more than a few drinks, was enough to help him forget his worries for a while and had brought out an altogether more convivial aspect of his nature.

Seeing his smiling, slightly soppy-looking face gave Flora pause for thought. She hadn't fathomed him out yet. Maybe he was just typically British: stiff upper lip, loosening up after a drink or two to reveal a more human side. She glanced across at the picture of the little girl on the desk and something twisted in her gut. Mr Homity had enjoyed a few hours to himself and now it felt as though she was going to rain on his parade. She wondered how he'd take the news that his son had trespassed into her room, not to mention the discovery of the rats. No wonder the man had seemed so uptight when they first met. She too might turn to alcohol if she were in his shoes.

'Miss Lanyon! I trust you've had a good day?' His consonants were slurred. 'Do have a seat.'

Flora smiled hesitantly as she joined him, perching awkwardly on the edge of the armchair opposite his own. 'Mrs Homity has done well. She ate all her breakfast and most of her lunch. She's sleeping at the moment.'

'Poor Agnes. She sleeps so much these days.'

Flora thought for a moment about Mrs Homity's reluctance to take her medication, and Mr Homity's insistence that she must have it. There was something in his tone which suggested sarcasm; that he was not perhaps entirely sorry that his wife seemed to be fading away. His eyes drifted to the wall above the mantelpiece. Flora followed his gaze to see a striking photograph of a young Mrs Homity with laughing eyes and a beguiling smile, her arms wrapped around a small black spaniel who was staring up at her adoringly. Her cheeks were full and round, a far cry from the gaunt, angular face that had been carved by the passage of time.

'She was all of twenty-three in that picture. Can you imagine? Seems like a lifetime ago . . .' He shook his head wistfully. 'I was so proud to call her my wife. So beautiful. Not a care in the world. But that's life for you. Crushes the spirit, unless you're one of the lucky ones.'

He turned to Flora, fixing her with his unnerving dark eyes. 'Few of us are in the end, Miss Lanyon. As I'm sure you know.'

Flora felt conflicted. His words, his pensive expression had softened her. She found her resolve beginning to waver. But she had come here for a reason and she still needed to say her piece.

'Mr Homity, I wonder if I might have a key, please. To lock my room.'

'What?'

He drew back his chin sharply, his brow creasing into a frown. He regarded her quizzically for a moment, then sat up a little, leaning forwards to shakily place his brandy on the table, but misjudged the distance and the glass teetered precariously on the edge. At once, Flora shot out a hand to steady it, sliding it into a more stable position. She was glad her reflexes hadn't let her down for once. But before she could withdraw, Mr Homity's hand was upon her wrist.

'Whyever would you want a key, you stupid girl? Don't you trust us?'

There was a threatening edge to his voice. His bony fingers were cold and Flora felt them biting into her. The stench of alcohol and stale cigar smoke was overpowering now. Flora's stomach turned over as the odour invoked terrible memories of Uncle Roger. Suddenly she was ten years old again, defenceless and frozen by fear. And then she thought of Iola. She would never have allowed herself to be intimidated in such a way, not by anyone. Summoning courage from somewhere within, Flora jumped to her feet, shaking herself from his grasp. Mr Homity seemed startled, as though he had swiftly come to his senses.

'Forgive me. I didn't intend to . . .' Leaning back, he pasted on a smile, his eyes darting. He straightened his collar, seeming suddenly more sober.

'A key, you say? I'm sure there must be one somewhere. I was . . . a little surprised by your request, that was all.' He nodded, his voice reduced to a mutter. 'Yes, yes. We shall find you a key.'

Flora mumbled her thanks and scurried from the room. All intentions of explaining in righteous indignation about Hector's intrusion had dissolved the second the old man's flesh had come into contact with her own. The hateful way his eyes had locked on her as the façade of cordiality had dropped. She stood in the hallway for a moment, taking deep breaths to compose herself. Suddenly she felt totally exposed. Totally alone. There was no one anywhere in the world she could turn to.

Flora thought of Mum, and wondered what she would have made of it all. Tears spilled from her eyes as she thought again of Iola, her enviable strength and feistiness; how she had always fought her battles for her.

But that had been a very long time ago.

CHAPTER 22

Little Hambley, November 2001

Flora jerked awake, her heart pounding inside her ribcage. The room was in darkness. She lay still for a moment, disorientated, trying to collect her thoughts. Turning to look at the illuminated dial of her alarm clock, she saw it was only two o'clock. Rufus, curled beside her pillow, was stirred by her movement and gave a small, drowsy chirrup. Flora stroked his head, reassuring him. She wondered if she'd cried out in her sleep. Mum had said that she often did. She hoped the Homitys hadn't heard her, if so. Gradually, she began to feel calmer, remembering where she was – and who she was now. That she was alone in her bed.

That Uncle Roger was a distant memory.

Her mouth felt horribly dry and she sat up, reaching for the glass on the bedside table. Flora took a few sips, the water icy-cold from the bitter temperature of the room. Slipping from the bed, she padded across to the bathroom, shivering in the frigid air. Still unfamiliar with her surroundings, she switched on the light en route, glancing down to where she'd strategically placed Mum's old dressing gown across the door the night before. She remembered Mum telling her that, if you were unable to lock a room, it was a good way to stop any unwanted visitors gaining access. It would have to suffice until a key was found, and she wasn't at all convinced Mr Homity would try too hard to locate one.

As she washed her hands under the freezing water, she remembered her unsettling encounter with Mr Homity that evening. A sick feeling churned in the pit of her stomach. This arrangement wasn't going to work in the long term. Her employer made her skin crawl and his son was obviously unbalanced. She would stick it out as long as possible, until she'd accrued a little cash, and then she'd move on. But more importantly, until she had found something that might lead her to Iola.

Flora climbed back into bed and lay, wide awake now. Maybe she could go down to the library, look for a book; something to take her mind off everything. But she had no desire to wander around this house in the dark. During the day it hadn't been quite as bad, but the scrapes and groans as the building settled for the night unnerved her. The very age of the place and the thought that generations of the Homity family had lived and died there. Possibly even in the room where she slept. As Yaz had implied, there might well be ghosts. But more than anything, the thought that either Mr Homity or Hector might be given to nocturnal wanderings made the hairs on her arms stand on end.

No. She must stay where she was, wait until dawn.

She fidgeted and turned from one side to the other, everything dancing in circles through her consciousness. Mum. Home. Iola. And now this place – this *awful, desolate* place. She hated it: the cold, the draughts. The creaking floors; the gloom. If she wanted to stay sane, she had to keep that knowledge in the front of her mind: that this was just a temporary arrangement. That soon, it would all be a distant memory.

Eventually, exhausted by the jumble of her own thoughts, Flora wriggled deeper into the bed and drifted off once more. But as she slept, she dreamed of a laughing little girl, white-blonde hair streaming behind her; the laughter becoming almost hysterical as she sought a hiding place from her playmate. The sound of small feet tripping urgently across the footbridge echoed in her ears. Flora woke once more, confused, her heart hammering. The laughter seemed distant now, but suddenly very real. Was it coming from somewhere in the house?

The door handle was rattling. She held her breath, fully alert now. Someone was trying to get into her room. It was still pitch dark, but there was no mistaking the sound. She was no longer dreaming. Flora lay stock-still, praying that the dressing gown would do its job. Eventually, after three or four attempts, whoever was on the other side of the door gave up. Shuffling footsteps moved away and grew gradually fainter.

Flora could feel blood pounding in her head. She strained to listen for evidence of anyone close by, still unable to move. Her hands were balled into tight fists around the bedcovers, her fingers rigid. It took several minutes to convince herself that the danger had passed – for the moment, at least. What the hell was going on? And what would have happened if the door had actually opened?

This was intolerable. Gradually, as her fear began to subside, it was replaced by anger. Without knowing any details about the previous carer's reasons for leaving, Flora understood all too well how the girl must have felt, particularly as she'd been young and inexperienced. She assumed it must have been either Hector or his father outside her door, and the idea of coming face to face with either of them while lying helpless in her bed was appalling. But with the way in which Mr Homity had met her request for a key, it was clearly inadvisable to confront either of them. The thought of any man invading her private space filled her with a cold, sickening dread, but whatever the Homitys' motives were, they seemed stranger and perhaps even more twisted than anything she'd encountered in the past, somehow. She realised she was in an extremely vulnerable position. There was nobody here to look out for her. She was entirely at their mercy.

But she needed to quell these feelings of panic, to stick it out for a little while longer. She was going to have to be brave: braver than she'd ever thought she could be. Shake off the timid persona that had held her back all her life. She would bide her time, bed in. Get to know the lie of the land. Because in spite of everything, she still had a gut feeling that Iola had been here at some point, and that someone or something in Little Hambley would lead her to her friend. She had to know exactly what had gone on in Mill House before and this was the best chance she would get.

CHAPTER 23

Stretmore, July 1980

The following three weeks were the longest of Flora's life. There was no sign of Iola. No one had heard from her; the police were suspicious that she might have tried to contact Stevie or Carly, although they swore they knew nothing. Mrs Oakley had rung several times to see whether there had been any news. Even Mum seemed concerned, since Flora was so subdued.

And then, at eight o'clock one Sunday evening, the phone rang. Flora had just packed her school bag ready for the morning and run a bath. She rushed to the top of the stairs, in time to see Mum picking up the receiver.

'Hello? *Hello?*'

Mum stared at the handset for a moment then replaced it, shrugging. She looked up at Flora. 'Nobody there.'

'Wrong number, maybe.'

Flora was pretty sure who'd been at the other end of

the line. She felt a mixture of excitement and guilt. On her way to school the very morning the policeman had later quizzed her about her friend, Iola had been waiting to meet Flora at the end of Ostleton Road. And she'd asked her to cover for her. This was the first time in her life Flora had told bare-faced lies to anyone in authority and she hadn't been comfortable with it at all. But Iola was her friend and in an intolerable situation. And she owed her. Big time.

At first, Flora had begged her to come clean. She'd told her all about the Oakleys; how they were good people, willing to offer her a home. But Iola had had other ideas. Even while Doreen was alive, she'd often spoken to the squatters living on the corner of Ostleton Road. They were an eclectic bunch, three men and two women in their early twenties. They all had lots of piercings and tattoos and wild hair. Mum said they were druggies and wasters, but two of the men were well educated – university drop-outs, disillusioned with society. They were all kind and not judgemental, Iola said – and disliked authority every bit as much as she did. They grew their own weed and scraped enough money between them to survive. The women were originally from Ireland. They would sell friendship bracelets and braid people's hair for a few pounds. Sam and Ed, the two older men, were talented artists, and produced the most amazing pavement drawings. They often brought home a hatful of cash at the end of the day. The third and youngest, Jez, who was actually just nineteen, came from a privileged background. He'd been a pupil at the prestigious Rugby public school. His wealthy family had disowned him when he became a Rastafarian. Apparently, he had a substantial amount of money in the bank, left to him by his grandfather, but was unable to touch it until he turned twenty-one. He claimed that, once he had his inheritance, he'd buy another, better house with it that they could all share.

When Iola told them about her predicament and how vile Smithfield House was, they'd invited her to move in with them. They were the perfect 'family' for her, she'd said; no rules, no curfews. She could just be herself – and be free to do as she pleased for once.

'No one ever bothers them. And they're really cool. They don't care if I go to school or anything. Nora, one of the girls, has shown me how to make friendship bracelets – it's dead easy – so I can make a couple of quid doing that. I can just do my own thing, keep my head down, hide out there till I'm sixteen – it'll only be a few months. Then the social will have to house me. And in a couple of years, Stevie and Carly can come and live with me again. I can't go back to Smithfield House, Flo – I hate it. It's the pits.'

And so, extremely reluctantly, Flora had kept Iola's secret. The two women, Nora and Aoife, seemed to find it a huge joke and made a wonderful job of disguising Iola with make-up and a long wig they'd found in one of the bedrooms; dressing her in the loose, hippyish clothes that they themselves wore and which suggested she weighed at least a stone more than her petite frame actually carried. They even spray-painted her signature monkey boots purple, her favourite colour, which seemed to delight Iola more than anything. She'd danced around in them, declaring she would never wear anything else now. They were so *her*. On the street, no one would ever have recognised her; not even her own mother.

But in any case, Iola spent most of her time inside the squat, making friendship bracelets and hanging out with her new 'crew', as she'd started to refer to them. On several occasions, Flora managed to call in to see her on her way home, telling Mum she was going to an after-school club. The house was a dump: bare floorboards, net curtains so filthy you couldn't see through them, but it all seemed very laid-back as they sat around on old cushions, chatting and drinking herb tea that Nora would make using an old camp stove. But Flora was uneasy about the others' influence and concerned that Iola was behaving differently. She even seemed less concerned about Stevie and Carly, saying they were being well looked after now and it was one less thing for her to fret about. Flora knew they smoked joints freely in the squat: she suspected Iola was joining in and it worried her.

What worried her more was Jez's apparent interest in her friend – and she noticed Iola's eyes seeming to float towards him all the time, too. He was good-looking – coffee-coloured skin framed by dreadlocks, and expressive dark eyes. His hand always drifted to her arm when they were talking and it stayed there a fraction too long. It made Flora uncomfortable. She didn't want to say anything to Iola, but she felt Jez was too old for her. After all, Iola was still only fifteen. Men and older boys expected more – and it tied Flora's stomach in knots to think that Iola might be coerced into something she wasn't ready for. Taken advantage of and then dumped. Her poor friend had already experienced enough upset in her life – she didn't need any more.

About ten days after moving into the squat, Iola

announced excitedly to Flora that she was going to get a tattoo. One of the older men, Sam, had acquired inks and a needle and had etched a beautiful butterfly into Aoife's shoulder. He had offered to do one for Iola – and for Flora too, if she wanted. Initially, Flora had been aghast. Apart from anything else, the thought of what Mum would say terrified her. But Iola wasn't giving up.

'Go on – what would you have, if you got one? A bird? A flower, maybe?'

Without thinking, Flora had said, 'I don't want one – not right now. But if I ever have a tattoo when I'm older, it'll be of a hare. Of Ostara.'

And that was it. Iola wouldn't let up. *She* would have one too – it was the *perfect* idea. Flora had once told her what Mum had said about Ostara. Since moving in with her 'crew', Iola had recently got into all this mystical New Age stuff, joss sticks and crystals and the like. Nora and Aoife knew all about Ostara, too. Suddenly the idea of a shapeshifting hare had inflamed her imagination.

'Sam's a brilliant artist. Go on, Flo. Live a little.'

Once Iola started to work on her, it was hard to resist. And so, arriving home two days later from 'after-school club', Flora found herself sneaking into the bathroom to admire Sam's handiwork on her wrist. It had been so sore, and had taken far longer than she'd expected – but Iola had held her hand and encouraged her all the way. Her own tiny, perfect Ostara. She would have to make sure she wore long sleeves in the house or Mum would go berserk. At least the rubber gloves would hide it.

But the knowledge that she, Flora Lanyon, the speccy, boring geek in class 4K with only one friend, who couldn't catch a ball or run to save her life, had actually got a secret, beautiful tattoo, gave her more of a buzz than she could ever have imagined.

She absolutely loved it. But she still didn't love the fact that her friend was doing other 'stuff' in that house and it was keeping her awake at night. Things in the squat were far too free and easy, and the others didn't seem to think there was anything wrong with sharing a spliff with Iola or giving her alcohol, despite her age. Flora knew Iola was drinking, and though she didn't really approve, had more or less accepted it. But Iola had slipped into the conversation that Jez had sneaked her into the local dive of a pub, The Jack and Jester, a few times, too. She obviously found it exciting: as though the risk of being recognised by someone gave her a thrill, but Flora was concerned that if Iola had too much to drink, she might say or do something to give herself away. And then this whole set-up would come crashing down around her ears.

The under-age drinking was bad enough. But Flora had been suspicious when they'd all been sitting around talking one day and Jez had casually handed Iola a small square of paper, winking.

'Save it for later,' Flora had heard him say in a low voice. Iola had giggled, her fingers clasping his for a moment. Flora looked on disapprovingly as he locked eyes with Iola and stroked her cheek. Open displays of affection made her uncomfortable anyway, but this just felt wrong.

Before Iola slipped the paper into her pocket, Flora had time to see that it was a tiny picture of a pink elephant. Despite the innocent-looking cartoon drawing, it niggled at her. The more she saw of Jez, the more she disliked him and the girly, flirty side he seemed to bring out in Iola. It was so unlike her.

'What was that bit of paper Jez gave you?' she'd asked, as she was leaving shortly afterwards. Iola had been cagey at first.

'Nothing much. Just a little present.' She gave a silly half smile, glancing back into the hallway from behind the front door. Flora felt suddenly annoyed. 'Well it was *something* – I could see from the look on your face.'

Iola had sighed. 'It's an LSD tab. You dissolve them on your tongue. It's amazing. Takes you right out of yourself, you know?'

Flora's stomach turned over. 'What the hell are you taking that for? It's dangerous stuff, Iola. You don't know what it might do to you.'

Iola had shrugged and dismissed her concerns. She said everyone else was doing it, and where was the harm. It was just a laugh.

But alarm bells were ringing more loudly than ever for Flora now. She'd been watching Jez like a hawk and he was becoming more and more demonstrative towards Iola, sitting with his arm around her shoulder, stroking her hair and whispering things into her ear. While Iola appeared to be lapping it up, all Flora could think of was where it might lead – and what might be happening when she wasn't there, especially if Iola was high. Why would a nineteen-year-old boy genuinely want a girlfriend so much younger than him? Something felt really off about it all.

Less than a fortnight later, Iola's perfect arrangement appeared to have come to an abrupt end. That same Sunday evening, within the hour, the phone rang out again – and this time Flora got there in time. Iola sounded really strange, her words disjointed. Flora thought at once that she'd been drinking.

'I'm – I'm outside the hospital, Flo. Jez made me . . .'

'Are you okay? What's happened?'

'Not feeling too good . . .' There was an odd gurgling sound, as though she was swallowing something. 'I – look, tell you tomorrow. Gotta go.'

There was a clatter followed by the empty buzz of the dialling tone. Flora felt sick. She wondered what on earth Jez had made her friend do. Up until now, her worst fear was that he might have just been using Iola, that he would dump her when he got bored, leaving her devastated. Or, God forbid, pregnant. But now, Flora's imagination was running wild. She'd heard tales of men getting girls hooked on drugs, forcing them onto the streets to sell their bodies. Had that been his game? Had something gone horribly wrong and Iola had been beaten up by some pervert? Flora was desperately worried about her friend. And there was no one she could tell about it.

All night she had tossed and turned, her anxiety building. It felt as though Iola's life was spiralling out of control and there was nobody to rein in her behaviour. However much she tried to reason with her, Flora knew it would make no difference. Iola was clearly dazzled by Jez, who was exerting what Flora believed to be a malign influence on her friend. Even if nothing really serious had happened to Iola on this occasion, where was it all going to end?

Flora realised with sudden clarity that she was the only one who could step in and save Iola – and there was just one way she could think of to do it. But she needed to act now, before it was too late. Setting her alarm for five o'clock, she wriggled beneath the bedclothes, her stomach fluttering with apprehension and excitement.

The following morning, there were two police cars and a patrol van parked outside the squat at the end of the street as Flora walked up to school. She drew in her breath as she recognised the back of Iola's head in an unmarked silver car, pulling away around the corner. She crossed the road and watched from the other side as, one by one, the squatters were led to the vehicles, the three men into the wagon, one of the women into each car. She saw Nora turn and hoick a mouthful of spit into the face of the police officer who was trying to push her head down to get her onto the back seat.

It confirmed what Flora had originally thought, despite Iola's insistence that they were a decent lot. Everything Mum had said about them must have been right. They were no good. She was glad she'd got up early to make that call. She didn't know why Iola was at the hospital but it must have been something pretty bad, judging by her voice. She shuddered to think what had happened to her. She only hoped that it wasn't too late for Iola to recover from the trauma.

Maybe now Iola would be able to live with the Oakleys and have more stability in her life, a better example to follow. Flora had agonised over the decision, but now she knew she'd done the right thing. She'd acted to protect her friend. It was the only way she could think of to get her out of there and, most importantly, away from Jez's influence.

But of course, she could never tell Iola.

*

Iola didn't go to live with the Oakleys. She said it was kind of them to offer, but their home was too far out and she wouldn't be able to walk to school or see her brother and sister often enough. And so she was sent back to the misery of Smithfield House. By Wednesday, she was back in school as if nothing had happened. Flora hadn't spoken to her since the phone call and was anxious to know she was okay.

'I tell you, Flo, if I find out who called the filth . . .' She'd shaken her head angrily as they met outside the gate that morning. 'Nora and Aoife are going back to Ireland. The lads are all heading for the coast. I'm going to miss them all so much.' Her eyes filled with tears.

'What actually happened though? Why were you at the hospital?'

'Jez made me go. I sniffed this stuff Sam got from somewhere – dunno what it was, but I had a bad reaction. Jez was really worried about me and he walked me there. But the fresh air livened me up in the end, so I just went back to Ostleton Road to sleep it off. And the next thing I knew, the cops were hammering on the door.' Iola shook her head, wiping her eyes on the cuff of her jacket. 'Jez is the best thing that's ever happened to me. I love him, Flo. And thanks to some fucking busybody, I'll probably never see him again.'

CHAPTER 24

Little Hambley, November 2001

Flora was exhausted for those first few days at Mill House. By bedtime, she felt sick with fear, terrified to submit to sleep after the attempt to enter her room during the night, which happened a further two nights running. She tried not to dwell on what might happen if the attempts were successful.

But it wasn't like it had been with Uncle Roger. She felt certain of that. Instead, she had visions of waking with a pillow over her face or hands around her throat. If the intruder turned out to be Mr Homity, she was convinced from the way in which he looked at her that he actually meant her harm. She'd fished a thick piece of cardboard out of the bin and wedged that under her door for good measure. Thankfully, along with the dressing gown, it was doing the trick and she began to relax a little. She wished she had something that would prevent access to the room during the day, while she was otherwise engaged. But apart from her diary, there was little else in there that might be of interest to anyone, as far as she could tell. She just hated the thought of Hector, or anybody else, rummaging through her things. It almost made her want to fumigate everything. And she was anxious about poor Rufie, although she'd overheard Mr Homity warning Hector in a low voice to 'stay away from that cat'. Interestingly, she had noticed, if his father gave him any kind of orders, Hector appeared to obey him to the letter, even if reluctantly.

In addition to the unwanted nocturnal activity, after the incident in the library, Mr Homity seemed even more hostile than before. At least, his wife felt like an ally, even if she was often confused, and Rita too, although her visits weren't as regular as Flora would have liked. She'd debated whether to confide in Rita about her worries but any time she'd mentioned anything about Hector and the fact that he was so unpleasant, she seemed quite dismissive as though it was almost to be expected.

Hector was definitely very odd. Maybe he was genuinely ill in some way, but that didn't stop Flora from feeling unnerved by him. Although – if it *was* him trying to get into her room, it could be under his father's direction. Mr Homity seemed to exert an uncanny hold over him. After the way her belongings had been disturbed, it was quite feasible that Hector had been looking for something specific.

But what?

*

Flora now had the hurdle of the first seven days at Mill House behind her and, though still on her guard, was cautiously settling into a routine. By prior arrangement with Mr Homity, she had taken two half days' holiday instead of one full one that first week, not knowing what she would do with so much time and nowhere to go. She needed to get her bearings first; find out more about the area. And when the opportunity arose, explore the rest of the house.

This arrangement suited Mr Homity perfectly, he'd said, and he had taken over the care of Mrs Homity on the Tuesday and Friday morning, leaving him free to meet with his friend for a late lunch the one day and dinner the other. On the Wednesday, he'd been out for the whole day again. Flora noticed how much more pleasant he seemed on these occasions, when he had an outing to look forward to. She was more than glad when he was no longer on the premises, and did her best to avoid him on his return. Even if he was more cordial, all thoughts of sympathy towards him had evaporated after his behaviour that evening in the library. And as the days passed, he appeared to have conveniently distanced himself from the memory of her request for a key.

Hector was invariably rude whenever she met him, on the stairs or passing in the corridor. More often she would see rather than hear him, the sombre classical music blasting from the annexe a sign that he was at home and psyching himself up for whatever it was that he liked to do. She dreaded to think.

Flora had never mentioned the fact that he'd been into her room that day, either to him or to his father. Nor that one of them had tried repeatedly to gain entry to her room while she slept. And she definitely wouldn't tell poor Mrs Homity. She was terrified of the repercussions; of what Hector or Mr Homity might do if she let it be known that she was aware they were up to something. She needed this job and, moreover, as much as she would have liked to run for the hills, she needed to muster every ounce of courage she possessed and ride it out until she could find out the truth. As uncomfortable as her predicament was, she felt forewarned now, and made sure the dressing gown and strip of cardboard were placed across her bedroom door each night. She had also found a substantial short branch when walking Mrs Homity through the woods and managed to sneak it into the house, concealed by the blanket's fringe, on the tray beneath the wheelchair. It now lay under her bed: a cudgel, a comforting arm's length away, should anyone make it past the makeshift barrier she'd created. Needless to say, Mr Homity had never brought up the subject of the key again, and after his previous reaction, drunk or otherwise, she decided not to raise it herself.

Nighttimes were all much the same. Mrs Homity was exhausted by the evening; her concentration levels and ability to communicate were noticeably impaired. But the old woman had been, for the most part, much brighter on the days when Flora oversaw her morning care. It was as if her husband's company set her off on the wrong foot, and she was subdued and muddled then for most of the day. Flora began to think that his company, his suffocating, controlling behaviour, drained her somehow.

Most days that week had been cold but dry, enabling Flora to take Mrs Homity for a walk through the woods on three occasions. After returning from their most recent outing they had spotted Hector marching across the footbridge towards the main house. Flora tucked the wheelchair behind the trunk of a wide oak tree and, concealed from view, they watched him for a few moments. His shirt sleeves were rolled up; he was swinging his arms and seemed to be talking to himself quite earnestly, pausing occasionally to wave his hands in an animated fashion.

Mrs Homity had shaken her head when he finally disappeared through the front entrance. She turned to look at Flora, her brow knitting.

'I do wonder sometimes, you know. About Hector. Do you think he looks more like me, Flora? Or Abey?'

Flora thought of Hector's thick, unruly hair; his heavy-set brow and bulbous, protruding eyes. His large, solid-limbed physique. Both Mr and Mrs Homity were small and slight: she, grey-eyed with fine bone structure; her husband, sharp-jawed and aquiline-nosed, his own dark eyes small and deep set.

'I don't think he's much like either of you, to be honest.' Flora laughed lightly, having learned that Mrs Homity had quite a sense of humour. 'Maybe he's the milkman's.'

Mrs Homity gave a wry smile. 'Yes. Maybe he is.'

*

Wednesday morning, Flora took Mrs Homity's breakfast up to her at 8.15 a.m. The old woman's GP was due to make a house call that morning, to check on her and whether she needed her medication tweaking. Again, she seemed far more alert than she had later the previous day.

Mr Homity had eaten breakfast in the kitchen and appeared, looking slightly peaky after his latest 'meeting' with Kenneth, just as his wife was finishing the last of her porridge. He came across to the bed and leaned in to peck her on the cheek. Flora thought she saw Mrs Homity flinch slightly, but the old woman summoned a small smile. He nodded towards Flora a touch sheepishly.

'Good morning, Miss Lanyon. I believe I told you that we're expecting our new GP, Dr Chabra, at ten o'clock – he's been very punctual so far. If you could have Agnes showered and ready by then, please . . .' He turned to address Mrs Homity, smiling thinly. 'I think I'll have a little walk into the village first, my dear. I could do with some fresh air. I'll see you shortly.'

The atmosphere in the room seemed to lighten the moment he left. Mrs Homity appeared immediately more relaxed.

'Oh well, I suppose we'd better get me spruced up, then. Dr Chabra is quite a dish, you know. I think I might even have a squirt of my best perfume today.' She gave Flora a wink. 'Come on, let's get the ablutions over with and then I can arrange myself to my best advantage.'

Flora managed a grin. Mrs Homity was still able to enjoy a joke, despite her predicament. Her medication remained untouched for the time being, just as she requested each morning Flora had been in charge. Although she was aware that dementia symptoms could fluctuate wildly in the earlier stages, Flora wondered about the marked contrast in her cognitive ability before and after taking the pills. She wondered too what Dr Chabra's take on it all was. She wanted to ask him about the Amiodarone. She'd been wracking her brains, trying to remember what it was for. She had asked Mrs Homity, but the old woman had seemed confused and said she just took what she was prescribed.

Soon, Mrs Homity was washed and dressed, wearing a plaid woollen skirt and a lilac cashmere sweater that she had picked out herself. She sat in the wheelchair in front of the bay, her hands in her lap, the fluffy slippers on the footplate making her emaciated legs appear even thinner. She gazed thoughtfully out of the window.

'I think Abey will probably be meeting Kenneth again on Friday, now that you're here to look after me,' she announced suddenly. 'He used to see him quite regularly before, but it's been difficult for him to get out much since the last young lady left. They're definitely making up for lost time now, though.' She continued to stare straight ahead, twirling a strand of hair between her fingers. 'Kenneth is the perennial bachelor. A real man's man. Never settled down. He went abroad for a few years; somewhere exotic, I believe. He doesn't come here these days. I'm not sure why. Or if he does, he never comes up to see me. I haven't laid eyes on him in a long while.' She seemed to ponder this for a moment, then tilted her face towards Flora with a sudden smile.

'I do hope you'll be staying, Flora. I very much enjoy our little walks.' She reached out and pressed Flora's hand with her cool, smooth palm, lowering her voice. 'Probably best not to mention them to Dr Chabra, either. I'm sure Abey must take a lot of his advice about my welfare from him. He mightn't approve.'

Mr Homity appeared suddenly in the doorway, a newspaper tucked beneath his arm, looking a little less green around the gills than he had earlier. He walked across to join his wife.

'Lovely morning out there. Very chilly, but bright. I've blown away a few cobwebs.' He hovered awkwardly for a moment, glancing at his watch, then peered out of the window. 'Ah, here comes Dr Chabra. Right on time.'

Mrs Homity locked eyes with Flora briefly, the hint of a smile playing on her lips. Dr Chabra was indeed very handsome, tall and immaculately dressed, with a neat beard and brown eyes like fathomless pools. He breezed into the room, carrying a battered tan leather case.

'Good morning, Mrs Homity! Mr Homity.'

He greeted his patient with a broad smile, nodding politely to Mr Homity and, putting down his bag, extended a firm hand towards Flora, which she shook shyly.

'Krish Chabra. You must be Mrs Homity's new nurse. Pleased to meet you.'

She thought of Mrs Homity's description of the doctor. *Krish the Dish*. She prayed she wasn't blushing.

'I'm Flora. Flora Lanyon. But I'm not actually a nurse.' She felt suddenly inadequate and awkward. And plain. So very plain. She ran a hand self-consciously over her unruly hair.

'Well, as good as.' He smiled again, revealing perfectly even white teeth. He turned back to Mrs Homity, who was beaming from ear to ear. 'I'm relatively recently qualified, so quite new to all this myself. I'm sure between you and Mrs Homity here, you can help me out.'

'Shall we do the necessary, then?' From his case, he produced a stethoscope and blood pressure monitor, and proceeded to move the chest-piece across the old woman's frail ribcage, asking her to take deep breaths, then moving to her back.

'All sounding nice and clear. Can I have a quick look in your mouth and your eyes?' He took out a small torch and asked Mrs Homity to stick out her tongue, then to follow the beam back and forth with her gaze.

'Perfect. Just your blood pressure and temperature now, then that's all the prodding over with.'

He made notes of the readings and packed away his equipment once more.

'Fit as a butcher's dog.' He gave her another smile. 'And how are you in yourself, young lady? How are your energy levels?'

'Not so bad today, Doctor. All the better for seeing you.'

Dr Chabra grinned. 'I'm sure you say that to all the chaps. And your mobility? Would you say it's any worse, or much the same?'

'It seems better in the mornings, I'd say. Maybe because I'm less tired.'

Mr Homity was observing the proceedings critically. He looked on, stony-faced.

'Agnes is usually such a stoic, Doctor, but she's showing signs of discomfort more and more. I wonder if you might increase her pain relief dosage? Or perhaps prescribe something . . . a little stronger?'

Dr Chabra's brow creased in concern. 'Is that right, Mrs Homity? Do you feel your pain medication isn't working as it should?'

Mrs Homity looked anxiously from her husband to the doctor. 'I'm not so bad, really I'm not. It's only the odd day when I feel a little . . .'

'Come now, Agnes,' Mr Homity interrupted. 'I know when things are bad for you. It worries me to think you're suffering in silence.' His face was close to his wife's now, a rigid smile on his lips. 'Do be honest with the doctor. You have to help yourself too, you know.'

'I can certainly increase the dose if it would help.' Dr Chabra looked dubious. 'But unfortunately, there can be undesirable side-effects from the stronger pills, so it's inadvisable unless it's absolutely necessary. And the fentanyl should only be used if things ever get particularly bad. I really would err on the side of caution if Mrs Homity says she's coping at the moment.'

'With the greatest respect, you're not that familiar with Agnes's condition yet. And you aren't seeing her on a daily basis.' Mr Homity's voice had taken on a granite edge. His head had begun to wobble in agitation. 'I know my wife, Dr Chabra, and I say she needs something more to keep her comfortable. I really must insist.'

Flora was startled by the sudden aggression in his manner. She looked from Mr Homity to his defenceless wife, wondering whether she ought to say something. From everything she had seen, this simply wasn't true. Then she thought about her contract and the words stuck in her throat. She felt spineless and ashamed.

Mrs Homity seemed browbeaten. She kept her gaze fixed on her husband's flashing eyes.

'Perhaps Abey's right, Dr Chabra. I . . . I do get confused sometimes. I'm sure he knows what's best for me. I suppose it wouldn't hurt to have something a little stronger, just in case.'

The doctor rose, snapping his case shut. His eyes narrowed as he addressed Mr Homity.

'I'll leave a prescription with the chemist in the village. It should be ready to collect later this afternoon. But please, only as and when needed.' He darted a look at Flora, who felt her cheeks bloom. 'I wouldn't want Mrs Homity to become dependent on these drugs. They're better reserved for chronic rather than intermittent pain, and from what I've seen of my patient today, she seems quite bright. Brighter, in fact, than a lot of other ladies her age.'

He clasped Mrs Homity's hand in his own, smiling down at her worried face. 'I'll call again in a fortnight to review things. In the meantime, you see how things go. Don't feel any pressure to take the stronger tablets if you don't need them. Only you know what's going on in your own body.'

Dr Chabra straightened, turning to Flora. 'You're in charge,' he said, rather pointedly. 'Keep an eye on her, won't you, and let me know if there's any change?'

Flora nodded, her cheeks warming again as his eyes scanned her face.

'Good day, Doctor. And thank you. Do let me show you out.' Mr Homity was already at the door, ushering him from the room.

Flora watched from the window as there was a brief exchange between Mr Homity and the doctor on the path below. Mr Homity came back into the house and Dr Chabra began to walk slowly away, glancing back up towards where she stood. He appeared vaguely perplexed.

Flora looked at Mrs Homity, parked in the middle of the room like someone stranded in a dinghy on a huge expanse of sea. All the earlier spark had vanished. The old woman was staring emptily into the distance, her expression resigned. Flora thought of all the times she should have been braver in the past and how things might have turned out so differently if she had. She *had* to be decisive for once. Taking a deep breath, she turned back and rapped loudly on the window. The doctor paused, casting a glance over his shoulder to locate the source of the noise.

Gesturing to him to wait, Flora indicated that she was coming down. As quickly as she could, she hurried downstairs and, praying not to bump into either Mr Homity or Hector, made her way outside to meet the doctor on the footbridge.

'Is everything okay?' He smiled uncertainly.

'I just wanted to ask you – about Mrs Homity's meds. As I'm supposed to be giving them all to her, I wanted to be sure what it is she's actually taking. She says she has something called CMT?'

'That's right. Charcot-Marie-Tooth. It's a progressive condition that affects her nervous system. The damage can affect patients' ability to walk and use their hands.'

Flora nodded. 'My mum had something similar. She couldn't walk at all in the final stages.' She felt a knot rise in her throat as she thought of Mum, lying there helplessly, her face contorted with pain.

'*Please, Flo. Please.*'

Flora dug her nails into her palms, trying to shut out the memory. The interminable nights, holding Mum's hand; trying to soothe her. The constant pleading which had gradually begun to wear Flora down.

Dr Chabra tipped his head sympathetically. 'I'm sorry to hear that. Neurological conditions can be extremely debilitating. It's so distressing for family members, watching a loved one deteriorate like that.'

Flora couldn't bear it when someone was kind. She didn't deserve it. And pity always brought the tears closer to the surface. She gave a small, dry cough.

'Mum took gabapentin for years – for her neuropathy. I haven't seen any of that in Mrs Homity's medications, but I notice she's taking something called Amiodarone? I know I've heard of it somewhere, but can't remember what it's for.'

'Yes, Mrs Homity should be having gabapentin, too. You're quite right. I was trying to familiarise myself with her medication before I came here today. I felt sure it was on her repeat script. But Amiodarone?' The doctor frowned, shaking his head. 'Absolutely not – she shouldn't be having that at all any more. It should have a big red warning sign on the packet for someone with nerve issues. My predecessor, Dr Houseman, must have prescribed it originally. He retired, a couple of months ago now. Great bloke, but very old-school. Probably not up to date with current thinking.' He grimaced.

'When the CMT was diagnosed, the Amiodarone should have been withdrawn from her immediately. I read up on it only recently for another patient. It's used to control arrhythmia, but can have a seriously negative effect on the nerves. There are far more suitable drugs available for Mrs Homity's heart. She's already prescribed a low-dose beta-blocker – and strictly speaking, she probably doesn't even need *that* half the time. The heart condition is only mild – a touch of angina.'

'But it's definitely one of her daily meds,' said Flora. 'I checked the packets – the most recent prescription for it was only issued last week. And I haven't seen any beta-blockers, either.'

Dr Chabra looked confused. 'That makes no sense. I'll double-check with the pharmacy, make sure they took it off her repeat list. But in the meantime, please make sure she doesn't have it again. I'll chase up the propranolol. And the gabapentin. We're trying to help the poor woman, not send her into rapid decline.'

Flora paused. She looked back at the house. 'Mr Homity – he seems a bit, I don't know, keen for her to take her painkillers. She seems so much more, well, *awake* when she hasn't had them. Like a different person. Do you think perhaps . . .' She wasn't quite sure how best to voice her concerns.

The doctor rolled his eyes and smiled. 'From what I've seen, I'd say our Mr Homity is a man used to being in charge – and irrationally overprotective of his wife. Which is entirely understandable, given her age. And he's not getting any younger himself, of course. I think the best we can do is humour him but take our guidance from Mrs Homity. Now you're here to oversee things, I'm confident she's going to be well looked after. I believe the last young lady was a bit, well . . .' He whistled and gave Flora a knowing smile.

'Do you know anything about the last carer? I wondered what actually went on; why she didn't stay long.' She watched his face, anxious for some insight.

'I don't, to be honest. I've only been here a couple of times – I met her just the once. She seemed a bit of a nervous sort. Maybe . . .' He chewed his lip. 'You've met Hector, have you?'

'Yes. I've met Hector.'

'Me too. Briefly. Enough said.'

But it wasn't enough. There was so much more that Flora wanted to know. She drew in a deep breath.

'I don't suppose – you didn't ever see another girl here, did you – a visitor? About my age – small; tattoos, lots of piercings?' Her fingers crossed, she willed him to give her a positive answer, hoping she didn't sound too desperate.

Dr Chabra cocked his head. 'No, I'm afraid not.' He smiled at her quizzically. 'Sounds an unlikely house guest for the Homitys, from what I've seen of them. Was she anyone important?'

Deflated, Flora shook her head. 'An old friend of mine. It was a shot in the dark, really. I just thought; well, hoped . . .' She trailed off. She was drawing a blank at every turn and it was demoralising.

'If I do see anyone like that, I'll be sure to let you know.'

'Thanks.' Flora mustered a diffident smile.

'Anyway,' Dr Chabra went on, 'going back to what we were saying, I'm sure with all your personal experience, you'll cope much better here than the previous carer. Hopefully between us, moving forward we can manage the situation and improve Mrs Homity's quality of life.'

'Speaking of which, what do you think about her getting out into the fresh air? She wants me to take her for walks but her husband doesn't seem to think it's good for her.'

The doctor lifted an eyebrow. 'Really? I think it might be exactly what she needs – providing she's well wrapped up. Who wants to be stuck looking at the same four walls, day in, day out? Go for it, I say.' He glanced at his watch and pulled a face. 'I'm sorry, but I really have to go. Three more home visits to make before lunch and then I'm back at the surgery this afternoon. It's still taking a bit of getting used to. But please, don't hesitate to call me if you're worried about anything else.'

Flora nodded. 'Thank you. I will. You say the new prescription will be ready to collect this afternoon?'

'Yes.' Dr Chabra's brow knitted. He pursed his lips. 'Hmm. I'll see if I can speak to Dr Houseman, see if he knows anything about the family dynamics. Mr Homity may be genuinely concerned about his wife, but he was a bit pushy today for my liking. We want to make sure he's not just trying to exert his control over her. Some men can be like that, I know.'

Flora stood for a moment, watching as he hurried off across the bridge, turning to wave before disappearing down the slope towards the main road. Slowly, she made her way back into the house, her mind whirring.

CHAPTER 25

Stretmore, September 1980

The summer holidays came and went, somewhat dismally. The new school term had begun and moving into the fourth year, everything felt different. Since leaving the squat, Iola had become distant, and she and Flora began to drift apart. Iola stopped calling for her, or waiting after school to walk up the road together as they'd always done. Even in school, Iola didn't hang out with her any more. She would still say 'hi' and sit at the back with her in Maths if she actually bothered turning up for the lesson, but that was about all Flora could hope for.

It had broken Flora's heart. Leaving the squat and losing touch with Jez, plus the 'survival of the fittest' ethos at Smithfield House, had hardened her friend; turned her into someone she no longer knew. Iola seemed to have capitulated and adopted an 'if you can't beat 'em, join 'em' philosophy, gravitating towards some of the least desirable residents of her new home. Flora had heard they were known for shoplifting sprees and it worried her that Iola would get caught and into serious trouble.

Flora had been absent from school since Friday with a stomach bug. Although fully recovered, without meeting up with Iola to look forward to any more, she had been in no rush to return. Mum eventually insisted she go in, saying the longer she stayed away, the harder it would get.

A buzz was going through the classroom at Wednesday morning registration. Animated whispers were being exchanged. Flora was intrigued. She tapped the shoulder of the girl sitting in front of her to ask what was going on.

'I thought you were good mates with Iola? Haven't you heard?'

'Heard what?'

And then the girl proceeded to regale her with the whole sorry tale: that Iola had viciously attacked one of the boys at Smithfield House two days earlier. The police had been called and Iola removed from the home.

'Dunno what the kid did. Iola's a bit of a headcase, I know, but she really went mad this time. Kicked the crap out of him.' She sniggered. 'She can certainly handle herself, considering how small she is.'

Flora was horrified. 'Is the boy all right? What about Iola?'

'Oh, he's all right. Pride dented more than anything, I reckon. He's a real shit from what I've heard. Probably asked for it. But they're booting Iola out of that home for good now. Sending her to some "Community Home with

Education" as they call it, somewhere near Birmingham. You know, what they used to call an approved school.'

'Birmingham? But that's miles away.' Flora's voice came out as a wail. She felt hot tears prick her eyes.

'Yep. Nearest one with any room, apparently. Poor old Iola.'

Poor old Iola. Flora felt sick. Iola had been happy in the squat, even if it wasn't an ideal situation. She'd still been coming to terms with losing her mum. However bad Flora had thought it at the time, the arrangement was infinitely better than what went on at Smithfield House. She realised that now. What kind of person would ring the police anonymously to say people were dealing drugs from the house on the end of her road when it really wasn't true? From everything Iola had told her later, though Jez's morals may have been dubious, she was never at any real risk from him. He'd been kind, Iola had said. Never tried anything on with her.

What on earth had she done?

Flora's own stupid, hysterical reaction to Iola's circumstances had ultimately brought this about. She should have talked to Iola properly, voiced her concerns. As on so many other occasions in the past, she had acted rashly without really thinking it through. And it was always someone else who carried the can for her poor judgement. She felt overwhelmed with guilt. None of this would have happened if she hadn't made that call. Iola was being sent away and any hope she'd had of rekindling their friendship had been dashed.

At that moment, she felt as though her whole world had collapsed.

And she'd brought it all on herself.

CHAPTER 26

Little Hambley, November 2001

After parting company with Dr Chabra, Flora had hoped to get back upstairs before she was missed. Her chest tightened at the sight of Mr Homity approaching down the passageway from the kitchen, apparently deep in thought. She looked from left to right, her heart pounding. There was nowhere to hide. Flora drew herself back against the wall close to the entrance, praying that he would go into the library and she would be spared an uncomfortable interrogation. But Mr Homity continued towards the foot of the staircase. Suddenly, his gaze drifted to where she was standing, stopping him in his tracks. Flora stood immobile, like a wild animal mesmerised by the glare of headlights. She tried desperately to find some explanation for her presence, but her tongue felt thick, unable to articulate one word.

The tendons twitched in Mr Homity's jaw, his eyes

narrowing. He cast around sharply, possibly checking whether they were alone. Flora felt herself shrivel inwardly. How she wished that Dr Chabra had not already left. Fists clenched at her sides, she held her breath, preparing herself for some sort of outburst.

Oddly, although he had clearly been startled and less than pleased to see her there, Mr Homity's mind was plainly on something far more important. He cleared his throat, adjusting his tie unnecessarily.

'Ah. Miss Lanyon – if you could collect Agnes's prescription later this afternoon, I'd be grateful. I have paperwork to catch up on after lunch and don't want to be disturbed.' He ran his tongue along his lip. 'Erm – would tomorrow be a suitable day for you to take free this week? I was hoping to go out for the day again on Friday. There's a . . . a race meeting in Cheltenham. I haven't been able to attend in a long while.' His head began to oscillate slightly as he waited for her response.

'Yes, that's fine.' Flora felt every muscle in her body slacken with relief. She forced a smile. 'Are you – will Hector be coming with you?'

'Hector?' He gave a fluting laugh. 'Oh no, Hector has no interest in horses. Not if they're alive, anyway.'

Flora's pulse skipped momentarily as the telephone in the library began to ring out. Mr Homity's unblinking stare was still fixed on her face. He hesitated briefly, as though considering ignoring the call, then turned abruptly and disappeared through the door, closing it behind him.

Flora strained to hear the conversation on the other side of the thick wall, but Mr Homity's voice was too low and muffled to discern a single word. She exhaled deeply. Taking a moment to compose herself, she made her way towards the stairs once more, her mind ticking over. She felt sure he was up to something.

Mrs Homity had managed to wheel herself over to the window. She turned her head as Flora came back into the bedroom, frowning slightly.

'What did you want to speak to Dr Chabra about?'

'Oh, it was just to check something about your meds. He seems really pleased with how you're doing, you know.' Flora nodded encouragingly. 'And' – she closed the door behind her quietly, lowering her voice – 'he's *more* than happy for you to go out for walks. In fact, he's actually quite enthusiastic about the idea.'

Mrs Homity brightened, pulling herself up a little in her chair. 'Really?' Just as quickly, her face clouded again. 'We still mustn't tell Abey, though. I'm sure he'd find some reason to object.'

'Well, Mr Homity just told me he'll be going out again on Friday. So we'll keep everything crossed for a dry day.'

Although prepared to comply with Mrs Homity's wishes, Flora felt uncomfortable about this covert arrangement. The thought of the contract and the threat of dismissal was never far from her mind. She was still desperate to track down Iola – and if she was forced to leave Little Hambley, she worried she might miss a golden opportunity to find out where her friend had gone. A chance meeting with Stevie all those months ago had set Flora on this path. So far, she had nothing but that and her own instincts to go on. It had lifted her spirits for a while when Stevie had said Iola was going to write to her. At the very least, the intention was there. Flora might have been more cautious about searching for her friend if she thought she would get a frosty reception. But she was bolstered by Stevie's words, hoping there was a real chance she could fix things between them.

She considered now, if her hunch was right, what Iola would have made of Mr Homity. Because the more Flora saw of the man, the more uneasy he made her. She wondered just what was going on in his head. And if he cared for his wife as much as he claimed to, why would he be so opposed to her doing the things she wanted to? It was completely baffling.

*

Having settled Mrs Homity down for her afternoon nap, Flora put on her coat and scarf and made her way into the village. It was icily cold; almost 4 p.m. and the sun was already starting to dip. She hadn't yet had an opportunity to explore and was excited about getting out of the house for a while. The slightly higgledy-piggledy pavement looked as if it had been scrubbed, with not a scrap of litter in evidence. Old-fashioned street lamps glowed on either side of the honey-stoned high street, which was filled with an array of independent shops – none of the pound shops or chain stores she was used to at home. Lights shone invitingly from their windows, one beautifully dressed with unusual ornaments and colourful lamps; side by side, two expensive-looking boutiques, the first selling ladieswear, its neighbour, children's (no price tags on anything); another displayed more types of cheese than she'd known even existed. Tempting cakes and scones were arranged on a tiered china stand in the window of a small tea shop, which seemed to have a constant flow of people in and out of its door.

There was a store selling art supplies and stationery, a shoe shop offering bespoke, hand-made footwear, and a gentlemen's tailor. All catering very much for those with a healthy amount of disposable income. There was no shortage of well-turned-out customers milling about; tweed caps and Barbour jackets appeared to be very popular with the older clientele, Flora observed. Most of the younger generation were fresh-faced and conservatively dressed, with few hoodies or oversized trainers in evidence. The people who passed her smiled in a friendly manner, but Flora felt conspicuous and dowdy in Mum's old British Home Stores coat and the same tatty boots she'd worn for the last four winters.

At the far end of the street were the more mundane establishments. A post office and newsagent; a hardware store and a grocer's. Right at the bottom, Flora could see the green neon cross of the chemist. As she approached, she noticed fairy lights twinkling through the leaded windows of the building on the corner opposite.

The hand-painted sign outside swayed a little, despite the lack of breeze. It bore the picture of a Jack Russell, a ruff around its neck, staring up at a sinister-looking man dressed from head to toe in a multi-coloured costume adorned with bells, his face concealed by a grinning carnival mask. He was brandishing a stick, a miniature version of himself dancing on the end.

The Jack and Jester.

Nothing like the shithole where Iola used to hang out, all tar-brown ceilings, beer stains and ripped seats. But a pub with the same name. What a coincidence.

But Flora didn't believe in coincidence.

At once she thought again of something Iola's brother Stevie had said. She felt the hairs rise on the back of her neck. *A village in the back of beyond. Something about a water mill . . .*

'Oh, hi! How's it going?'

Startled, Flora realised someone was talking to her. She stopped in the pharmacy doorway and turned to recognise not a woman as she'd first thought, but the teenage girl, Yaz, she had spoken to on the bus, the day she first arrived in Little Hambley. The girl's purple fringe peeped from beneath a rainbow-striped woollen hat and she wore a long, fake fur pink coat. A stark contrast to the sober dress-code of the local residents Flora had seen so far.

'Hello again! All good, thanks. I'm just picking up a prescription for Mrs Homity.'

Yaz nodded. 'Just been to get my mum's antibiotics. She's got tonsillitis.' She held up a small plastic bag, looking slightly pained. 'How've you found them then, the Homity lot? Is that Hannibal as creepy as everyone says?'

Flora hesitated. She didn't want to divulge too much about her employers. She didn't really know Yaz, and it wouldn't do for anything she said to get back to Mr Homity. And more than anything, she didn't want to find herself on the streets. Not just yet, at least.

'They're not so bad once you get to know them. Mrs Homity is very sweet.'

'Yeh – but what about *him* – the weirdo?'

The girl's eyes grew large, eager for some gossip. Flora wasn't going to be the one to give it to her.

'Hector's okay, actually. I've been pleasantly surprised all round, to be honest.' She cringed slightly as the lie left her lips.

Yaz looked deflated. 'Oh. Just goes to show you can't always believe everything you hear. No ghosts either?'

Flora smiled. 'Nope. No ghosts, I'm afraid. Not that I've seen, anyway.'

'Never mind. I s'pose it's better for you though, staying there and that.' She paused. 'You met their cleaner yet?'

'Rita? Yes. She seems nice.'

Yaz pulled a face. 'That's not what I've heard. She's my nan's neighbour. She seemed all right when she first moved here. Acts like she's the bee's knees now, though. My nan's asked her a couple of times what they're like up there –' she flapped a hand in the general direction of Mill House. 'Last time, she nearly bit her head off and said it was none of her business. My nan says you'd think she'd signed the bleedin' Official Secrets Act.'

Flora thought about her own contract. A cold sensation prickled along her spine.

'Well . . . there doesn't seem to be much to tell anyway – from what I've seen. Maybe Rita was just . . . having a bad day.'

The girl shrugged. 'Who knows. Just sounds like a stuck-up cow to me.'

Flora was about to leap to Rita's defence when the girl's face suddenly brightened.

'Aww – how's the cat, by the way?'

'He's settled in fine. I'm thinking of getting him a lead so I can take him out for a walk.'

'Really? Oh cool, I'd love to see that! There's a pet shop further up the road –' She waved a hand past the chemist's to where the street lights petered out. 'Not far from where I live. The arse end.' She grinned. 'I bet they sell 'em.'

'Cheers.'

'Anyway, gotta go. See you again, maybe.'

'Yeah. See you.'

Flora watched her walk away, feeling slightly wistful. Yaz reminded her so much of Iola; the self-assured way she carried herself, that cocky little strut. But her words about Rita had sowed a niggling seed of doubt. The woman had seemed perfectly pleasant. Perhaps, like herself, Rita was terrified of anything getting back to Mr Homity. There was always that possibility.

Flora went into the chemist's, collected the prescription which was already waiting, and came back out onto the street. Staring over at the pub, her mind began ticking over again. *A village in the back of beyond*. And a familiar name, that to an outsider might seem like a beacon in the dark: a home from home. She thought of Rita: warm, funny Rita and how she had come across as hostile and uppity to Yaz and her family. It didn't fit with how she had found her. It didn't fit at all.

Flora glanced at her watch. Mrs Homity would need supper in about an hour and a half. She should have just enough time.

Looking from left to right, she crossed the road and, pushing open the door, walked in. Forty minutes and two Cokes later, she was back on the pavement, heady with excitement from what the barman had told her. And the conviction that Iola had been drawn like a magnet to a pub with the same name as the one she frequented all those years ago.

CHAPTER 27

Stretmore, October 1982

Two years went by with no contact from Iola. Flora's life revolved around caring for Mum, whose health and mobility were gradually deteriorating, and attending college, where she had enrolled on a secretarial course. Although she had no real idea of what other work she might be suited to, Flora knew this was not what she wanted to do with her life, and she found the typing difficult, but the careers officer at school had persuaded her it might lead to a job further down the line.

She would see Stevie in the street occasionally and ask how Iola was getting on. It sounded as if Iola's phone calls were few and far between, but she'd left the Community Home and had moved into a flat in Birmingham with a lad she'd met. Stevie said he was a loser. He and Carly saw one another in school, but not much apart from that. He seemed almost indifferent about it all and it made Flora sad. The family unit that Iola had been so desperate to keep together had all but disintegrated.

Flora had lost all hope of ever seeing her friend again. She might as well have been on the other side of the world. Flora would stare at the little hare engraved into her wrist. It was the only real evidence that her bond with Iola had ever existed.

And then, out of the blue, late one Saturday afternoon, a knock came at the door. Flora groaned. She wondered if it might be Jehovah's Witnesses again. They always seemed to call at the weekend. She didn't really want to talk to them, but it felt rude giving them the brush-off and she would usually finish up stuck on the doorstep for half an hour or more. But she'd better answer the door, in case it was someone else. Something important.

Through the glass, Flora could see the solitary figure of a young woman. Maybe not Jehovah's Witnesses, then. They usually called in pairs. She wondered if it might be someone trying to sell Avon or something. She opened the door, preparing her usual, *I don't really need anything just now, thank you* speech.

Flora's jaw dropped. She had to do a double-take. She hardly recognised her friend, who had grown her hair and filled out. A gold stud sparkled in the centre of her lower lip, a matching hoop was threaded through one eyebrow and the thorny stem of a tattooed rose climbed her neck. But if nothing else, the purple monkey boots would have given her away. Iola stood on the step, grinning widely and carrying a Virgin Records bag in one hand and a bottle of Thunderbird wine in the other.

'Hello, stranger. Long time no see! Thought I'd look you up. Well, you gonna ask me in or what?'

And just like that, they picked up where they had left off. Flora had been hesitant about bringing Iola into the house, but Mum was in bed asleep. And God knew she'd missed her friend so much.

They sat on the living room floor, playing Bob Marley and David Bowie on low on Mum's old turntable and catching up as though Iola had just been on holiday for a fortnight. Flora had so many questions she wanted to ask her. Where to even start?

She learned that the boy at Smithfield House had said something unforgivable about Doreen – something which Iola didn't even want to repeat. Suffice to say, she'd seen red and launched herself at him. She wasn't sorry for what she'd done – the bastard deserved it, she said emphatically. Although she regretted the outcome, she told Flora that, in a way, it had probably done her good. Given her space to sort everything out in her head.

But Iola was remorseful for the way she'd behaved after leaving the squat.

'I was in *lurve* – or at least I thought I was. Wallowing in it; couldn't think of anything else – and look where it got me.' She grimaced. 'But I've grown up a lot since then, Flo. Actually got myself a job in a record shop – just part-time. Found a really cool fella – no strings attached. Done a lot of thinking, too. You were a good mate and I shut you out. I'm sorry.'

Flora felt her insides fold. *She* was sorry?

How could she possibly tell Iola what she'd done – about *everything* she'd done? Without a word, Flora put her arms around her. They squeezed one another for a moment, then pulled apart, laughing at the awkwardness of it all. It was time to look forward now, not dwell in the past.

Suddenly the future seemed a whole lot brighter.

CHAPTER 28

Stretmore, June 1983

From then on, it was as though the last two years had never happened. When she wasn't working, Iola came over to see Flora at least once a fortnight over the weekend, and on these occasions they would usually go into town for a couple of hours in the daytime, for drinks and a catch-up. For Flora, such outings were an important outlet. She hated college and hadn't really gelled with the other girls on the secretarial course, whose conversation seemed to revolve around the fit boys in the carpentry workshop and the latest fashions. It wasn't that she didn't like boys. Not really. But they never gave her a second glance, and on the rare occasion that one actually spoke to her for whatever reason, she became so flustered and tongue-tied, she wished the ground would swallow her up. It was easier to look aloof and avoid eye contact, and thus any potentially uncomfortable encounters. She kept herself to herself and, much as she had been throughout her school life, remained a lonely figure. Life with Mum could be hard at times, and being stuck at home so much, it was easy to forget that there was another world out there.

While Iola was outgoing and chatted freely to others whenever they went out, Flora always hung back and almost hid behind her friend. Iola tried to encourage her to drink alcohol a bit more, shake off her inhibitions. But Flora didn't much like drinking. It didn't agree with her; she found it just made her feel light-headed and tired rather than relaxed. Whenever they went to the pub, she preferred sitting at a quiet table sipping a Coke while Iola drank sweet cider; just her and Iola, talking about anything and everything. She was totally at ease in Iola's company and it was the only time she could really be herself.

Flora's favourite Saturday afternoons were the ones when Iola wasn't in the mood for booze. They would go instead to the cosy, old-fashioned coffee shop in the town square, the waft of freshly ground coffee almost intoxicating as they entered. The friendly waitress had got to recognise them and always gave the pair a warm welcome.

Cappuccinos, and Iola's cake of choice: huge Chelsea buns, which they would eke out for hours, sitting at the table in the window. It became a bit of a ritual. The waitress obviously realised they couldn't afford to keep returning to order more, but never asked them to move on.

Recently, Iola had made more of an effort to re-establish her connection with Stevie, which pleased Flora. Occasionally, he would meet up with them and join them for coffee. Stevie still lived with the same foster family and had grown into a sensible, pleasant lad. Neither Iola nor Stevie saw much of Carly, but on the few occasions Iola and her brother got together, they still had an obvious affection for one another. They were chalk and cheese in appearance: he, tall and well-built now, conventional in his choice of clothes; Iola, small, slight, and outlandish as ever. Their talk often turned to Doreen and things that had happened when they were young. Sometimes they would laugh, but Flora could sense the underlying sadness that reliving the past brought to the surface; for Iola, especially.

One wet Saturday in early summer, they had all been sitting next to the steamed-up window and Iola was subdued. Although usually upbeat, sometimes she would get like this: reflective and angry. It would have been Doreen's birthday a few days earlier and her mum had clearly been on her mind more than ever. Flora could empathise, knowing how sad she felt around the time of Daddy's birthday. She often wondered what he would look like now; how her own life would have turned out if she hadn't lost him so young.

Iola sat, staring at the table, picking chunks of icing off her bun and dropping them absently back onto the plate. She let out a long sigh.

'I'm sure if our Warren hadn't been taken, Mum might have turned a corner eventually. Don't you think so, Stevie? D'you ever wonder how differently our lives would have been if she was still with us?'

Flora didn't want to dwell on the what-ifs. She felt her cheeks warm whenever the subject of Warren's kidnapping was raised. She could think of nothing positive to contribute and sat in awkward silence, fixing her gaze on the café's 'Specials' board and hoping that Stevie would steer the conversation in another direction.

Stevie was more pragmatic. He puffed out his cheeks. 'Look, when I think back now, I reckon Mum was on a course of self-destruction anyway. Warren being taken just made it all happen sooner rather than later.' He shrugged. 'You've got to admit, she couldn't look after any of us properly, let alone herself. Yes, it was terrible, what happened with Warren. And bloody awful the way things panned out for Mum. But I think we've all turned out okay, all things considered.' He shot Flora a look that seemed to ask for her input but she could only manage a weak smile. This really wasn't any of her business, and she didn't want to get dragged into a discussion about the Chappells' family history – and certainly not about Warren.

Iola went very quiet. She dropped her eyes, fiddling with one of the cardboard coasters for a few seconds, her lips pursed. Flora wasn't sure if she was annoyed with Stevie or if she realised deep down that what he'd said was probably true. And the truth hurt. A moment later, she excused herself and headed for the bathroom.

With Iola gone briefly, Stevie dropped his head to his chest. 'Shit. I think I've upset her.' He leaned across the table suddenly, his eyes scanning Flora's face earnestly.

'She puts on this front, our Yol, but she's a bit of a lost soul underneath it all. Probably hit her the hardest of all of us when Mum died. I think she's built this rosy-coloured picture of her in her mind. S'pose it makes it easier to bear.' He smiled sadly.

'Yol's never had any other proper friends – always kept people at arm's length. I'm glad she's got you, Flo. If you ask me, that lad she's with is a real no-hoper.' He glanced across the café to see Iola reappearing from the

Ladies', shaking his head as he stooped suddenly to pick something up from under the table.

'I mean, Christ's sake – look at this.' He waved a five-pound note in the air, rolling his eyes. 'She earns next to nothing and she dropped a bloody fiver when she got up. Total scatterbrain. She'd lose her own head if it wasn't attached. Yol needs someone with a bit of common sense to look out for her. Someone like you, who actually cares about her.'

Flora had swelled with pride. She was beyond glad that Stevie thought her friendship with Iola so important. But as Iola re-joined them, her expression downcast, Flora's brief feeling of joy was sullied by the resurgence of gnawing guilt that lurked inside her: the knowledge that she had let Iola down. That she wasn't the perfect friend Stevie believed her to be. That maybe Iola deserved someone better.

Iola's on-off boyfriend, Levi, with whom she'd shared a hovel of a bedsit for the last six months, was decent enough but showed little drive or interest in finding work. Iola would shift from being madly in love to angry exasperation, frustrated that he was content to drift through life signing on and blowing his dole money in the pub over the weekend. Stevie had been right: he *was* a loser.

One warm Friday evening, Flora had arrived home from college to find Iola on her doorstep, her face streaked with tears.

'I've left him, Flo. I'm sick of having to pay for everything. I don't earn a fat lot myself and Levi's never got a penny to his name. He's never gonna change. My boss has a string of shops, so I've had a word and got myself a transfer to Rugby. Can I crash here for a couple of nights till I can find a flat?'

Flora knew Mum wouldn't be happy. But she also knew that much of the time these days, she was drowsy with medication and retreated to her room to rest, and if Iola was quiet and careful, she could probably get away with sleeping on her bedroom floor without Mum even knowing. And Flora had to step up to help her friend.

'Just a couple of nights, then. That's all. And house rules – no fags, no loud music.'

Iola had grinned. 'Scout's honour.'

True to her word, within two days, Iola had found a flat-share in town with a couple of girls a few years older than them. She had little stuff to move, other than what she'd brought with her from Levi's place in a holdall. But she was keen for Flora to meet her new flatmates and they were throwing her a sort of 'welcome' party. And naturally she wanted Flora to be there.

Flora was uneasy about attending. She didn't 'do' social gatherings and felt uncomfortable around people she didn't know. But Iola insisted, saying she was her oldest friend and she needed her.

'Lighten up, Flo. You might even enjoy yourself.'

Flora didn't tell Mum it was Iola's party. Instead, she said some people from college were having a few drinks in town and she had been invited along. Mum seemed pleased.

'I'm so glad you're mixing with your college friends, Flo. A nicer bunch I'm sure than your usual crowd.'

Flora bristled. Her 'usual crowd' was Iola, and Mum knew it. She had given up trying to persuade Flora not to see Iola, obviously hoping things would fizzle out naturally over time. But it wasn't going to happen.

Flora had put on make-up and attempted to style her naturally curly hair, which was a disaster. In the end, she covered it with a headscarf, tied in what she hoped was a trendy knot. She pulled on a baggy Bob Marley *Catch a Fire* T-shirt over a pair of skin-tight jeans that she'd bought in the sale from Chelsea Girl, and beige desert boots she'd picked up from the market. She'd frowned at her reflection in the bedroom mirror as she was about to leave to catch the bus. The glasses. They ruined everything, but she needed them. It was so frustrating.

Flora arrived early, or so she'd thought. She was hugged effusively, then whisked round by an ebullient and obviously tipsy Iola, anxious to introduce her to everyone. The flat was already heaving. It was only 7 p.m. and the gathering was just getting off the ground, but already people seemed drunk. The windows were wide open, the air stuffy with smoke and the smell of weed. Reggae pulsed from a ghetto-blaster brought in by one gangly lad with spiky, dyed orange hair, who was getting slowly stoned, sitting cross-legged in a pungent cloud on a floor cushion in the corner of the small sitting room.

Abandoned by Iola, Flora drank the can of strong white cider she'd been handed far too quickly, then went to grab another. She didn't much like the taste, but felt so awkward that she needed a prop. Soon, with four cans consumed in quick succession, the room was spinning and she felt slightly queasy. She stood with her back to the wall, looking round for Iola, but she had disappeared into the kitchen. Everyone else seemed to be talking and laughing. Flora felt like a fish out of water and totally invisible. As usual. She was tempted to slip away. Iola probably wouldn't even notice.

The boy who'd been sitting in the corner got up and swayed across the room to join her where she stood against the wall. Typically, Flora would have wanted to curl up into a ball if a boy approached her, but the building feeling of nausea had begun to override everything else.

'Hi. You into Marley, then?'

'Hmm? Oh. Yeah.'

'Wicked.' He offered her a blast of his spliff.

'No. Thanks, though.'

The boy shrugged. 'Suit yourself.' He took a deep drag, then looked her up and down with interest. All Flora could think of was getting outside for some fresh air. She couldn't see, let alone think, straight.

Before she knew what was happening, the boy had grabbed her by the hand.

'Come on. Let's get outta here.'

He pulled her into the corridor, past the bathroom where she could hear someone throwing up, down into a small bedroom. Everything was a blur. The door closed behind them. It was mercifully quiet. The boy smiled crookedly, his eyes half closed and dreamy-looking. Flora felt spaced-out. She glanced round, wondering what was happening here.

He sank onto the bed, pulling her roughly after him, then turning her over so that he was on top. Flora barely had time to think before his mouth was on hers, his tongue forced into her throat. She could feel one hand snaking its way inside her T-shirt, over her breast, the other pressing down between her legs.

And she screamed. She became hysterical, hitting out, raising her knee hard against his groin. The boy fell back, suddenly stunned into a state of sobriety.

'What the *fuck*—'

Before Flora knew anything else, the door burst open. Iola came tearing in. She took one look at Flora and began to rain blows onto the cowering boy, whose arms were wrapped protectively around his head. Eventually she stopped, standing back, her eyes burning with anger.

'Stay the fuck away from my mate, you scumbag.'

The boy wobbled to his feet. He wiped the blood dripping from his nose with the back of one hand and staggered to the door. He turned to look back at the pair of them, at Iola, whose arms were now wrapped around the weeping Flora.

'Pair of lezzers,' he called angrily, as he disappeared back down the corridor. Iola got up and closed the door. Flora was shaking from head to toe. Adrenaline seemed to have negated the sedating effects of the alcohol. But now she really did want to be sick.

'You okay?' Full of concern, Iola sat beside her on the bed, taking her hand. 'The *bastard*.'

'I – I need to go. I can't . . .'

She looked at Iola through her tears then and knew. That she would never, ever be able to go with a boy. That for her it was unthinkable. Not after what had happened to her all those years ago. Even the thought of sex that wasn't forced on her made every muscle, every nerve in her body clench with repulsion and fear.

But it didn't really matter. She didn't need a boy. All she needed was Iola.

And Iola would always be there for her.

CHAPTER 29

Stretmore, February 1984

In the months since the party, Iola had become incredibly protective of Flora, as though she'd suddenly woken up to her friend's vulnerability. She had moved into a different flat, sharing with one quiet, teetotal girl who was studying to be an architect. Drugs were no longer on the agenda and Iola had even toned down her drinking. She seemed to have become a responsible adult almost overnight and Flora was delighted. She had worried for so long about what might become of Iola and it seemed she no longer needed to. She had grown up.

It was Saturday morning. Last night had been particularly bad. Mum had complained of terrible pains in her hands and feet, with Flora kicking herself for forgetting to collect her pain relief from the pharmacy, since it meant neither of them had had much sleep. She and Iola had planned to go into town for an hour or so later in the day, but now she felt shattered. Iola was reaching to knock at the front door just as Flora was returning home from the chemist.

'Got to dash upstairs – Mum really needs her painkillers and she's run out. Stick the kettle on and make yourself a drink if you want. You can bring it up and wait in my room till I've seen to Mum. Shouldn't be long. But *please* don't make any noise.'

Iola raised her thumb. 'I'll be quiet as a mouse.'

Flora climbed the stairs, two at a time, to Mum's room. Seeing Mum lying there, her face twisted with pain, was like a punch to the gut. She helped her to sit up in the bed, Mum's complexion ashen as she gulped down the medicine. Flora knew when things were especially bad, as Mum only asked for the liquid morphine if she couldn't cope with the pain. She sat beside the bed, holding Mum's hand, watching anxiously until gradually her face began to relax.

'D'you want a cuppa?'

Mum shook her head, smiling faintly. She closed her eyes, her breathing growing slower and more even. It was such a relief to know that she wasn't suffering any more – for the time being, at least.

Flora crept from the room, closing the door quietly behind her. She crossed the landing. Through the gap in her own bedroom door, she grinned at the sight of Iola's purple boots dangling over the edge of the bed.

'It's okay, I think she's settling again now. The meds kick in pretty quickly . . .'

An awful cold feeling surged through Flora's veins. She realised she had gone out in such a rush to collect the medication that she'd left her wardrobe doors wide open, the contents laid bare for anyone who cared to look. Lined up in chronological order on the top shelf, the outward-facing spines of the journals containing more than a decade's worth of her thoughts and deeds. And Iola wouldn't have been able to resist sneaking a look. Flora felt every ounce of strength drain from her as her eyes fell on the diaries scattered across the floor, one opened on Iola's lap where she sat. Her friend's focus was trained firmly on the pages, her fingers tracing the same lines, over and over; lines scribed all those years ago in Flora's own spidery, childish hand.

'So, you've always shared everything with your beloved Ostara, then?' Iola lifted her eyes slowly to meet Flora's, her expression a mixture of incredulity and anger.

'I . . . it's just . . .' Flora could find no words. There was nothing she could say to make amends for what the girl must have seen.

'What the *fuck* have you done, Flo?' Iola spoke quietly at first, the hiss of rage beginning to build. 'What kind of freak are you?'

She jumped to her feet, thrusting the book beneath Flora's nose. Her face was white with fury, her mouth twisted into a snarl.

'Do you have *any* idea of the damage you've caused? What you've put me and my family through? You and your airy-fairy ideas. You stupid, *stupid* bitch!'

'I'm so sorry. So, so sorry . . .' Flora began to sob uncontrollably, her whole body quaking. She wanted this all to be a bad dream, one she'd wake from any minute and heave a grateful sigh of relief. But it was painfully, torturously real. She'd dreaded, agonised over, the possibility of this moment for so long. She had been found out.

Flora sank to her knees, covering her face with her hands as hot tears coursed down her cheeks. 'I couldn't – you have to understand . . .'

'*Understand*? Are you fucking kidding me? Oh, I understand all right. That you're a coward and a weirdo and you wormed your way into my life and pretended to be my friend, and all the time . . .' Iola flung the notebook across the room, her dark eyes ablaze. Flora shrank back, fully expecting her to throw a punch as she lunged towards her.

Iola bent down, one arm raised; her chin stopping just inches short of Flora's head. Hurt, contempt, anger: every emotion running through her was etched into Iola's face as she glowered down at her.

'And to think I've always stuck up for you. I even lost sleep, worrying about you after that party. *Poor old Flo*. I should have "Mug" tattooed across my forehead. I can't believe I've been such an idiot. Well, you're on your own from now on. Don't ever come near me or my family again, d'you hear. Not *ever*!'

The bedroom wall shook with the reverberation of the door as Iola kicked it on her way out. Flora listened as she thundered down the stairs, fully expecting the glass in the front door to have shattered from the force with which it had been slammed. Still shaking, she got up and went out onto the landing, peering down into the hall. Through the frosted pane, she could see Iola's furious silhouette disappearing at speed up the path.

'Flo?' Her mother's voice, weak and drowsy, came through the wall. 'What was that noise?'

Flora cleared her throat. 'It's okay, Mum. Just a lorry going past. Go back to sleep.'

She stood for a moment, weeping silently, her back pressed against the landing wall. Why the hell hadn't she been more careful – kept the diaries locked away somewhere more secure, hidden from view? She thought in shame of everything written in there, every bit of evidence about her failure as a human being. As a friend. It didn't matter that she'd only been a child. She had never felt so utterly wretched. Iola was right: she was a coward. A total waste of space. The only true friend she'd ever had wanted nothing more to do with her now. And who could blame her? At that moment, she was tempted to hurl herself from the banister.

But then what would become of Mum?

CHAPTER 30

Little Hambley, November 2001

Although Flora had wondered previously what on earth she would do with a whole day to herself, she now had a focus. The chill air in her bedroom wasn't conducive to a lie-in; she had been awake since 6.30 a.m., wrapped in the bedclothes, the tip of her nose like an ice-cube. Eventually, she decided it was pointless trying to go back to sleep and launched herself reluctantly from the bed. After feeding Rufus and cleaning out his litter box, she washed as quickly as she could under the weak spray of the shower, its jet alternating between bracing and scalding hot. She dressed warmly in clean jeans and a roll-neck sweater and made her way downstairs. The clock in the hall chimed in the hour. Still only eight o'clock. It was going to be a long, but hopefully insightful, day.

Mr Homity was coming from the kitchen, a mug of

something steaming in his hand, his tongue flicking in concentration between his opened lips. He was almost slithering along the corridor; or at least, that was how it seemed to Flora. She had never forgotten the feel of his hand on her arm, cold and clammy. It made her skin crawl whenever she encountered him.

'Good morning, Miss Lanyon.'

For some reason, despite her request, he still refused to call her by her first name. Maybe it seemed too familiar; too friendly.

'Have you any plans for the day?'

'I thought I might go for a walk this morning, explore a little. Maybe have a look in your library later, if that's okay?'

'Of course. I'm heading there myself now, just to enjoy my coffee, then I'll be going up to see to Agnes. She was still asleep when I looked in a few minutes ago, so I thought I'd take a quick break before the onslaught. No peace for the wicked.' He smiled thinly.

Flora shuddered a little. She wished him a good morning and went to make herself tea and toast in the kitchen. After, she washed up the breakfast things and looked out of the window. It was a dull, grey day. A spectral layer of mist hung ominously over the pond. The curtains to the annexe were still drawn, so Hector probably wasn't up yet. It seemed he rarely emerged before eleven o'clock. Flora was more than happy about that. The presence of one Homity male was quite enough at any one time. Apart from playing music loudly, she wasn't sure what Hector actually did all day – and after speaking to Rita, was equally unsure whether she really wanted to know. But she needed some excuse to knock on his door in a short while. She would have to think of a plausible reason.

What the barman in The Jack and Jester had told her had been going round and round her head. The chatty, tattooed woman he'd described, with the facial piercings and purple boots, who'd sat at the bar two summers ago, commenting that the pub was about as unlike her local as it was possible to be. And how, after a few drinks, she'd leaned in and said she was keen to get a good look at the young man living up at Mill House; how she'd tapped her nose and wasn't saying any more at that point, but that he should keep his eyes and ears open for some interesting news about the place very soon.

But no news had emerged. And the barman hadn't seen the woman again.

Flora put on her coat and boots and took a stroll down to the village again. It appeared different in the harsh morning light; starker, somehow. She reached the high street and glanced from left to right. Unfolding the sheet of paper she'd been carrying in her pocket, she reread the name. From the Yellow Pages, it was the only B&B she could find actually listed in Little Hambley itself. She looked around. An elderly, round-shouldered woman in a long, camel-coloured overcoat and brown felt fedora was crossing the street a short way ahead. She smiled and nodded as she passed by, raising her walking stick a few inches off the ground in greeting.

'Excuse me,' Flora called after her. The woman stopped and turned slowly.

'Yes?'

'I wonder – do you live round here?'

'Born and bred.' The woman's eyes drifted with interest from Flora's shoulders to her footwear. Flora shifted uncomfortably.

'I'm looking for a guest house – Lime Tree Lodge? Would you happen to have any idea where it is, please?'

'Ah. It used to be a little way up there – just on the outskirts of the village.' The old woman pointed with her stick in the opposite direction to the pub. 'Towards the church, on the right. The couple who ran it came from Canada originally, but the lady sold up and moved back to be with her family after her husband passed away; in August, if I remember rightly. Such a pity. It's a private residence again now.'

'Oh.' Flora's heart sank. 'That's a bit of a blow.'

'Oh dear – were you looking for somewhere to stay? There's a very nice hotel just off the high street. Quite reasonably priced, I believe.' The old woman's sharp blue eyes seemed to be drinking in everything about Flora's appearance and it made her squirm.

'No, no. I was looking for someone who might've been staying in the B&B, actually. Or at least, hoping to find out where that person could have gone. Never mind.' She thought for a moment. 'Are there any other guest houses in the village?'

'No, I'm afraid not.'

Flora blew out a long breath. 'Oh well. Back to square one, then.'

'That's a shame. Well, I wish you luck. Are you just visiting Little Hambley?'

'I'm actually living in at Mill House, caring for Mrs Homity.'

The old woman's face lit up. 'Dear Agnes! How is she

doing? We used to be great friends. I haven't seen her for, ooh, at least a year; maybe more. I'd heard her health wasn't too good and did try to call on her once, but Abraham wasn't very forthcoming. Said she was resting and didn't even ask me in. No visitors welcome up at that house these days, it would seem.' She raised an eyebrow.

'She's not too well at all, I'm afraid. That's why I'm helping to look after her.'

'I'm very sorry to hear that. Poor soul. She's had so much to contend with over the years.' She shook her head sadly. 'I suppose you know what happened to Xanthe, do you?'

'Yes. She told me all about it. So sad.'

'Such a happy, lively little girl. A terrible tragedy. She would have been the same age as my own daughter, had she lived. I'm a great-grandmother now. I don't expect poor Agnes can even hope to have grandchildren, with that son of hers.' She pulled a face. 'An odd chap, if ever I met one.'

Flora smiled weakly. She looked round as a middle-aged man wearing a checked, peaked cap walked past, nodding and smiling to the old woman, who returned the gesture, watching for a moment as he moved along the high street. She turned back to Flora.

'I'm sorry, I didn't introduce myself. I'm Marjorie – Marjorie Clewes. I knew Agnes well when we were girls. Sad that we've lost touch. Happens so often as one gets older, I suppose.'

Flora shook her outstretched hand. 'I'm Flora; Lanyon. I've only been here a few days. Still finding my feet, really.'

'Yes. Yes, I suppose it must take some adjustment, moving in with complete strangers. But Agnes is the loveliest person.' Marjorie paused. 'And how is Abraham?' The tone of the woman's voice had altered – almost imperceptibly, but there was a definite edge to the question. 'I don't often walk into the village these days, but I've only seen him out once or twice over the last couple of years. He's always in such a hurry. Never was very sociable.' She put a gloved hand to one side of her mouth and leaned forwards. 'They were an unlikely match, those two. Between you and me, I always felt Agnes could have done much better for herself.'

Flora wasn't sure how to respond. 'Mr Homity seems . . . a very private person. I think his health must be reasonable, as he's still able to look after Mrs Homity on my days off, which is why I'm here and not back at the house.'

'Hmm. Well, I do hope he's caring for her properly.' She looked thoughtful. 'But at least she has you to keep an eye on things.' She raised a hand to wave at someone suddenly, her face breaking into a smile. 'Must fly, I'm afraid. I'm meeting my daughter for coffee and I've just seen her Land Rover pull up. Enjoy your free time, young lady.'

'Thank you. Enjoy your coffee! Nice to meet you.'

'You too – Flora, wasn't it? Please give my love to Agnes, won't you. Tell her – tell her I hope she feels better very soon.'

Flora knew that wasn't likely, but decided not to elaborate about Mrs Homity's failing health. There seemed to be little point. She watched for a few seconds as Marjorie carried on up the high street, then, feeling suddenly directionless, turned despondently and trudged slowly away from the village and back towards Mill House. As she reached the stone steps, the bleak sight of the old building backed against the grey sky brought the prickle of gooseflesh to her arms and neck. She stopped for a moment, suddenly and inexplicably overcome by fear, her eyes drinking in everything about the place: the dark waters where a child had once drowned; the annexe and its waterwheel; the dense, eerie woods that concealed a chapel and its graveyard. Every instinct she possessed told her she needed to cut her losses and get away from there. But she couldn't. Not yet. There was something important she needed to do before she could move on. The need to find Iola and make things right had become almost an obsession.

It was still only quarter past ten. While waiting for Hector to surface, Flora decided to make herself a coffee and take it into the library. She didn't expect to find anything useful in there, but hoped there might be something worth reading to distract her from her situation and the oppressive atmosphere within the house. She intended to choose a book then smuggle it back to her room, to cuddle up with Rufie and try to block out the world for a while.

She hated having nothing constructive to do – and the fact that she had no one to do anything with. She'd never really dwelled on it before. Not often, anyway. She'd been so used to being busy caring for Mum for most of her adult life that free time wasn't something she was accustomed to – or relished. And now there were so many regrets to lament, compounded by the grief of losing Mum and her only real purpose in life. Here she was, in her thirties, with no friends or family; no home of her own, nor any prospect of meeting someone who'd want to share their life with her. She hated the way she looked; hated her self-consciousness and clumsy gait, and the fact that her eyes, while her best feature (or so Mum had always told her), would always be hidden behind glasses. Contact lenses would never be an option – the optician had suggested she try them once, but she'd found them intolerable. So without the means to buy anything more flattering, she was stuck with the same, owl-eyed frames she'd worn for the last decade, and they put years on her.

Flora couldn't face writing in her diary today. It had always been one way of helping her make sense of stuff; an outlet to express herself since she had no one to confide in. But her thoughts as she wrote them now only seemed to bounce back at her cruelly, reminding her of her many mistakes; of everything she'd lost. Of the uncomfortable position she was in. Every time she put pen to paper, it was making her more unhappy than ever. She hoped and prayed that her time at Mill House would soon be in the past.

The library was cold. Mr Homity had obviously not thought it worth lighting a fire, as he was only going to be in there briefly. With only a small window at the far end opposite Mr Homity's desk, the contents of the room were in shadow. It felt gloomy; almost threatening. Flora switched on the light and scanned around. Satisfied there was no one lurking in any recesses, she entered more confidently. But where to even start looking? She decided to work from left to right. Trying hard not to spill any of her coffee, she walked slowly past the bookshelves, clutching the mug in both hands.

She was unsurprised, given Mr Homity's meticulous nature, to find everything catalogued in alphabetical order in each of the three wide sections across the back wall. Reference; fiction; non-fiction. All with helpful subcategories. She homed straight in on the fiction and started with the bottom shelf. She looked up at the dizzying height of the wooden ladders and felt woozy, deciding she would have to select something from lower down, whether it offered the best stories or not.

Her heart gave a little jump as her eyes fell on a whole shelf, only a quarter of the way up, devoted to folklore. She quickly finished her coffee and cast around for somewhere to deposit the mug before taking a closer look. On the table in front of the fire was a small stack of coasters in a silver holder. She went across to take one, lifting her eyes to the portrait of Mrs Homity hanging above the mantelpiece as she did so. Along the marble shelf over the fire were four other framed photographs, interspersed with two liver and white ceramic spaniels, one facing left, the other right. A large brass mantel clock ticked away slowly in the centre. One picture was of Hector from when he must have been about twelve, stiff and grim in his school uniform, his hair slightly dishevelled. There was a black and white image of a small, smiling baby with a halo of white curls, clutching an old-fashioned rattle. *Not* Hector, Flora assumed. Another was a group picture from Mr and Mrs Homity's wedding, with the happy couple glued together and beaming in the foreground. She wondered if Marjorie Clewes had been a guest.

But it was the last picture that drew her gaze and made her catch her breath. Carefully, with quivering fingers, she lifted it from the shelf to take a closer look. A fading colour photo of a sharp-featured man in a wide-lapelled seventies-style brown suit with flared trousers and a huge-collared, open-neck shirt, posing casually against the bonnet of a Daimler Sovereign. His dark hair was combed to one side and covered his ears, the tan Hush Puppies he wore crossed at the ankle. Her eyes took in every pixel of his face; every minute detail of the shiny blue vehicle.

The polished chrome grille. The RAC membership badge. She peered more closely at the registration plate. The letters *R* and *F* could easily have been altered with black tape or a marker pen to the *B* and *E* she had engraved on her memory. But the last three characters were identical.

And she knew, with absolute, horrific certainty, then; that everything she'd suspected was true. Without a shadow of a doubt. Because here was the man she had expected to answer the door when she first arrived at Mill House.

And here was the same blue car that, all those years ago, had whisked away little Warren Chappell.

CHAPTER 31

Little Hambley, November 2001

Carefully removing the picture from its frame, Flora read and reread the handwritten words on the back. *Kenneth – Cheltenham 1972*. She stood staring in disbelief; for how long, she wasn't sure. Thoughts tessellated in her mind and the image they formed was an ugly one. *Kenneth Ogilvy*. Had Mr Homity's close friend been the man who had taken Warren? But why?

Eventually, she replaced the photo in its frame and, grabbing her coffee cup, stumbled from the library, her heart racing. She went back to the kitchen, all the while turning over what she had just discovered. From the window, she was surprised to see Rita's old bike, with the basket attached to its handlebars, propped up against the far wall. She washed the mug and was about to place it on the draining board when, as if from nowhere, a magpie landed on the sill, tapping loudly at the glass with its beak. The mug fell from her hand, landing on the stone floor and smashing into several pieces. Just as quickly as it had appeared, the bird tilted its head and took flight, landing on the apex of the annexe roof.

One for sorrow.

That was what Granny Jean had always said. A bad omen. A shiver of dread passed through her.

The curtains in the annexe twitched. So, Hector was up, then. Although slightly terrified at the prospect, Flora was more determined than ever to go inside. But after the shock of the photo and now the magpie, she needed to compose herself first. She found a dustpan and brush in the cupboard underneath the sink and swept up the shattered fragments of the mug. She decided to go and look for Rita. What Flora wanted more than anything right now was the company of someone – *anyone* – who wasn't connected directly to Mill House. Someone *normal*. Despite what Yaz had told her.

She followed the sound of the vacuum cleaner and, climbing the stairs, found Rita hoovering the landing. She looked round to see Flora standing there and smiled, switching off the machine.

'Morning.'

'Hello. I didn't think you came on Thursdays.'

'No, it's not my usual day, but we're visiting hubby's sister in Devon for a couple of days next week, so I'm doing a bit extra before we go. Everything okay? You look like you've seen a ghost.'

'Bloody magpie just landed on the window ledge and frightened the life out of me. I smashed a cup.' Flora wasn't sure whether to mention the photograph.

'Don't worry. They've got plenty more.' Rita studied

Flora's haunted face, her brow creasing slightly. 'You sure that's all it is?'

Flora nodded, glancing sideways. 'Will you – are you cleaning at Hector's today?'

'It'll get a quick once-over when I've finished up here.' She nodded towards the bedrooms. 'I'll give Mrs Homity's room a good bottoming when he comes out; change her sheets and stuff. Takes Mr H a while to sort her out these days, but he says he still wants to do it while he can.' She chuckled suddenly. 'Eww, that sounded a bit iffy, didn't it!'

Flora laughed nervously.

Rita cocked her head and gave a half smile. 'You been in Hector's den yet? Seen his exhibits?'

'No. I haven't been invited yet.' She paused, remembering the clause in the contract. But this was important. 'Erm, I did wonder: seeing as you have to go in at some point today – could I come with you? I'd rather not go on my own.'

''Course you can.' Rita paused. 'Isn't it your day off, though? Thought you'd have wanted to get out for a few hours.'

'I – I just wanted a restful day today. I was going to get a book from the library and put my feet up for a bit.'

'Whatever floats your boat. I'm not much for reading, myself. Always gives me a rotten head. I can just about manage a few pages of *Woman's Own* when I'm at the hairdresser's.' She rolled her eyes. 'Anyway, I'll crack on here and give you a shout when I'm done. So you'll be in the library, then?'

Flora thought for a moment. 'Yeah. See you down there in a bit.'

Rita moved further along the landing and resumed her cleaning. Flora paused outside Mrs Homity's room. Despite the noise of the hoover, she could hear Mr Homity's voice filtering through the wall. The words were muffled, but the tone was impatient. A brief silence, followed by his wife's quiet, pleading response. Flora wondered what was going on; whether Agnes was resisting her medication again. Poor woman.

Flora popped her head round her own bedroom door to see Rufus stretched out beneath the window, cleaning himself. He looked up briefly, then resumed licking his hind leg diligently. Guiltily, she thought how bored and lonely he must be, shut in the room all day. She was about to go across to give him a fuss when something caught her eye, pulling her up sharply.

Her suitcase, which had been pushed completely under the bed, was jutting out. Just a little, only a corner protruding. But enough for Flora to know that it had been moved. She drew in her breath. On hands and knees, she slid the case out and lifted it onto the bed. The steel clasps which held it shut were stiff and it always hurt her fingertips to pop them open, but she was so focused on what she might find that she didn't notice.

Her eyes took in every visible crevice of the case. An effort had obviously been made to replace things as they were, but her belongings had definitely been disturbed. Frantically she rifled through, trying to see if anything was missing. Not that she had anything worth taking. The few budget toiletries she had were already on the bathroom shelf. Any clothes she owned were cheap and functional, and much of what she'd brought with her had once belonged to Mum, who'd been the same size as Flora until all the weight had dropped from her. It helped to keep Mum close, somehow; wearing things that still smelled of her. Of home.

She fumbled open the tote bag in which she'd wrapped her diary and a single, frayed cardboard wallet of old photos. Flipping over the first page of the notebook, she felt a surge of blood to her head. There, at the bottom corner, faint but distinctive, was a thumbprint.

Who did it belong to? And more importantly, how much had they seen?

CHAPTER 32

Little Hambley, November 2001

Still reeling, Flora went slowly back down to the library. She felt nauseous. Desperate to clear her mind, she returned to the folklore section and selected the book with the most appealing cover and title she could find – *The Portal to Albios* – but it was a futile exercise. She sat at the table near the hearth, but without a fire the room was cold and uninviting. She stared at the pages without absorbing one word, her eyes drifting constantly to the photo on the mantelshelf. It was impossible to relax: someone had been snooping through her things and she felt even more exposed and vulnerable than ever.

'Right then, ready for the experience of a lifetime?'

Flora started at the sound of Rita's voice, almost falling off the chair. She turned to see the woman standing, watching her from the doorway, a plastic toolbox containing various cleaning implements and products suspended from one hand. Flora wondered how long she had been there.

'Shall we?'

Flora closed the book, forcing a smile as she joined her.

'Did you find anything worth reading in there? All looks ancient to me.'

'There's plenty actually, but I couldn't really concentrate for some reason. Lots going round my head at the moment.' She darted another look at the man in the photograph; the blue car. *That same blue car*.

Rita looked at her curiously but said nothing. Together, they walked back through the dingy hallway and out into the damp morning air.

'Just say you're helping me if he asks,' Rita told her as they climbed the slippery steps to the annexe. The rush of water was louder than ever; the white surface bubbling angrily. Flora could feel the chill of ozone as they stood at the entrance. Normally she would have found it exhilarating, but today it felt like some sort of threat. A warning.

As if he'd heard someone approaching, Hector suddenly switched on his music. The eerie introductory notes of *Danse Macabre* whined from the other side of the door, the strings getting louder as he turned up the volume. Flora winced.

'Jesus Christ.' Rita pulled a face, hammering on the varnished oak door with a heavy fist. 'It's a wonder he's not deaf.'

Flora was amazed Hector could actually hear the door above the din, but within seconds he had flung it wide. His tartan dressing gown was flapping open and he was brandishing a conductor's baton in one hand. His hair was wild; his eyes even wilder.

'Can't you see I'm busy!'

'And a good morning to you, too.' Rita, unperturbed, led the way past him into the hallway, beckoning with her head for Flora to follow. There was a closed door to their left and another straight ahead. Beneath their feet was the original terracotta-tiled flooring, with plain magnolia walls throughout and old, dark beams visible above their heads; a full-length, frameless mirror hung next to a row of brass coat hooks to their right, which held just one heavy brown overcoat and a peaked cap. Adjacent to this was the entrance to the music room. Through the open doorway, Flora could see a music stand in the centre of the floor on a sort of plinth, and huge speakers hanging in the corners. Hector stepped back against the wall, staring after them as they entered.

'What's *she* doing here?'

'Who's she? The cat's mother? Flora's helping me.'

He eyed Flora suspiciously. 'Why? You normally manage perfectly well on your own.'

Rita tutted. 'Not that it's any of your concern, but I need to be quick today. I've got other things to do. You know I don't usually come on Thursdays.'

Flora confirmed this with a solid nod of her head, glancing uncertainly at the stick he was wielding. Hector gave her a look of pure contempt.

'But her job's to help Mummy. Why isn't she doing that, if that's what she's paid for?'

'It's my day off. I didn't have anything on, so I offered to help. I'm sure Rita would do the same for me.' Flora shot a pleading look at her companion.

'Absolutely.'

Hector glowered at them both.

'We'd better get on, then.' A hint of a smirk on her lips, Rita winked briefly at Flora. 'Don't mind us. As you were.'

'Whatever.' He pushed past them sullenly, disappearing back into the room from where the music was still playing and slamming the door behind him. There was a brief respite, and then the screech of violins started over from the beginning.

Flora looked around. The narrow passageway they'd passed through had brought them out into a sort of low-ceilinged anteroom, about five feet square, with yet another door opposite them. There was a low, dark-stained bookshelf to the right, on which sat a sizeable glass dome containing a small, cross-eyed tawny owl with pitifully sparse plumage. Its twisted talons dangled in mid-air above a wire stand, around which several feathers appeared to have been recently shed. To the left, a glass case which ran the width of the wall held a misshapen, badly stuffed muntjac deer, no more than three feet in length and maybe two feet tall, the dried leaves and twigs surrounding the creature clearly an attempt to create a woodland setting. The eyes, bulging from their sockets, resembled dried horse chestnuts; the misaligned jaws fell slightly open to reveal tusks protruding at an unnatural-looking angle.

'Dear God.' Flora pulled a face.

'You ain't seen nothing yet. Just wait till you get into his hobby room.'

Flora followed Rita through the next door into a room at least double the size of the previous one, and what she assumed was the main living area. The magnolia theme continued. A black wood-burning stove stood beneath the arch of the old brick fireplace which occupied one corner, its flue pipe disappearing into the chimney. On the opposite side of the space, below the large window which overlooked Mill House, a sagging brown Dralon three-piece suite spread itself out around an ancient bulky TV set upon a teak cabinet. Several copies of *Taxidermy Monthly* magazine were scattered across the floor in front of the settee, along with two crushed beer cans and an empty crisp packet. Only one example of Hector's handiwork had found its way into here: a mangy-looking Yorkshire terrier, sitting up to beg from a patchwork leather footstool just inside the door, the poor thing's uneven eyes staring as if it had just received an electric shock, its mouth preserved in an eternal, lopsided snarl.

'He was the original victim,' Rita remarked. 'Apparently after his first pet was stuffed professionally, Hector thought he could do just as good a job himself. And after that there was no stopping him.'

Flora's eyes took in every detail of the disfigured dog. 'Just as well he doesn't rely on it to make a living.'

'Brace yourself. The hobby room's through here.'

Rita carried on through the narrow archway at the far end of the room. They had to duck a little and appeared to have come to a dead end. It was darker in here: a windowless, exposed brickwork square beyond which a short flight of steps descended to a grey metal door. The temperature had dropped noticeably. Flora felt a shiver of dread. It was as though they were entering a crypt. She looked on apprehensively as Rita turned the handle.

The heavy door had some sort of seal around it and made a swishing noise as it opened. They were hit by a blast of chilled air and an overpowering chemical smell. Flora clapped a hand over her mouth and nose. Rita raised a hand to the wall and a cold, white beam of fluorescent light flickered into action.

Flora surveyed their surroundings, her eyes widening in horror. In the centre of the windowless room stood a wide, stainless-steel-topped workbench, covered with various surgical implements, glass jars, a tape measure and lengths of wire. Laid out next to a plastic tray containing some sort of liquid was a mean-looking electric drill.

From a chain attached to the ceiling, a partially skinned pheasant dangled by its feet. The bird's plumage was turned inside out; the head, stripped of feathers and flesh, was separated from the body and lying on its side on the table below, next to the fanned-out wings. On a wooden board to the far end of the bench lay the opened-out, flattened skins of two white rats, most likely the ones Flora had discovered in the freezer.

The room, at least eight feet by six, was filled with glass cabinets piled in tiers along the two longest walls, containing a variety of dead animals. The smallest cupboard at the top was devoted to frogs and toads; grass snakes, a couple of salamanders. Others held birds: a sparrowhawk; robins, starlings, wood pigeons, magpies. A jay. But it was the mammals that looked particularly bizarre. Two foxes, an adult and a cub; a badger; a large tabby cat; rabbits, stoats, moles, hedgehogs. Grey squirrels. All stuffed in unnatural-looking poses, ill-positioned eyes staring horribly; not one looking remotely as it would have in life. The scene was grotesque.

Rita looked at Flora and screwed up her face. 'I told you.' She pointed to her temple with her finger and described a circle. '*Not all there*,' she mouthed.

'Now I know *exactly* what he does all day.' Flora shuddered. 'Where does he get them all?'

'I know some have expired naturally – on the road; or killed by other animals and that. But let's just say quite a few have been helped on their way.' Rita tipped her head forwards, looking straight ahead. Flora followed her gaze, which settled on a large, military-style camouflage net, spread out across the back wall. She pulled in her chin, swallowing hard.

'You mean . . .?'

'He's got some sort of chemical mix – instant death, apparently. Uses it to keep a steady supply; you know, when he hasn't found anything he wants. Mr H orders the stuff in for him from some pest control place up north.'

Flora covered her mouth in shocked disbelief. Bad enough that Hector had chosen such a gruesome pastime, let alone the fact he actually killed innocent animals for the purpose. And that his father actively supported his behaviour.

Her eyes travelled unwillingly to the viscera of the pheasant. 'Can we get out of here? It's giving me the creeps.'

Rita nodded. 'Just thought you ought to know what you're dealing with. I don't *think* he'd do anything, but . . . well, probably best to keep a close eye on that cat of yours.'

Flora's stomach clenched. She felt the need to keep Rufie safe more keenly than ever. The thought of what Hector might do if he was left alone with him made her blood run cold.

CHAPTER 33

Little Hambley, November 2001

They went back through the living room. Hector was still conducting, a rousing rendition of 'O Fortuna'. Rita tutted and led the way into the other room off the hallway, which turned out to be a kitchenette – bare brick walls and the same terracotta floor, a stainless-steel sink, white melamine work surface with basic white units, an electric cooker badly in need of a wipe, and a small fridge.

Perfectly adequate for Hector, Flora thought. And perfectly manageable. A mug of cold tea, a skin forming over its surface, had been left on the draining board. A used butter knife and open jar of marmalade still remained on the worktop next to a half-eaten slice of toast.

Flora's eyes took in everything. Hector, she realised, was a slob. He had been fortunate enough to be provided with his own place and it seemed he almost treated it with contempt. On the far side of the room the door was ajar, a spiral staircase visible on the other side. She wondered, with a shudder, what delights lay in the other parts of the house.

Rita seemed to have read her mind. 'I'll clean up in here. You go and have a look upstairs, if you like – he's got a great view from his bedroom window.'

Flora moved towards the door and let out a shriek.

'Oh, I forgot to say – you don't mind spiders, do you?'

Rita's warning came too late. In the vestibule at the foot of the stairs stood a large terrarium, set on the top level of a two-tiered metal stand. From the midst of the foliage and soil a furry black and orange tarantula, at least the size of a large man's hand, had emerged.

Although she wouldn't have wanted one as a pet, Flora wasn't unnerved by spiders as a rule, as long as they weren't too close; at least, not the regular, common or garden variety. But the sight of this striped creature scuttling from nowhere had caught her off-guard. And it was huge. Pinned to the wall, she watched as the thing began to scale the sides of the glass, leaving a silken trail in its wake. Flora froze for a moment. Thankfully there was a lid over the tank. She let out a long, slow sigh of relief, and leaned forwards to take a closer look. The Perspex case beneath was rammed with chirping, hopping crickets, all clearly destined to provide the spider with a tasty meal. Flora stared in horrified fascination as, with its front legs, the tarantula enveloped one of the unfortunate insects that had already been dropped into its enclosure and began to devour the poor thing alive. It was a gruesome sight.

Still shuddering, Flora made her way hesitantly up the open wooden stairs. She found spiral staircases tricky to navigate and clung onto the cast-iron banister, placing her feet with care on the open tread. Immediately opposite the top of the stairs was a small, white-tiled bathroom with a basic white suite and a glass shower enclosure. At a glance, the towel bundled on the floor aside, it all looked infinitely more inviting than her own bathroom in the main house.

The landing was carpeted in a coarse coir which continued into Hector's bedroom, visible through the open doorway. Flora could see an unmade double bed, looking as if someone had been fighting in it, the pillows discarded on the floor at its foot. Clothes were scattered on and around a dark wooden rocking chair in the corner. Other items exploded from a tall mahogany chest of drawers, which stood against the wall next to the window boasting the wonderful views.

But the sound of running water drew Flora towards the room to her left with an almost irresistible force. She pushed open the door and gasped. The room was spacious but unfurnished. A beamed ceiling was supported in four places by sturdy oak columns rising from bare floorboards. The flooring disappeared on the far side of the room, replaced with a large, rectangular section of glass, which met a thick floor-to-ceiling glass wall. Flora walked across and placed both palms on the glass in awe. The sensation was surreal, like being suspended in mid-air, and it made her slightly giddy. She looked down at the frothing water below, which concealed the lower part of the hefty iron waterwheel. Both the wheel and its complicated-looking mechanism, which stood against the bare brick wall adjacent to the viewing window, turned slowly and steadily. Flora wasn't sure how they worked and wondered if they still served any real purpose. She'd had no idea this was inside the house. From outside, the exposed part of the wheel concealed the glass completely. She felt compelled to stand, motionless, staring down at the water rushing beneath the house. It was incredible; mesmerising.

Flora remained there for a few minutes, marvelling at the construction of the wheel and the genius idea of incorporating it into the interior of the building. It was a unique feature. She couldn't envisage either Hector or his father having had the imagination to propose such a thing. Perhaps she was wrong.

As Flora stared down into the depths, she thought she saw a flash of something mauve surface through the bubbling foam, but just as quickly it receded. Maybe a scrap of discarded paper or material had blown into the water and become caught in the paddles of the wheel. Mildly interested, she tried to locate the object again but it had vanished. Was it possible she'd imagined it, staring for so long at one spot as she had been? But then, there it was again: more of it revealed than before. And not a piece of paper at all, but something far more solid. Something oddly familiar. Flora gasped and peered downwards, but once more, the thing had disappeared from view.

Inexplicably she had the immediate sense of being watched. The back of her neck prickled uncomfortably. Spinning round, she fully expected to see Hector standing behind her. But she was quite alone. She shivered. It was that odd feeling; the one Mum would always describe as *someone walking over your grave*. She glanced back at the water and felt suddenly uneasy. For no reason that she could justify, Flora no longer felt comfortable being in that room alone. It was time to leave.

She moved across into Hector's room. The cacophony of violins boomed unrelentingly from below, a constant background drone. It put Flora on edge even more, and she prayed he would soon tire of it.

As she pushed the door to Hector's room wide open, Flora started, catching her breath at the sight of a small, light brown border terrier with a dark face, its ears slightly raised. Initially, she thought the dog was asleep. The animal lay prone, chin on its paws, on a sheepskin rug next to the bed. An engraved metal tag hung from the red leather collar round its neck. Flora approached gingerly, bending to read the inscription.

Toby. At once she realised that this must be the adored pet that Hector's parents had had stuffed for him, given pride of place in his room. It was far more realistic than his own attempts, but still macabre. She stood staring in distaste for a moment, then shook herself and picked her way past the furry little corpse over to the window.

The air in the bedroom smelled sour, and, ignoring the cold air, she opened the frame as wide as it would go and leaned out. There was indeed a fabulous outlook: Mill House and its wide pond, the road and occasional passing car below clearly visible; the church spire, even the rooftops of the buildings in the village. Being so high, every field and tree in surrounding Little Hambley was in sight, stretching for miles around the property. It was like being at the top of the world.

Music continued to thump through the floor. Flora

turned, scanning round the room in disgust, her eyes constantly drawn to the dead dog. That aside, she was appalled that Hector had left everything in such a squalid mess. He may have been privileged, but he hadn't been brought up well. It was almost as though he'd done it deliberately, knowing Rita would tidy up after him. Even though there was a wicker laundry basket in one corner, stinking socks and underwear had been piled just behind the door; chocolate bar wrappers and an empty tube of Pringles were discarded randomly on the floor on the opposite side of the bed to the dog, nearer to the window. The three half-emptied glasses of squash sitting on the mahogany bedside table had left sticky rings. It was a wonder he was able to care for his pet tarantula, since he seemed incapable of taking any responsibility for himself and his possessions. She was thankful he had chosen a spider and not another living canine.

Thoughtless and disrespectful. This was clearly the attitude fostered in Hector by Mr Homity. It made her blood boil. Poor Rita. She was trying to do everything in a rush in time for her holiday. She didn't need this.

Flora removed the tumblers and tipped the squash into the basin in the bathroom. Blobs of dried toothpaste were stuck to the bowl and the tap. She rolled her eyes. In disgust, she flushed the toilet, which Hector had clearly found a task beyond him. She rinsed out a cleaning sponge from the cupboard beneath the sink and wiped the little bedside cabinet. She glared round again in irritation, then pulled back the duvet and straightened the sheets. Retrieving the pillows, she remade the bed, then picked up and folded the clothes that had been strewn, placing them neatly on the chair.

With gritted teeth, she opened the chest of drawers and began to take out the things that had been so roughly shoved in, beginning at the top and working down. She folded T-shirts and vests, underwear and pyjamas, sweaters and cardigans, replacing them all in an orderly fashion. She hated anyone being so untidy and showing such little regard for their belongings, especially when they were all such good quality and clearly costly. Things that most hard-working people could never afford.

The slightly narrower bottom drawer was particularly jumbled. It seemed to be reserved for miscellaneous items, cufflinks, tie pins and such, all separated from their boxes. Hector's wallet. Old train tickets; theatre pamphlets from his boyhood. A miniature Eiffel Tower keyring. Old, hardened sticks of chewing gum. A tube of antiseptic cream.

Flora groaned. She wasn't prepared to spend ages sorting everything out only for Hector to trash it all the very next time he opened the drawer. She made a half-hearted attempt to put things into some sort of order and was about to close the drawer when something caught her eye.

There, tucked beneath an old pantomime programme, a glimpse of colour right at the back stopped her in her tracks. She knelt down, the harsh fibres of the carpet chafing her knees even through her jeans. Gingerly she picked it up, her heart quickening, blood filling her head. Purple, red and white. Any combination – but it always had to include purple. So painstakingly woven.

As Flora held the friendship bracelet in her hand, she recognised the handiwork at once. Her quivering fingers closed around the soft cotton strands. She sat back for a moment, collecting her thoughts. Unseen icy fingers seemed to be tracing a line along her backbone. Pocketing the bracelet, she got up and hurried back into the room containing the mill wheel. She peered down once again into the angry waters, her eyes fixed to one spot. She waited, holding her breath, afraid to blink. Then briefly, so briefly, a pop of colour, this time just a little more than the last, rose above the spume, disappearing again almost instantly. But visible long enough for Flora to verify what she thought she'd seen. Her heart turned over.

She hadn't known what, but something in her gut had told her that here was where she might find some sort of confirmation. She felt a glimmer of hope; then of fear. Because now she knew for sure.

That Iola, dear, reckless Iola, had once been in this house – or at the very least, outside it. That the flash of mauve rising from the frothing water was, as she'd suspected, one of Iola's omnipresent boots. Flora pictured her friend now, jeans rolled up, her bare feet dangling into the irresistibly cool water of the mill pond after making her way up there one day the previous spring, swearing loudly as she carelessly knocked the boot into the water. Leaning back on the grass to feel the sun on her face and dropping her bracelet where she lay. Flora could well imagine there might be an earring or two, even a jacket, belonging to Iola floating around there somewhere into the bargain. She never had taken much care of her possessions. And she must have owned about four lots of purple boots – 'back-up pairs' she called them. Iola was always losing things and she would just shrug it off.

'Chill out, Flo. It's only stuff. No one's died,' she would say, whenever Flora chided her in exasperation. As Flora remembered her words now, she thought how much truth there was in what Iola had said.

Stuff wasn't important. *People* were.

But if Iola *had* been to Mill House, where on earth was she now?

CHAPTER 34

Little Hambley, November 2001

Despite not having had her morning medication, Mrs Homity seemed more confused than normal. Flora found her less co-operative and heavier to move as she undressed her for her shower. She put on a plastic apron and wheeled the old woman through into the wet room, rolling up her sleeves in readiness. Each day, seeing Mrs Homity's fragile form was like a stab to the heart. It reminded her so much of Mum towards the end. The constant, heart-wrenching pleading.

'*Look at me, Flo. Please. I'm no more than a bag of bones.*'

Breasts like squeezed lemons sagged emptily across the ribs that poked through her skin like chicken bones. The old woman's stomach sank inwards down to hip bones which jutted painfully. She seemed to be struggling to hold her head up. Her arms flopped limply by her sides and it was an effort for Flora to lift them as she attempted to rinse the soap away. The old woman stared passively at the ground, her mind apparently elsewhere.

Mr Homity had breezed in earlier to see her briefly before leaving for the races. Although it was Flora's turn that morning, he was already in the bedroom when she came in and had brought his wife up a cup of tea. He'd sat on the edge of the bed making small talk for a few minutes, although Flora could see that he had one eye on his watch most of the time. She had watched him from the window, crossing the footbridge with a spring in his step. He'd raised a hand to give an exaggerated wave and she'd seen a silver car pull up on the road below. Her stomach clenched at the thought of him and Kenneth Ogilvy, swanning off on a jolly, drinking champagne and eating fine food.

Anger built inside her, seeing him so carefree. It felt as if he was content to leave his poor wife to rot in that house, waiting for the moment when she would no longer be his burden and he could do exactly as he pleased, every single day.

The sun was high and clear against the brilliant azure of the morning sky. Conditions were ideal for a blow in the crisp air. She would wrap Mrs Homity up warmly and take her out. Flora felt suddenly defiant. What did it matter if Mr Homity found her out? What right had he to keep Agnes from doing the things she wanted?

Back in the bedroom, Flora eventually managed to dress the old woman in clothes she had selected for her: a knitted jade-green twin set and thick, navy-blue trousers with an elasticated waist. Mrs Homity had shown no interest when she'd opened the wardrobe, simply staring across the room.

'D'you still want to go to the chapel today?'

'Hmm?' She lifted her face to meet Flora's gaze, her eyes foggy.

'We were going to go for a walk if it was fine, remember?'

'Ah. See Xanthe.' She smiled dreamily.

'Yes. To see Xanthe.'

Flora crouched beside the wheelchair and took Mrs Homity's hand in her own. 'Would you like that, Agnes?'

The old woman tipped her head a fraction. She patted the back of Flora's hand, examining it absently, turning it this way and that. There was a sudden shift, a glimmer of lucidity.

'Oh, a tattoo. Young ladies didn't have them in my day.' Mrs Homity jerked her head sideways, studying her with new interest. Her attention returned quickly to the tattoo on Flora's wrist.

'A little hare. Just like the other girl's. They must be popular, then.'

Flora felt unexpectedly faint. 'No, not especially.' She tried to gather her thoughts. 'I mean, tattoos are becoming more common, yes. But not of hares.'

She drew in her breath, searching Mrs Homity's face. 'Agnes, who's this other girl you mentioned?'

The old woman's brow puckered into a frown. She paused, tracing the outline of Flora's tattoo with one finger. 'I – I'm not sure. My memory . . .'

She sighed, locking eyes with Flora once more. 'It was the hare, you see. It reminded me.' She tapped her head in frustration. 'It's in here somewhere. It'll come to me soon, I'm sure.'

Flora straightened. She closed her eyes for a moment,

covering her mouth with both hands. She fought the urge to shake her into life, revive the memory.

'Try to think, Agnes. It's really important.'

Mrs Homity shook her head sadly. 'Just the little hare. That's all I can see.' She looked at Flora curiously. 'Why is it important? Is she someone you know?'

'Yes. I think she's someone I know – *knew* – very well.'

'I'm sorry.' The old woman began to wring her hands, her eyes filling with tears. 'I don't know what's wrong with me this morning. My head – so muddled.'

'It's all right. Don't upset yourself.' Flora squeezed her hand. 'You'll remember later, I'm sure. Come on – let's get you out before the sun disappears.'

Frustrated, she could only hope that a blast of fresh air would help to spark something in Mrs Homity's memory. She *must* have met Iola. Maybe – just maybe – there was a chance she might know where she had moved on to.

Even the trip to Xanthe's grave seemed to do little to improve Mrs Homity's clarity of thought that morning. Now and then she brightened fleetingly, but most of the time it was as if she had retreated into herself, mumbling a lot and not really engaging with Flora at all. Flora was puzzled, since the mornings were usually her best time and they'd had some quite reasonable conversations. She hoped Mrs Homity's dementia wasn't suddenly getting rapidly worse, as she knew could sometimes happen.

As they were returning to the house, from across the lawn, they saw Hector coming out of the annexe, walking towards Mill House. He was carrying something and appeared not to have noticed them. As they drew nearer, he crossed the footbridge and disappeared through the front door. Mrs Homity became agitated. She leaned forwards and then turned to Flora with a frown, her voice low and urgent.

'I don't want him in my house. He's an imposter, you know.'

'Pardon?' Flora felt a frisson: of shock, or possibly excitement; she wasn't sure which.

'Him. *That boy*. I don't know who he is, but he's not welcome here.'

Flora wasn't quite sure how she should respond. Part of her wanted to coax more information out of the old woman, but she felt that it would be wrong. It could just be her current confused state, after all, and she was becoming overwrought. 'Mrs – Agnes, that's Hector. He's your son.'

Mrs Homity grew angry. 'He is most definitely *not* my son. You should ask Abey about him. I'm sure they're in it together.'

'I think you're probably a bit muddled . . .'

'Muddled?' Her voice rose to a furious shriek, her hands gesticulating frantically now. 'I know *exactly* what I'm saying. Don't patronise me, girl.'

Flora looked around anxiously. 'I'm sorry, Agnes. But please, try to calm down. You mustn't distress yourself like this.'

'But he's *not* my child, I tell you! Why does no one ever listen to me? I've seen the evidence – here, in this house. I can show you proof!'

Try as she might, Flora found it impossible to pacify her. The old woman continued to rant about what an awful boy Hector was and how someone must have stolen her real son. That he was some sort of changeling. Thankfully, by the time they got into the house, he was nowhere to be seen. Even though she disliked Hector, Flora didn't want him to hear the things his mother was saying. But more than anything, she feared a horrible confrontation, dreading to think how the volatile Hector might react if he heard his mother calling him an imposter. She wasn't sure what he was capable of.

They took the lift up to Mrs Homity's bedroom. She was calmer by now, fatigued from both her excursion and her outburst. They'd been out for well over an hour. Flora changed the old woman's incontinence pad and helped her back into bed. She went to pick up Mrs Homity's medication box from the dressing table, but was surprised to find the first dose missing. She could only assume that Mr Homity had taken it upon himself to give it to her when he brought up the tea. No wonder she hadn't seemed her usual self. Flora felt undermined, but angry too that he'd insisted on his wife taking something she was clearly resistant to and that seemed to make her feel worse rather than better.

Mrs Homity fell asleep quickly. Flora slipped from the room and back into her own bedroom. She sat on the bed next to Rufus and took out her diary, mulling over the strange things that the old woman had been saying. How it was all tying in with what Flora had begun to suspect herself. How Mrs Homity knew that Hector wasn't her real son and that she could prove it.

That she'd seen *evidence*. And it was somewhere in that house.

Dear Ostara, Flora wrote. *I think I'm closer to finding the truth.*

CHAPTER 35

Little Hambley, November 2001

With Mrs Homity sleeping soundly and no danger of her husband reappearing for several hours, Flora was prepared to take a risk. From her bedroom window, she'd seen Hector walking away from the house once more, over towards the trees. She was thankful they hadn't bumped into him earlier, or she'd have had some explaining to do. And she was even more grateful that he hadn't heard the terrible things his mother was saying about him. So far, she had managed to time Mrs Homity's outings to when he was otherwise engaged, busily conducting, or dissecting, or whatever other bizarre pastime took his fancy.

She moved stealthily along the landing to the room at the far end. A china plaque bearing Xanthe's name, next to a twee cartoon depicting a plump, apple-cheeked little girl bending to feed a kitten, still hung on the door. Flora knew that this had once been Xanthe's nursery. She paused outside for a moment, feeling slightly dizzy, almost as though she was about to commit a crime; to desecrate something sacred. But that was ridiculous. She only wanted to see Xanthe's room; that was all. To have some understanding of who she had been; this lovely, sunny little girl who had left such a hole in Mrs Homity's life. Although, knowing the terms of her contract, Flora was all too aware that to do so was risking her job. But she *had* to know what lay beyond that door. She knew that, along with many of the other rooms, Xanthe's was out of bounds to her, but wondered if there was a specific reason for Mr Homity's insistence on this – or whether it was just another example of his desire to control.

She was surprised to find the room unlocked. As she entered, Flora put a hand to her mouth. Everything was spotlessly clean and had been preserved perfectly, as though waiting for Xanthe's return. The walls were decorated with scenes from nursery rhymes: Little Miss Muffet. Bo Peep and her sheep. Humpty Dumpty. The small bed was made up with a counterpane decorated with hand-stitched pink rosebuds. A child's midnight-blue nightdress, spangled with golden moons and stars, was neatly folded atop the pillow and a fluffy white toy cat with a peachy little nose placed just below. A quick look beneath the bed revealed only an old-fashioned chamber pot, painted with flowers to match the bedspread.

More embroidered rosebuds covered the long voile curtains draped at the window, which were pulled back around a beautiful grey rocking horse with a flowing white mane and tail. The small white bookcase on the wall opposite the bed was filled with picture books; a white shelving unit held cute animal ornaments, dolls and other cuddly toys. Stepping cautiously across the pale pink carpet to the left of the bed, Flora pulled open one of the double doors to the little wardrobe. It was crammed with dresses and coats; party shoes, sandals, boots. Everything Flora could only have dreamed of as a child. Her eyes moved over everything as she parted the clothes carefully, looking sharply from top to bottom, left to right. She slid open the chest of drawers, releasing the scent of fresh laundry: underwear, tights and socks, nightdresses and woollens, all neatly folded. All ready for a little girl to climb into the very next day. Someone – presumably Rita – must have washed everything recently. It was bizarre.

Flora lifted every item, taking care not to disturb the order of anything. She closed the drawers, then leafed through the books. Her hand hovered over the sketch pad which had Xanthe's name in large blue letters across the front, written neatly in the child's own hand. She slid out the book and turned the pages slowly. The artwork made her think of Iola's wonderful elephant sketch, which had impressed her so much. And Xanthe would have been younger still. The drawings were remarkably detailed and accomplished for a five-year-old. Flowers, insects, animals. Even a picture of Mill House. But the strange picture on the back page halted her abruptly. What did it mean? Flora stood looking round uneasily, gooseflesh prickling her arms. She replaced the book, her mind whirring.

The room was like a shrine, frozen in a 1960s time-warp for all eternity. She almost expected Xanthe to skip in at any moment; that it had all been a terrible mistake – that she was still very much alive and had just been out to play. A sudden, terrible image flashed through her mind: of Xanthe's lifeless little body, laid out on that bed for one last time before she was put into her coffin. The thought made her feel faintly nauseous.

With everything that Mrs Homity had been saying earlier, Flora had half wondered whether there might be something relating to Hector in that room. She didn't know what she'd expected to find exactly; Mrs Homity's words had been jumbled, but she was quite adamant that the evidence she spoke of lay somewhere within Mill House. She'd been so earnest about the fact that Hector wasn't her son. There was no evidence here regarding Hector that Flora could see. But had Mrs Homity perhaps found something else? Or maybe Flora herself was putting two and two together and making ten.

Taking one last look around, Flora decided that, with regard to what Mrs Homity had alluded to, Xanthe's room didn't appear to hold the answer and could be ruled out. Ensuring all was left as she'd found it, she retraced her steps, then went back out onto the landing and closed the door.

'What the hell are you doing?'

An angry voice from behind almost stopped her heart. She turned to find Hector standing at the top of the stairs, his face stony. Where on earth had he appeared from?

'I – I was just . . .'

'You were snooping, weren't you? Why would you want to look in there?'

He approached, glaring, chewing the inside of his cheek. 'You're only supposed to go into Mummy's room. You've no business poking around in my dead sister's nursery. It's out of bounds. Even *I'm* not allowed in there. Daddy said so.'

His eyes, burning with curiosity, drifted to the closed door. Flora studied him with sudden interest. She sensed an opportunity.

'I was just replacing something on the shelf. Your mother asked me to.' She knew that Mrs Homity wouldn't contradict her. She was too sleepy and confused.

'*What* were you replacing? I don't think I believe you.' He looked at her askance.

Flora thought of the drawings she had rifled through.

'A sketch book. Your mother wanted to show me how beautifully Xanthe used to draw for such a young child. She asked me to fetch it earlier and I've just put it back.'

Hector looked from Flora to the door. Something glinted in his eyes suddenly. 'Okay. Show me, then.'

'But you just said it's out of bounds. *I* had Mrs Homity's permission to go in, but I wouldn't want you to get into trouble.' She paused, watching as his face clouded. He seemed suddenly hesitant.

Flora lowered her voice conspiratorially. 'I won't say anything. It can be our secret.' She gave him a slow wink, waiting with bated breath for his reaction. Relief surged through her as he responded with an excited whisper.

'Okay. Our secret.'

Flora held open the door and watched as Hector, glancing nervously over his shoulder, entered. He peered round, his eyes wide.

'So, where's this book, then?'

Flora went to the bookshelf and took out the sketch pad she'd found, handing it over. She watched as Hector turned the pages, a slight frown on his face. Xanthe had definitely had a gift, Flora thought sadly, as for a second time she regarded the drawings that the little girl had once so carefully created. She recalled that Mrs Homity had actually once mentioned her daughter's love of nature and flair for art. It was tragic that she'd never lived to realise her full potential.

Hector didn't even reach the end. Snapping the book shut, he thrust it back towards Flora. He seemed almost peeved.

'I wouldn't have expected anything else. She was wonderful, wasn't she? Pretty, clever; loved by everyone.' His tone was bitter. '*Perfect* little Xanthe.'

Something seemed to take over Hector. His whole demeanour changed in an instant. He began to stamp round the room, opening then slamming the wardrobe doors, picking things up and replacing them roughly. He swept a hand across one of the shelves, angrily knocking a fluffy rabbit and a teddy bear to the floor, then turned to Flora, eyes ablaze, his mouth twisted in undisguised resentment.

'If she had lived, I'd probably never have been born. She was all they ever wanted. They were hoping for another Xanthe – but they got me instead. How very disappointing for them.'

Flora felt increasingly alarmed. Hector's voice was getting louder, more aggressive. His movements were becoming worryingly erratic, as though he might actually be on the brink of some sort of dangerous episode. She shrank back against the wall, concerned that being the nearest thing to him could make her the target for his ire.

'Hector, d'you think perhaps we should go downstairs?' She was trying to appear calm but could feel the tremor in her voice. She hoped he hadn't noticed. But Hector was paying no attention to her at all.

His eyes panned wildly round the room, his glare fixing on the rocking horse.

'I always wanted one of those when I was small. I begged my parents, time and again. Now I see why they didn't get me one. It would have reminded them of her, wouldn't it?'

Flora almost jumped out of her skin as he let out an anguished yell, lunging at the rocking horse and shoving it so hard that it tipped over sideways, knocking over the small lamp on the bedside cabinet. With both hands, he clutched at his head for a moment, tugging viciously at his hair in frustration. She watched him, fearful that he would injure himself, or launch an attack on some other inanimate object. Or worse.

But just as quickly as it had become inflamed, his anger seemed to subside. He sank down onto the bed suddenly, staring at the floor, rocking and mumbling to himself. Flora realised he had begun to count backwards from a hundred. Maybe this was some sort of strategy he'd been given: a coping mechanism. She looked on anxiously as, gradually, he fell silent, closing his eyes for a moment.

He rose abruptly and shook himself a little, smoothing down his tousled hair with one hand. It made little difference.

'I've seen enough. I want to go now.' His eyes trained firmly on the exit, he made his way from the room.

With trembling hands, Flora scooped up the stuffed toys, righted the lamp and rocking horse, then followed, exhaling deeply as the door closed on Xanthe's shrine. She wasn't quite sure what she'd just witnessed, but an enormous wave of relief washed over her, thankful that things hadn't escalated further. It seemed so odd that Hector had never been permitted to enter the room before; that he hadn't even attempted to, by the sound of things. Although she could imagine that he would take any instruction issued by his father very literally. But if it had been made less taboo when he was a child, maybe he wouldn't have had such an extreme reaction. Seeing his crestfallen expression now, she actually felt a bit sorry for him. Then she remembered the friendship bracelet, the boot glimpsed in the water, and the feeling vanished almost instantly. More than anything, she was desperate to quiz him about it – but was acutely aware that this was not the most auspicious moment.

He turned to her at the top of the stairs. 'You won't say anything – to Daddy? Do you give me your word?'

His tone was hard, but his anxious eyes told her she had the upper hand. Particularly after his inappropriate eruption.

'I told you. It's our secret. You have my word.'

He nodded, his shoulders lowering a fraction. 'Good. Anyway, I have things to do, as, I'm sure, do you. I think Mummy will be needing lunch soon.'

Flora watched as he took a last glance towards Xanthe's door, then careered down the stairs, disappearing along the hallway.

She thought of Xanthe's drawing at the back of her sketch book; of the innocently captured image that might mean so much more. Two men holding hands.

Daddy and Uncle Kenneth.

Was it simply the way in which a loving little girl wanted to portray her beloved father and his best friend? Or maybe, as Flora suspected, there was more to it.

*

Although less confused, Mrs Homity was in a strange mood that evening, restless and anxious. She ate little of the meal Flora prepared and kept watching the door of her room, almost as though expecting someone to walk in at any moment.

'What date is it today, Flora?'

'Date? November thirtieth, I think. Nearly heading into the festive season.'

At once her face clouded. 'Yesterday would have been Xanthe's anniversary. It's unforgivable of me. How could I have forgotten?'

Flora felt a twinge of remorse. Mrs Homity probably had little concept of time – she herself should have made her aware of the date. But after her visit to Hector's annexe, Flora had been completely preoccupied with her discovery of Iola's things. What it all meant.

'You mustn't upset yourself. You didn't actually forget at all. One day seems much the same as the next when you're constantly stuck in the house. I remember my mum . . .' Flora trailed off, thinking of Mum's words: that nothing had meaning any more. It didn't matter if it was Saturday night or Monday morning – she had nothing to look forward to. She never did anything, never went anywhere. That last year, she'd even refused to celebrate her own birthday, saying it was pointless. Flora had had so much time to reflect on it all since. The guilt was consuming her.

'I'll pick up some nice flowers when I next walk into the village. We can take them to Xanthe's grave. We'll take a bottle of water to pour into the holder.'

'Yes. Yes, that would be nice. Show her I haven't forgotten.'

'I'm sure she knows that, Agnes. She would understand.'

'Would she?' The old woman's eyes flooded with tears. 'Did she understand why she'd been left behind that day, why I didn't take her with me? I can't stop thinking about it. Even now. It feels as though it were only yesterday. The pain won't ever go away.' She shook her head, her jaw growing suddenly taut. 'It doesn't appear to have affected Abey in quite the same way. He moved on long ago. I don't think he even visits the chapel any more. Where are his flowers for our daughter? And where is *he*?'

'I think I told you – he said he was going to a race meeting – in Cheltenham?'

Mrs Homity gave an odd, bitter laugh. 'Is that what he said? He stopped bothering with it years ago, said it was a bore and a complete waste of time. He has no interest in racing. Nor in much else, if the truth be told. Oh Abey, what a tangled web . . .'

Flora was puzzled. Why would Mr Homity have lied about where he was going? Soon the old woman grew tired, her eyes becoming heavy and glazed with that familiar, empty look. Flora settled her down for the night, glad that she seemed to have forgotten her earlier anguish.

Flora went down to the kitchen to make herself a

sandwich and a cup of tea, then took it back up to her room. It had been a cold, crisp day and the night was clear and still. Seating herself on the ottoman, she stared up at the moonlit sky as she ate her sandwich, listening enrapt to the sound of an owl calling close by. Rufus was in a playful mood, chasing a pen which had rolled onto the floor. She watched him absent-mindedly, glad he was able to keep himself amused.

Flora drank the last of her tea then, rooting under the bed, fished out her diary. That was something she intended to buy – a padlock for her suitcase. In the meantime, still with no key to lock her door, she was being careful about what she wrote, in case it fell into the wrong hands and was somehow incriminating. She would fill in today's entry and then read for a while. She liked looking out at the night sky, but the draught from the window was making the room even colder, so she pulled the curtains across. As she sat on the bed, ruminating the events of the day, she heard deep-voiced laughter outside. Curious, she got up to peep through the gap in the drapes.

Mr Homity was on the footbridge below, in conversation with a man. They looked loose-limbed and slightly unsteady, as though they had been drinking. The man wobbled slightly and Mr Homity put an arm around his shoulders, leaning in to say something into his ear. There was more laughter, from both of them.

And then Flora had to do a double-take. Because the man took Mr Homity in his arms and kissed him. Not in a jocular way, but passionately, on his mouth. They remained locked together for a few seconds, before the man finally broke free, glancing over his shoulder towards the steps. He appeared to wish him good night, before staggering back over the black water and down towards the road, where a car was waiting to collect him. Mr Homity waved until it was out of sight, then retreated into the house.

Flora was stunned. So Xanthe's drawing did have another meaning. The child was only five: she wouldn't have understood, even if she'd seen something pass between Mr Homity and her 'Uncle Kenneth'.

But would she have told her mother?

CHAPTER 36

Stretmore, November 2001

Initially the remains in the cellar had been something of a mystery. The forensics analysis revealed that they were those of a large-boned Caucasian male, probably in his forties, around five feet ten, with poor dental hygiene. From the level of decomposition, it was apparent that he had been dead for at least twenty-five years. Sparse strands of dark hair still protruded from the skull.

The majority of the neighbours were of little help, having only lived in the area for a maximum of ten to fifteen years. Sheila Lanyon and her daughter had very much kept themselves to themselves. It seemed that the mother had been completely housebound in the last two years of her life. Her health had been in steady decline for more than a decade.

There was clear evidence of foul play, and they needed to find the recently bereaved Flora. From the diary entries over the last couple of years, clearly her pattern of thought had become more and more erratic. And the recent bombardment of correspondence from the gas board requesting access to the meter had obviously been a source of real angst to her. It sounded as though she might have been on the verge of some sort of breakdown. They had no clue as to where she might have gone, nor whether she had any knowledge of, or indeed involvement with, the unlawful disposal of the body.

The only person who seemed to know anything at all about the Lanyons was the elderly widow who had lived across the road from them for the last forty years. Sadie Malone was eighty-five; small, snow-haired and sharp as a tack. As Sergeant Kaur approached her front door, it opened before she'd had a chance to knock. The old lady had even boiled the kettle in anticipation of a visit.

DS Kaur settled herself in the proffered armchair beside the bay window in Mrs Malone's neat sitting room. Through the glass, they had a clear view of the Lanyons' home, still fenced off by blue and white tape. It made her slightly uncomfortable. Mrs Malone, on the other hand, in that accepting way often found in older people, was clearly unperturbed. She placed two mugs of strong tea on floral coasters on a small coffee table between both chairs, lowering herself onto the seat opposite the young policewoman. Sitting with her gnarled hands clasped in her lap, she began to speak without any prompting.

'You must understand, I didn't know Sheila well. She was always a very private person – at least, after she lost her husband. Terrible for her, it must have been.'

'Did she ever confide in you? Tell you what was going on in her life?'

'Well, no. Not really. But she'd always looked happy before. Always a cheery "hello" if you saw her in the street. It was like all the light was gone from her afterwards. All on her own with the little girl. It was tragic. I was seventy-four – our three were all grown up and settled with their own families – by the time I lost my Pat. I know I'll be joining him soon enough.'

'So, can you tell me anything about Mrs Lanyon's relationships after the death of her husband? Did she have many male friends?'

The old woman shook her head vigorously. 'Never. Not that I knew of, anyway. Or if she did, she must have smuggled them in after dark.' She laughed lightly.

'We're trying to establish the identity of one particular man. We think he'd have visited the Lanyons over twenty years ago. Please think – I know it's a long time ago. Was there anyone at all Mrs Lanyon could have been involved with? That might have visited or been staying at the house?'

Mrs Malone sat up sharply, her eyebrows high. 'Well now, how *silly* of me. Of course, there was that Roger. He completely slipped my mind. *Roger the Lodger* – that's what Pat and I called him. Pat would see him coming up the road after his shift. "There goes Roger the Lodger," he'd call to me.' She chuckled to herself. 'Roger Blight – yes, that was his surname. Miserable-looking bugger, he was.'

'So Mrs Lanyon had a lodger?'

'Well no, not strictly speaking. That was just our little joke. No, Roger was her older brother. Half-brother, if I remember rightly. She did tell me once, when I asked. He moved in a few months after Mr Lanyon died. I think

Sheila was struggling – with the bills and everything. I suppose she needed more income from somewhere. I didn't get the feeling there was much love lost between them.'

'So, this Roger – he actually lived in the house, then?'

'Yes. Yes, he must have been there four or five years, thinking about it. No idea where he went. Pat remarked one day he hadn't seen him for a bit. I asked Sheila and she said he'd moved out. I think she was glad, reading between the lines. And I did notice a nasty bruise on her cheek the once. Made me wonder – well, you know . . .' She stretched her mouth into a tight line.

'And Mrs Lanyon didn't have any other . . . lodgers, after that?'

'No. She was taken ill quite soon afterwards. In hospital for the best part of three months, poor woman. Young Flora was in a foster home for a while. I've never had too much to do with them, but I don't think things have been easy – for either of them.'

'Thank you, Mrs Malone. You've been most helpful.'

The officer rose to leave. The old woman eased herself from her armchair by the window to see her out.

'So, I take it you've found a body, then? Is that what all the commotion's been about over there?'

'We can't really say too much at this stage, I'm afraid. The investigation is ongoing. But thanks very much for your time and do contact us if you think of anything else that might be relevant.'

'He didn't have anything to do with the baby that was snatched, did he? That Roger? He certainly looked like a wrong 'un to me. Wouldn't have surprised me at all.'

The officer paused at the door. She turned round slowly.

'What baby was this, Mrs Malone?'

'The little Chappell baby. They never found him, did they? I know Flora got pally with the older sister when they went up to the big school.' Mrs Malone pulled a face. 'An unlikely pair, they made. She was a proper tearaway, by all accounts.'

Sergeant Kaur's heart quickened. 'When did this all take place? When the baby went missing, I mean?'

'Ooh – must be about twenty-five years ago now. Maybe more. Shocking business. You don't expect that kind of thing on your own doorstep, do you?'

The cogs in the young policewoman's mind had begun to turn. In such a small area, this all seemed a bit too much of a coincidence.

'Can I come back in, please? I think there are a few more questions that I need to ask you.'

Mrs Malone smiled. 'I'll make another pot of tea.'

CHAPTER 37

Little Hambley, November 2001

Sleep evaded Flora for several hours that night. She lay in the silent darkness, Rufus curled at her feet, staring at the ceiling, wondering exactly what she had witnessed. What it meant. She had gone over and over it in her mind, but there was no mistaking the nature of that embrace.

Were Abraham Homity and Kenneth Ogilvy more than just friends? Had that always been the case? She thought of poor Mrs Homity, trapped in a loveless marriage, her beloved Xanthe gone. The strain of caring for Hector. The more Flora considered the possibility, the more she became convinced that the old woman knew. What was it she'd said? *His trophy bride*. And now she was physically incapable of leaving. No wonder she'd referred to that room as her cell. Flora thought of what Mum had told her; about there always being someone worse off than yourself. How very true it was.

Her ears attuned to a sudden noise on the other side of the door, Flora sat up sharply, her heart quickening. There it was again. The floorboard on the landing creaked: slowly, very slowly, as though someone was shifting from one foot to another, placing their weight carefully. She caught her breath, straining to listen. Her head whipped round as the doorknob began to twist, a glint of brass in the pale shaft of moonlight seeping through the gap in the curtains.

She was overcome by sudden horror.

She'd forgotten to put the dressing gown across the door. Her mind had been reeling, still full of the sight glimpsed below as she'd closed the curtains earlier. How could she have allowed herself to become so distracted?

Quickly Flora lay back down, pulling the covers tightly around her trembling body, snapping her eyes shut. She felt Rufus stretch slightly, then settle once more. The door began to creep open. She lay rigidly as she became aware of someone entering the room, petrified her irregular breathing would give her away. She tried to steady the breaths; deep, deeper, as though she were in that profound, unstirrable stage of sleep. She thought of the cudgel beneath the bed but was paralysed by fear.

Flora half opened one eye, squinting as the bulk of a tall figure padded stealthily across the room. *Hector*. But what was he doing? He squatted close to the window, lowering himself to the ground. With one hand, he appeared to reach beneath the ottoman. Through the gloom it was difficult to discern his movements exactly, but he was definitely looking for something, groping around on the floor, moving his arm from left to right. After what felt like an eternity, he rose to his feet. He stood for a moment, his head turning this way and that, as though wondering what to do next.

Eventually he began to edge back towards the door. Flora quickly closed her eyes. Rufus jerked his head up, letting out an anxious bleat as Hector passed the bed. Flora lay, taut with fear. She felt her stomach coil into a tight ball as he paused, his thigh almost level with her face. He sniffed loudly. Flora wondered with mounting dread what, if anything, he intended to do. Relief washed over her as eventually he carried on his way, quietly clicking the door shut behind him. She remained motionless for a few seconds before daring to move. Her heart was still pounding. Easing herself up against the headboard, she peered towards where he had been kneeling.

What had he been looking for? Whatever it was, it was clearly very important. The fact that he'd tried her door during the night several times over the past week and felt the need to enter the room under cover of darkness told her it was something she wasn't supposed to know about. Was this the same reason he'd entered her room before? Had he been searching and not found what he'd expected to? From the way he had stood looking around, she suspected that the mystery item had evaded him yet again. Maybe he intended to try again later.

Flora slid from the bed. Quickly, she puddled the dressing gown across the door and switched on the light. She tiptoed across to the ottoman. At once, Rufus jumped down and came across to her, rubbing round her legs and purring. She stroked him gently, lifting him out of the way, then dropped to her hands and knees to look beneath the chest. There was a gap of around three inches under its base. She peered more closely and felt around but all she produced was dust and a spherical brass button, which she cast to one side. Surely Hector wouldn't have risked breaking into her room to look for a button? She looked down at her hands, now grimy from the floor. She got up, intending to wash them.

Seeing the shiny item, Rufus immediately thought that this was a game. He began to slide the button across the floor, darting after it and tossing the thing into the air with both front paws. He caught a claw on the deep hem of the curtain as he patted it beneath and fought to free himself.

'Silly boy,' Flora whispered. She crossed to the window, stooping to untangle him. But as she lifted the curtain, something fell from the folds of the heavy fabric. A flash of red and silver.

A key.

As quickly as he'd pounced on the button, Rufus, freed and now in playful mode, launched at the piece of red ribbon attached to it and proceeded to dribble it across the floor. Flora hurriedly followed him and retrieved the key from between his paws.

She turned it over in her hands, looking round the room. There didn't appear to be anything in the room with a lock, other than the door, and this key was far too small for that. Was *this* what Hector had been looking for? If Rufie had found it before, he'd have had a field day chasing it round the room on the slippery wooden floor. Maybe that was why it hadn't been where Hector had expected to find it.

For a brief moment, if it meant a halt to the attempts

to gain access to her room, she considered handing it over. But maybe not just yet. In the morning, she would try to find the lock that the key fitted. If Hector had been so furtive about looking for it, there was a good chance there might be something of interest on the other side.

And Flora's already smouldering curiosity had been ignited.

CHAPTER 38

Little Hambley, December 2001

Mr Homity had requested that Flora work another half day, to take over at lunchtime, allowing him to attend a meeting of the local Landowners' Association just outside Gloucester the following afternoon. He might be back late, he'd said, since some of the members were going for dinner afterwards and he felt it might appear churlish if he declined the invitation. She was more than happy, as it would be the ideal opportunity to see if she could find the right home for the key; even more so as Hector was going out for once, too. A quarterly medical appointment, apparently. She did wonder what this meant, but made no comment.

On her way to the kitchen the following morning, she passed Hector in the corridor as he came out of the library. He mumbled a curt hello, which in itself was unusual. As she reached the kitchen door, he turned and called after her.

'I say, you haven't . . .' Hector looked around furtively. He came back towards Flora and gestured for her to go through. Following her into the kitchen, he closed the door behind them. He seemed agitated.

'Is anything wrong?'

'I've lost something. That is, Daddy . . . Daddy has lost something. He asked me to look for it – has trouble bending down these days, he says. But I can't find it. I've looked . . . everywhere. For days, now. Just wondered . . .'

'You wondered if I'd found it?'

His previous attempts having proved fruitless, Hector had obviously given up on the idea of another search of her room. Flora was hugely relieved. It had been terrifying.

'Well, yes. Only I don't want him to know I've asked you. It's just . . . he gets very upset when he loses his belongings. It's been missing for over a week now, and . . . well, I don't like him to be cross . . . upset, I mean.'

'It might help if I knew what he'd lost. And where he might have lost it. This is a big house, you know.'

Hector began to pace, his eyes flicking constantly to the door. 'He did think it could have been upstairs. Possibly in your bedroom?' He studied her hopefully. 'Well? Have you? Found it?'

'Hector, you still haven't actually said what you're looking for.'

'A key!' He was becoming impatient now. He clasped his head with both hands. 'The key to Daddy's desk drawer.'

Flora felt her heart skip. She did her best to maintain a poker face.

'He says he'll have to get another cut if it isn't found. He'll be very cross if it comes to that; very cross.' He shook his head. Clearly making Daddy cross was something to be avoided at all costs.

'I can't say I've found a key, I'm afraid, but I'll certainly have a look. If it turns up, I'll let you know. Right away,' Flora added, seeing his eyes widen in despair.

'You promise? Right away? It's very important.' He lowered his voice. 'Daddy keeps important things in his drawer and it wouldn't do for the key to fall into the wrong hands. You do understand, don't you?'

'Absolutely. I'll be sure to tell you if I find it.'

'But you won't mention it to Daddy? I don't think he'd be pleased if he thought I was sharing his business with the hired help.'

The hired help? Flora gritted her teeth.

'No; I won't mention it to Mr Homity. Now if you'll excuse me, I haven't had any breakfast and I'd like to do my laundry, too, while I've a couple of hours to myself.'

Hector nodded. He seemed satisfied that Flora was to be trusted. She watched him leave. Moments later, he could be seen from the kitchen window as he disappeared at speed back into the annexe. She'd wondered whether to ask about his medical appointment, but decided against it.

The desk drawer. Flora felt a tingle of nervous excitement. She might let Hector have the key at some point; put him out of his misery. But not yet. Not until she knew exactly why it was so important for Mr Homity to find it.

The morning passed quickly. Flora was aware that once she had given Mrs Homity her lunch, she'd be sleeping like a baby in no time. The old woman was always much more tired and listless in the afternoons. Usually, Flora would fill this time doing Mrs Homity's laundry and preparing her evening meal. Filling in her time log. Today these were tasks she had already completed. The second Mr Homity and Hector were safely away from the premises, she would head straight to the library.

Within minutes of settling Mrs Homity down for her nap, Flora made her way downstairs. She had seen Mr Homity striding across the footbridge, Hector following behind. A taxi was waiting for them on the road below, to drop Mr Homity off first and then take Hector on to see his doctor in private rooms somewhere the other side of Gloucester. Even if Hector was only out for a couple of hours, it should give her more than enough time.

Even though she knew she was alone in the house, apart of course from Mrs Homity, Flora's heart fluttered with nerves. Supposing Mr Homity and Hector forgot something and returned? Supposing their appointments had been cancelled at short notice – or an accident in the lanes meant their way was blocked and they had to turn back?

She stood anxiously in the library doorway for several minutes, deliberating. But the longer she waited, the higher the likelihood of their returning before she had done what she needed to and the moment being lost. The more she procrastinated, the greater the risk of being caught in the act. Flora filled her lungs. It was now or never. Feeling the key in her pocket, she crossed to the desk. She seated herself on Mr Homity's chair, trying each of the four drawers, one by one, to ensure they were actually locked.

Two were open. There was little of interest within: stationery and envelopes. Books of stamps. Pens, Sellotape. A staplegun. A different key was needed to open the third. But slotting it into the final drawer, the key turned with ease. Flora held her breath as it slid open.

Inside were three stacks of papers: two of open, printed loose sheets; tied with string. The third comprised several blue A5 envelopes, tied with a length of the same red ribbon attached to the key.

With trembling fingers, Flora took out one of the bundles and placed it on the desk. She lifted the corner of the top sheet and flicked carefully through the pile. There appeared to be little of interest here: receipts; invoices for work undertaken in and around the house, dating back several years. A copy of the conversion plan for the annexe.

She replaced the pile in its original spot, then took out the bundle wrapped in ribbon. It was fastened with a neat bow. Taking care to remember exactly how it had been tied and the order in which the envelopes were stacked, she loosened the ribbon. There was no name, no address on any of them. Only initials.

A.H.

Abraham – or Agnes?

They had all been opened and replaced in their original envelopes. Gingerly, she lifted the flap of the first and took out its contents: two folded sheets of high-grade, unlined palest blue writing paper.

The address at the top merely stated: *Brompton, 23 December 1955*.

Flora cast an anxious look at the door. All appeared quiet – for the moment. She leaned forwards and began to read.

CHAPTER 39

Little Hambley, December 2001

My dearest A,

It is so hard not to be able to spend Christmas together. I am counting the days until we next meet. I do hope you like the gift. It was so hard to choose something for you and I wanted it to be perfect. I miss you every moment we are apart. I hope your Christmas is bearable and please keep in mind that ten days is not so very long – even if it will be a different year.

Look after yourself, my darling. You are very precious to me.

Forever yours,

K. xxx

K? *Kenneth?* Flora had to assume from what she'd witnessed that the recipient must be Abraham. She sat up, her mind reeling. She replaced the letter in its envelope and took out the next in the pile. Easter 1957. Much the same – mawkish; expressions of endearment and adoration. Nothing of any great significance. And still just initials.

One by one, she went through the letters, skimming the content of each. There were two or three a year, a catalogue of more than two decades of forbidden love. But the letters stopped abruptly in the November of 1975. She read the final one in full.

My dearest A,

It breaks my heart to write this, but we must not see each other again. It is too risky now – for both of us. And so it is with the greatest reluctance that I am going away. I have a flight booked tomorrow at seven thirty – I won't tell you where, as I know it will be too tempting for you to try to contact me. By the time you read this, I will have left the country. A clean break is best. You must try to carry on as though everything is normal. Raise the child and keep your counsel. I know you will give him a good life. Always remember it was for the right reasons. Goodbye, my sweet A.

I remain forever yours.

K. xxx

Flora read the letter, over and over again. The child – was he referring to Hector? Was this the proof that Mrs Homity spoke of? But there was nothing concrete here – the underlying meaning clear only to the sender and receiver. She rifled through the bunch once more hoping for some other clue, but she'd missed nothing. Frustrated, she retied the ribbon around the pile and replaced them in the drawer.

She lifted out the final sheaf of papers. The top one was an illustrated information leaflet, about six sheets thick, regarding the assembly and maintenance of Mrs Homity's wheelchair. Flora's heart sank. It didn't look as if there would be anything out of the ordinary in the pile, but Flora went through it anyway. Just in case. There was a typewritten, lined sheet with a list of Mrs Homity's various medications, with scribbled notes in the margin. *Amiodarone* was heavily underlined, along with the subtext: contraindications – detrimental to conditions of the central nervous system. The analgesics were underlined, with several large asterisks.

Fentanyl: causes drowsiness and confusion.
Naproxen: changes in vision, drowsiness, dizziness and confusion.
Thickener for liquids: risk of dehydration and malnutrition.

Was Mr Homity deliberately making his wife's condition worse? Flora had been suspicious of his motives for being so insistent about everything his wife must take. Rather than out of consideration for her welfare, was he actively trying to shorten her life? At the very least, it seemed he was trying to control her: silence her, even. The old woman had let a few things slip in her more lucid moments. The medication undoubtedly affected her memory and increased her levels of tiredness.

But what could Flora do with this information? The

sheet with its handwritten addendums could be interpreted as a husband simply researching what was best for his wife out of love and concern. There was no hardcore evidence here. But it screamed to her that something very sinister was afoot. She thought of Dr Chabra's reluctance to comply with Mr Homity's wishes about his wife's pain relief; of the doctor's obvious concern about the dangerous medication she had mysteriously been prescribed.

Replacing the information leaflet carefully in the drawer, Flora folded the last sheet and slipped it into her cardigan pocket, then hurriedly made her way to the door, turning briefly to ensure she had left everything as she'd found it. Although appalled, she felt suddenly bolstered by what she had discovered. She would write to Dr Chabra; send him the list. She was certain that he would find it every bit as disturbing as she did. Then Mr Homity's behaviour would have to be properly investigated.

And with the other information she intended to share with the doctor, anything else untoward in Mill House's past might just come to light, too.

CHAPTER 40

Little Hambley, December 2001

With the envelope to Dr Chabra marked *URGENT* now safely delivered, Flora had returned from her walk feeling strangely liberated. She didn't care that the snotty receptionist had looked at her as though she'd crawled out from under a stone. She would have liked to place it in the doctor's hands, tell him in person what she suspected, but as he was otherwise engaged, she'd handed it over at the desk, impressing upon the woman in an unfamiliarly assertive voice that it was extremely important: that he needed to see it *as soon as he was free*.

Flora was confident that this information landing on his desk would shock the doctor and hopefully trigger something momentous. And having acted so decisively for once, she felt somehow empowered. It gave her hope that she had grown as a person: that, in spite of everything, coming to Little Hambley might actually have made her stronger and better able to cope with whatever obstacles she encountered in future.

It had been good to get away from the house for a while, to feel the hustle and bustle of the village; to remind herself that there was life, *normal* life, away from her stifling existence at Mill House. She'd known it wasn't going to be forever, and she was frustrated beyond belief that she hadn't yet managed to locate Iola; but at the very least, her position had bought her time and also given her the chance to save a little money, so that eventually she'd be able to afford to rent somewhere and start afresh. She'd decided the Cotswolds was the perfect place to settle – she'd look for a similar village, but as far away from the Homitys as possible. Maybe the other side of Cheltenham. She imagined a tiny cottage built in golden stone, cosy and welcoming, with steps leading to the street and a neat square of garden at the back. She dreamed of living in the heart of a chocolate-box hamlet with friendly neighbours; artisan shops, not many cars – maybe a brook running through. A village hall, summer fetes with stalls and brightly coloured bunting.

She smiled to herself as she pictured it all in her mind's eye. It would be the icing on the cake if she had Iola to share it all with her. She hoped, *prayed* that she was nearer to finding her friend. And if her own efforts proved fruitless, telling Dr Chabra in the letter that she was certain Iola had been in Mill House searching for her long-lost brother, he might alert the authorities and *they* would find her, without the need for Flora to go directly to the police herself. Somehow, unburdening herself to Dr Chabra had cleared her mind. She was determined to be brave, ask Hector outright about her friend. She was even considering challenging Mr Homity about the letters she had found. About little Warren.

What was the worst that could happen? Ever since leaving Stretmore, she had feared the police catching up with her, but she couldn't run forever. She had done the right thing by Mrs Homity. Hopefully that would stand in her favour. Because she knew that, having just blown the whistle on her employer, come what may, her time at Mill House was coming to an end.

Breathless, she paused at the top of the steps and stared up at Mill House. It seemed less forbidding in the late afternoon light, a rosy glow glinting from the windows. Blackbirds swooped and chirped, signalling their intention to retire for the evening. There were only another three weeks until the shortest day of the year. Not long till Christmas. Her first without Mum. She thought back to their last one. The memory was painful and she tried to push it from her mind.

A chill was descending along with the sun, and Flora thrust her hands into her pockets, picking her way carefully towards the eerily still waters which belied the rapid movement of the leat, channelled from the weir concealed somewhere higher up the slope. Dwindling rays of light shimmered benignly on the pond's surface. Something made Flora glance up again at the house. She caught her breath. A figure stood, motionless, apparently staring down at her from one of the upstairs windows.

From her bedroom.

The sudden, awful realisation that it must be Mr Homity filled her with cold dread. What was he doing in there? Had he somehow found her out – that she'd been rifling through his drawers? That she'd been on a mission to reveal his despicable actions to the authorities? She knew she couldn't avoid him. Flora dropped her eyes, steeling herself as she continued, even more slowly than before, desperately trying to think of what she would say if confronted. Thank *God* she'd already taken the list to Dr Chabra. At least someone else now knew what was going on in that place.

Sudden movement to her right startled her and she looked round to see Hector emerging from the trees. She wondered if he'd been to the chapel. She could imagine him ranting at Xanthe's grave in a jealous rage; damaging it even, if he thought no one was watching. She hoped this wasn't the case. Despite their recent, albeit awkward, concord, his presence still made her uneasy and she felt something squeeze inside her chest. Seeing him in the flesh, her earlier resolve to question him began to crumble. Maybe she should wait until Dr Chabra, or someone else – anyone not connected to the Homitys – was present.

Flora pretended not to have seen Hector, continuing to climb towards the house and Mr Homity in grim but resigned anticipation of what might ensue once she reached her room, but Hector started to cross the lawn to meet her, picking up pace as he did so.

'Hello.'

She was surprised to see him smiling. Despite her continued antipathy towards him, she returned the greeting with a civil nod. He was carrying something under his arm, wrapped in a dustbin liner. He began to walk alongside her. An awkward silence played out for a few seconds until he spoke suddenly.

'You've got a strange walk, haven't you?' He arched his eyebrows, studying her feet with interest.

Flora was taken aback. 'I'm sorry?'

'I was just watching you – I hadn't noticed before. You look a bit, well, unsteady. Is there something wrong with you?'

'That's actually quite rude, Hector. As it happens, yes; I have a condition, called dyspraxia. It's more of a problem when I'm tired these days. But you really shouldn't comment on such things, you know. Haven't your parents told you that?'

'Told me what?'

'That some thoughts should remain in your own head. That occasionally, it's better to say nothing than to cause offence.'

He seemed to absorb this for a moment, his brow creasing in concentration. 'So have I offended you, then? I was just making an observation. I just wanted to understand why you walk the way you do, that's all.'

'Yes. Well, now you know.' Flora felt more exasperated than affronted. Clearly Hector had no comprehension of social niceties.

'Are you staying for good? You don't feel as if you've made a huge mistake any more, coming here?'

'What do you mean – a mistake?' So it had been him then, looking in her diary. She thought as much. She wondered if he'd reported what he'd read back to his father.

He faltered a little. 'I mean – you seem a bit less uptight than when you first arrived. I think Mummy likes you. More than that other girl.'

Flora felt suddenly light-headed. Was he referring to

Iola? But as he continued, oblivious, it became clear he was talking about Mrs Homity's previous carer, the one who had left in such a hurry. The one he had upset for some reason.

'She wasn't fit for the job. Daddy said she was too young, not enough experience. He said it was probably just as well she handed in her notice. Better that you're older, I'd say.'

This had clearly been a back-handed compliment, then. Maybe he was growing more accepting of her.

He frowned. 'I didn't mean her any harm. She made such a fuss. It was her hair, you see. It was so long; so golden. Like ripe corn. I just wanted a little of it, to keep.'

Flora's pulse began to race. 'What – what did you do?'

'I snipped a lock of it, when she had her back turned. Only a bit. She was looking for something in the pantry and I thought she wouldn't notice. But she started to scream; said I was completely mad and she couldn't stay in the house a moment longer. It was a total overreaction, of course. Stupid little cow.'

Flora's head swam with the image of a leering Hector, creeping up behind the girl's back with scissors raised. Small wonder that she had left in such a hurry. But thank God it was nothing worse. Hector was being extremely candid about it all. He clearly had no idea he'd done anything wrong. She tried to imagine how she would have reacted in the same situation. It must have been a terrible shock for the poor girl. At least he would have no designs on Flora's own short, dun curls. Probably best not to let him know what she really thought, though.

She drew in a long, steadying breath. 'Well, I've no

plans to leave. Not at the moment, anyway.' She tried to keep her tone light. Anxious to change the subject, she indicated the bin liner. 'What's in the bag?'

Hector gripped his bundle more tightly. He seemed suddenly agitated. 'I found it. In the woods.'

'What did you find?'

His jaw tightened. He shook his head, glancing shiftily towards the house.

Flora wondered if Mr Homity was watching their exchange and what might be going through his head. The thought was discomfiting. She turned her back on the house, to face Hector. 'I just told you about my dyspraxia. The least you can do is tell me what you've got there.'

Hector hesitated for a second. Slowly, he reached beneath his arm and began to unwrap the plastic, holding forth his discovery. Flora peered into the bag and recoiled. It was a dead hare, small – probably a doe, limp and with blood oozing from its throat.

'I'm going to stuff it later. We get plenty of rabbits, but I've never found a hare before. It will make a wonderful addition to my collection.'

'But you mustn't!' Flora looked again at the poor creature in horror. She thought of the grotesque, badly stuffed menagerie in Hector's hobby room, then suddenly of Ostara; of the myths that her mother had told her when she was a child. Of how, years ago, hares were buried with reverence alongside humans.

'Hares are magical – sacred, even. You can't trap her in a glass case for people to gawp at. It's wrong. You should bury her. Let her bones go back into the earth where she belongs.'

Hector looked indignant. 'But I found it. It's mine.'

'She is *not* yours. And if you cut her open and mutilate her, you'll bring bad luck on yourself. Don't say I didn't warn you.'

Flora began to walk quickly away from him, suddenly sickened by his vacant eyes and warped mentality. He may not have been able to help it, but she couldn't bear to be around him a second longer.

'Wait! What sort of bad luck?'

Flora looked back to see his worried face staring after her. She smiled inwardly. 'Who knows? But I wouldn't tempt fate, if I were you. I really wouldn't.'

Hector stared at the animal, clearly torn by the possibility of being besieged by ill fortune. 'But what should I do with it, then?'

'How about taking her back into the woods where you found her? I'm sure you could find a nice yew tree to bury her under.' Flora realised she had his attention and was in full flow now. 'They're supposed to help the soul on its way. You might even say a prayer and a few words of apology, for good measure.'

'Will you help me? Look for the best place to bury it – I mean, her? I – I didn't know. About the bad luck, I mean.' Hastily, he re-wrapped the hare in the plastic, his eyes darting anxiously to the trees.

Flora saw that her words had actually sent him into a blind panic. It was as though he'd become suddenly childlike, incapable of reason. She'd heard about the association with yew trees and the dead; she wasn't entirely sure about the luck thing herself, but it felt satisfying that she'd been able to exert some sort of influence on Hector; put the wind up him a bit. However, the suggestion of going into the woods with him alone was not something she wanted to entertain.

'I – I have to check on Rufie. I'm sure you're capable of finding a yew tree by yourself. You don't need me to . . .'

His face reddened, his eyes flashing with sudden anger. '*You're* the one who's insisting it should be buried. I'm not a tree expert. You have to help me.'

'But –'

'If you don't, I'll tell Daddy I saw you in Xanthe's room. He'll be furious with you. And you wouldn't like *that*, would you?' His voice had lowered to a hiss. Flora's stomach turned over. She thought of Mr Homity, waiting in her room. Waiting, at the very least, to admonish her; she was certain of it. Flora didn't want more fuel added to his flames.

She drew in her breath.

'All right. Go and find a spade. I'll wait here.'

Within minutes, Hector returned, a shovel in one hand and the hare, now wrapped in a beige cotton throw, under his arm. Flora had been hovering anxiously by the path into the copse, deliberating as to whether accompanying Hector into the darkening woods or an encounter with his father was the lesser of the two evils. How she wished she had timed her return from the village differently.

'I thought the blanket was perhaps more respectful than the bin bag,' he said, watching Flora for a reaction. 'You know, like a shroud.'

She wondered about his logic, but simply nodded. He was obviously taking it very seriously, which was a start. Hopefully it would divert any attention from her.

'Right then. Where did you find her?'

'Through there. Close to the chapel.'

They walked in silence, side by side, along the dirt path. Beneath the canopy of green overhead, the late afternoon light had all but deserted them. Flora felt increasingly apprehensive. What on earth had she been thinking, agreeing to go alone into the woods with Hector? She stole a glance at him, but his expression was determined, all his focus plainly on the task ahead. She had to maintain an air of some sort of authority, behave as if she was in control, but was fearful of him having another irrational outburst.

The light levels increased a little as they reached the graveyard wall, but it was still dimmer than Flora was comfortable with. As if reading her thoughts, Hector laid down the spade and pulled a small flashlight from his jacket pocket.

'Here. This where I found her, right here.' He switched on the torch, pointing with his foot to a patch of grass a couple of yards from the gate.

Flora looked around, frantically searching for a suitable tree for Hector to dig beneath so that his task would soon be complete and she could go back to the house, even if it meant facing Mr Homity. Her eyes fell on a huge, majestic yew, gnarled with age, its knotted roots spreading out around it like a skirt. It seemed the perfect place for anyone to be laid to rest, with views over the graveyard and so close to where the hare must have made her nest.

She waved a hand. 'Right there – I think that would be the perfect spot.'

Hector propped the torch next to the tree so that the

beam fanned out across the ground like a floodlight. He laid the hare down carefully and, taking up the spade once more, aimed it at a spot between the long, wavy fingers of the roots.

'Here?'

'Yes. Right there.'

Flora stood picking at her lip as Hector took off his jacket, hooking it from an overhanging branch. He rolled up his sleeves and began to dig with enthusiasm, but the task proved arduous. The ground was hard, smaller roots snaking below needing to be sliced with the blade of the shovel to clear the way.

'Are you sure this is the best spot?' Slightly breathless, Hector ran the back of his now grimy hand across his forehead, straightening for a moment.

'Certain. I told you: yew trees are magical. But that will do now. Let's put her into the hole.' This was taking far longer than Flora would have liked. The sooner she got out of there, the better.

'No, it needs to be deeper. So the foxes can't get at her.' He continued to displace the earth, his face grim with determination.

Flora's heart sank. She scanned their surroundings with unease, discomfited by the eerie stillness and being so far from the house as dusk approached. Why had she ever suggested burying the hare? Whatever was she thinking?

Stamping her feet, she wrapped her arms around herself, trying to rub away the creeping cold. All the time, Hector puffed and blew. He muttered now and again under his breath, apparently oblivious to her presence. Flora watched in desperation. He was getting completely carried away. After around twenty minutes, he had created a hole deep enough to come up to his waist. The light was fading fast now and the temperature had plummeted further. He stood back, cheeks glowing in the torchlight, and put down the spade.

He looked up at Flora, encircled by the mound of dirt and sinewy strips of roots he had created. 'I think this will probably do now.'

Flora's whole body had been rigid with anxiety. Relief flooded through her. 'Yes; yes, that's perfect.'

All she wanted to do was complete their mission and get back to the house, back into light and warmth, as quickly as possible. It had all been a terrible idea. Hector held out his arms to receive the bundle containing the hare. Flora's arms still stiff with tension, she passed it to him, then lifted the torch to illuminate the area as he laid the animal on the ground.

'Wait – what's that?' Something in the hole had caught Flora's eye.

The light flicked over a shred of something pale blue, incongruous against the deep brown of the soil.

Flora leaned forwards to get a better look. What appeared to be the corner of a piece of fabric was protruding from the earth behind Hector's shoe. He twisted round to see what she was looking at, stooping to pull at the material.

As he did so, it began to unwind. Soon he was holding a long strand of fine, wavy wool. The more he pulled, the more appeared. He wrapped the filthy skein around his hand, stopping to look up at her for a moment, his brow knotted with confusion.

'Use the spade to clear the earth away,' urged Flora.

Despite her instinct to get out of the woods, she was curious to see what he had uncovered. 'Whatever it is, you're unravelling it doing that.'

Hector retrieved the shovel and began to scrape away the soil around the wool. Flora watched, intrigued. Soon, what appeared to be the remnants of a blue shawl or blanket began to appear. But as Hector tugged and it was freed, it became clear that something else was concealed beneath the wool.

Caked with soil, a small rubber teddy, the kind that would have been commonplace in a baby's pram maybe forty years earlier, fell to the ground. But it was what tumbled out with the bear that almost made Flora's heart stop.

'Oh, good God. Is that . . .? It is! A skull!' Hector sounded almost triumphant. He cast the spade to one side and bent down, grabbing the thing and cupping it in both hands. He looked up at Flora, then back at the tiny, fleshless head, his eyes wide. He dragged one foot along the ground, turning over other fragments of bone that had been released from the blanket.

'Well, it looks as though somebody else got here before us.' He turned the skull over in his hands, examining it in morbid fascination. 'Funny shape. Looks like an alien. What d'you think it is? A monkey or something?'

Flora's throat seemed to have seized up. She opened and closed her mouth, the horror of what she was seeing rendering her momentarily speechless.

'No,' she whispered eventually. She was shaking from head to foot now, a wave of nausea surging through her. 'For God's sake, Hector, can't you see? That's no animal. It's a little baby.'

CHAPTER 41

Stretmore, December 2001

Mrs Malone's testimony had set them on the right track. The absence of any dental records was telling, but evidence of an old surgery to fuse discs in the spine had helped the police to confirm via medical records that the remains were in all probability those of Sheila Lanyon's half-brother, Roger Blight. They'd managed to track down where he had been working in the mid-1970s. Several of his former colleagues, one in particular that he'd struck up a friendship with, had since passed away, although two men they did manage to locate verified the fact they hadn't seen much of Roger since he'd lost his job in the local foundry at some point in 1975, but couldn't be certain exactly when. People had wondered as to his whereabouts, but no one appeared to have officially reported him missing: Sheila had told anyone who'd bothered to ask that she believed he'd found work elsewhere and moved up north.

DS Kaur breezed through the double doors clutching a blue cardboard folder. Her head was spinning after a morning spent interviewing. Any sympathy she might have felt for the victim found in the cellar at 29 Ostleton Road was diminishing rapidly. Seeing DI Baines with knitted brow, poring over something, she hovered a short distance from his desk. She had been surprised to learn that, as a young DS, he'd actually been involved directly with the Chappell family after the abduction of the baby, Warren. He'd seemed quite emotional to be reminded about it all and clearly the fact that they'd never found the baby, particularly with what had happened to the rest of the family in the aftermath, had weighed heavy on him. Whether or not there was any connection with the body in Ostleton Road or the Lanyon woman wasn't clear, but DI Baines seemed to be taking it all very personally. He was an old softie really.

DS Kaur watched him fondly for a moment, before placing the folder in his in-tray. She stood back a little and waited for his reaction.

'Erm – the full report's in from pathology for Roger Blight, sir.'

Inspector Baines looked up from his desk hopefully and put down the pen. 'Anything interesting?'

'An injury consistent with a heavy blow to the head. Fractures to the left humerus and scapula – possibly sustained post mortem. Could have happened when he fell down the cellar steps.'

Baines arched an eyebrow. 'Or when someone pushed him.'

'Well, he didn't wrap himself in that rug.' Sergeant Kaur rolled her eyes. 'It's just whether what happened was an accident or an act of malice. From everything I'm hearing, he wasn't too popular. We could really do with finding Flora Lanyon. She'd have only been a kid at the time, but I reckon she's the only one who might be able to shed any light on what went on in that house. We managed to trace Blight's ex-wife. She'd had no contact with him for over forty years. And she seemed less than grief-stricken to learn he was no longer with us. Sounds as if he was far from a top bloke.' She pulled a face. 'Liked a drink a bit too much and quite handy with his fists, apparently.'

Baines rubbed his chin. 'Maybe he got handy with the wrong person.'

'Only the mother and daughter living there, from what we can gather. The old neighbour – Mrs Malone – said they never seemed to have visitors. No other men over the threshold since the husband passed donkey's years ago, from the sounds of things.'

'Well, it's not impossible she could have missed someone, unless she had binoculars on the place twenty-four/seven. Blight could've brought someone back with him after a few beers, had a falling-out.'

Sergeant Kaur nodded. 'We're hoping the diaries might throw something up.'

The inspector sat up. 'Diaries?'

The sergeant groaned inwardly. 'Sorry, sir. I should've said. Forensics found these boxes in one of the wardrobes at the house. Full of notebooks that Flora Lanyon had been writing in since she was a kid. They're going through them all now, but there's so much it won't be a five-minute job. So far, most of it's waffle by the sounds of things, but you never know . . .'

'Well, thanks for keeping me in the loop. Eventually.' He looked at her obliquely. 'In the meantime, let's see if we can't find our Miss Lanyon. No leads at all, you say?'

'No, sir. I'll keep you posted if there's any developments.'

'You do that, Sergeant. And go and have a word with Forensics – see if they've managed to find anything useful in those diaries. Sounds as if the time frame we're really interested in would be about '73 to '76, going on the suspected time of decease.' He looked at her pointedly. 'You might even like to give them a once-over yourself. Might speed things up a bit.'

DS Kaur thought of the number of boxes she'd seen earlier in the Forensics department. Her heart sank.

She squeezed out a small smile. 'I'll get onto it right away, sir.'

*

The diaries offered a disturbing insight into Flora's state of mind in the months leading up to her mother's death and also revealed what life had been like for her as a young girl. Between Sergeant Kaur and the Forensics officer tasked with examining the remaining notebooks, it had taken days to sift through the information; painstakingly, line by line. Much of it was mundane beyond belief. Years of what someone had eaten for tea, what the weather had been doing that day. What had been on television. At the beginning there was little of real interest, the musings of a lonely child with an overactive imagination, given to flights of fantasy. All quite poignant, but nothing really significant.

But woven into the narrative, hints of something else

festering below the surface gradually started to seep through. Something very dark indeed.

DS Kaur found it emotionally draining. She couldn't shake the case off at the end of the working day as she was usually able to. Everything she'd read kept going round and round in her mind and it was keeping her awake at night. She had begun to feel as if she actually knew Flora, and her heart went out to her. It seemed as if happiness had eluded the woman her whole life. The sergeant had fought back tears more than once, particularly when reading the excerpts from when Flora was a child.

Kaur set aside the sections she felt were particularly salient and photocopied them, going over any passages which might prove helpful with a highlighter pen. Some made for uncomfortable reading. But soon a full picture of what had actually happened at 29 Ostleton Road had begun to emerge. And of the shadow the monstrous Roger Blight had cast over the lives of Flora and her mother. While as a police officer upholding the law Sergeant Kaur couldn't condone the wilful taking of a life, she wondered if she herself would have acted any differently under such unthinkable circumstances.

The entries stopped abruptly three days before the gas board officials had gained entry to the property and made their grisly discovery. It was as though poor Flora Lanyon had disappeared off the face of the earth.

But DS Kaur was more determined than ever to find her.

CHAPTER 42

Stretmore, 27 October 1975

Built in the latter part of the nineteenth century, Ostleton Road had once been deemed a desirable suburban location. But the tall, three-storey red-brick homes that stood proudly along the tree-lined avenue had gradually become swamped by the prefabricated social housing and high-rise flats thrown up around them after the Second World War, and soon the road's status had levelled to that of the newer ones in the vicinity. Many of the houses had fallen into disrepair and some even stood empty, with missing slates and boarded-up windows. Squatters had moved into the house at the end of the terrace, only five doors down, after its elderly residents had died. Rats could often be seen weaving amongst the debris discarded in the front garden.

Mercifully, David had made at least some provision for Sheila and their daughter, in the event anything should happen to him. Sheila had never had to deal with the financial side of things: David had always taken care of everything and she'd been happy to let him. At least he'd had the good sense to take out insurance and make sure the mortgage would be paid if he went before her. She'd often wondered if he'd had any inkling of what might happen to him – some sort of premonition. She'd heard that people sometimes did.

Sheila had tried hard to maintain number 29 after her husband's passing, but, with only a meagre widow's pension and the few pounds from her little cleaning job at the local community centre, it was an uphill struggle, even without the mortgage. Heating such a large house was an expense beyond her means and she felt humiliated by continually having to ask at the corner shop for a few extra days to pay for her groceries. But she really didn't want to move. This was the house she had shared with her husband since the day they'd married, where they'd made so many happy memories. Where she'd brought Flo into the world.

And then one day, right out of the blue, her half-brother Roger had turned up. She wasn't even going to invite him in, but somehow he had insinuated his way past her into the hallway and, once he was inside, he wasted no time in making himself at home. She felt angry with herself and helpless. She should have stood her ground right from the start and given him his marching orders. But she was weak; she knew that. And he scared her. Always had.

He had wheedled and pleaded at first; told her that she was his only living relative, that he'd had a row with his landlord and had to leave his bedsit. He had nowhere to go. He needed a bed for the night. Maybe two, at the most. That he would bung her a few quid towards the housekeeping. It was with the greatest reluctance that she had eventually agreed to show him to her spare room. But she quickly realised that it had been a huge mistake.

Roger was nine years her senior. He had been her father's son from a previous marriage. Left a widower at the age of thirty-eight, her dad had been in a hurry to remarry: more, it would seem, for a replacement mother and carer for his son than a wife and companion for himself. Sheila's parents' marriage had been less than blissful and her own childhood marred by the suffocating male influences in her life. Her father had been controlling and surly. And Roger was a chip off the old block.

Now, here she was, sharing her roof with the man who had made her formative years a misery. Her own mother was long dead and she had no close friends; no one she could turn to for support of any kind. It sickened her to admit it, but she had gradually allowed herself to become financially dependent on Roger. She'd told herself that it would be a short-term solution; that it was preferable to going into the red. That she could put up with him for a while. She was still a young woman, relatively attractive. Hopefully it wasn't too late to find someone else to share her life with when she felt ready. But until that time, she had a house to run and a daughter to feed. And even though she loathed the man, Roger's contribution was helping to keep their heads above water.

Flo was a delightful child but not without complications. At least, that was how Sheila had begun to think of the girl's various issues. She'd always expected that Flo would outgrow her clumsiness; that she was perhaps just a late developer in many ways. It had never concerned her too much before, while Flo's dad was alive. But without his support, coupled with the daily battle to keep Roger from flying off the handle for one reason or another, her daughter's problems had become more apparent – and more of a strain on her nerves. Roger was a bully by nature and had now made Flo the focus of his irrational ire. Sheila felt exhausted by it all.

This uncomfortable arrangement, she'd thought, she'd *hoped*, would last a few weeks – a month or two at the most. She should have known better. Because here they were, almost five years on from the day he had wormed his way in. She'd tried her best to protect Flo, really she had. If only the poor kid could be a bit less . . . *quirky*. It broke Sheila's heart that her daughter seemed to have no friends; that mealtimes aside, she spent every spare moment hiding in her room. She had become quieter and more subdued of late; moody, even. Sheila wondered with increasing concern if there was something, other than the usual, troubling her. But whenever she asked if everything was okay, Flo would shrug and say she was fine. She was a closed book.

Though that Monday morning, Flo had come down to breakfast, pale and drawn, the skin around her eyes dark and almost bruise-like. Sheila studied her daughter. She looked utterly miserable, as though she hadn't slept for a week.

'You all right, love?' Sheila had crossed the kitchen and put a hand to Flo's forehead as she sat at the table. The girl flinched at her touch and shrank back.

'I'm *fine*. Stop asking me all the time.'

Sheila frowned. 'Maybe I should make you an

appointment to see Dr MacLean. You look so pale these days. Maybe you're, I don't know, anaemic or something.'

'No!' Flo's eyes widened in alarm. 'I don't need to see the doctor. I told you, there's nothing wrong. I'm just – just a bit tired, that's all.' Her voice was sharp, and a touch too loud. Her eyes swivelled anxiously towards the door. Sheila followed their trajectory.

'It's okay, he's already left.'

Sheila pulled up a chair next to Flo and took her hands in her own across the table. She searched her daughter's face. Something in Flo's haunted expression made her stomach turn over.

'You're quite sure – that there's nothing worrying you? You can tell me, you know. Have you . . .' *How to put it delicately?* 'I know it's a bit soon perhaps, but have you started your periods? Some girls get them very early. I was almost thirteen when I first got mine, but that's not to say yours mightn't come sooner.'

Flo's lower lip began to tremble. She dropped her gaze and withdrew her hands from her mother's.

'I don't know, Mum.' Her voice was small, almost a whisper. She wrapped her thin arms around herself, plucking anxiously at the bobbly sleeves of her cardigan, and looked up suddenly, staring into Sheila's eyes earnestly. 'How would I be able to tell?'

Sheila had been mortified. She realised she'd never actually sat Flo down and explained to her about the birds and the bees. Never prepared her for what could happen to her body as she approached adolescence. She had always assumed Flo would pick things up from the girls at school, or that they'd be taught all about them by their teacher. Yet again, she had let her down.

'Do you – have you noticed any bleeding at all? *Down there*?'

Flo's cheeks flushed scarlet. She dropped her eyes. 'No.' She rose abruptly, scraping her chair across the floor. 'I'd better go. I'm going to be late.'

'Flo . . .' Sheila looked on helplessly as she moved towards the door.

'Leave me alone, Mum. I'm all right. Stop fretting.'

Minutes later, the front door slammed. Sheila rushed into the hall to see her daughter's forlorn figure through the glass, lolloping down Ostleton Road, her head bowed, satchel trailing. A knot formed in Sheila's throat. She grabbed her coat and hurried after her. Flo looked round, stony-faced, as she caught up, but said nothing. They walked in awkward silence. As they reached the gate, Sheila leaned forwards, pressing her lips to her daughter's cheek. Flo accepted reluctantly, but didn't return the gesture. Sheila watched, her hands clasped across her chest, as Flo carried on across the playground, her head still lowered.

Sheila was even more worried now. There was definitely something else going on with Flo, she was sure of it. Roger was a tyrant who delighted in tormenting the girl, and it was hard for her sometimes: Sheila knew that. She remembered all too well how he'd been with her when *she* was a child and cursed the day she'd been forced to let him back into her life. *Their* lives. Lately Flo had become surly and short-tempered and it wasn't like her at all.

Maybe it wasn't just Roger. Sheila hoped Flo wasn't being picked on in school again. Things had never been easy for her, being a little different as she was. Kids could be cruel. Or maybe it was no more than that: an age thing. Hormones. Puberty was a tricky time; Sheila remembered the anguish she'd gone through herself. There was always the danger, too, that Flo might go off the rails if she wasn't steered in the right direction. She'd always been such a good girl, but some sort of deep-seated anxiety could easily be a tipping point. More and more kids seemed to be out of control these days.

Whatever was at the back of it, the only way Sheila could help would be by finding out what the problem was. So, after dropping Flo off at school, she went up to her bedroom. Steeling herself, she reached beneath the mattress and wrangled out the notebook, smiling wistfully at the picture of the hare. She remembered the day she'd given it to Flo, how her little face had lit up. Sheila sat down on the bed and turned the cover, leafing through to the most recent entries.

And she began to read. Sheila suddenly realised she was shivering. She glanced across at the little alarm clock on Flo's bedside table. She'd been sitting there over an hour, staring at those few shocking lines.

Dear Ostara, He came into my room again last night . . .

The words seemed to dance on the page in front of her.

So now she knew. She couldn't unsee what she had just read. The shocking, unthinkable detail of what had been happening to poor Flo. It was far worse than she had feared. Roger had always been cruel; that much she knew. But this – *this* . . . Sheila was flooded with a whole range of emotions: anger, revulsion, sorrow. Fear of what damage had been done to her daughter, physically and emotionally.

Sheila hated herself for being so stupid. She'd been totally wrapped up with what now seemed trivial worries; about money and running the house, and keeping everything ticking over. How could she not have noticed what was going on under her own roof? She had let this happen: allowed that monster into their home.

As she thought about him, she could barely contain the fury building inside her. She balled up her fists with blinding rage and sheer loathing. He would never lay another hand on Flo. Not while Sheila had breath in her body.

Because, sure as hell, she wasn't going to sit back and let her beloved daughter suffer in silence.

Not any more.

CHAPTER 43

Little Hambley, December 2001

'Hector, we have to call the police. I don't know what's gone on here, but it's not right. No one buries a baby like that unless they've got something to hide.'

Hector continued to handle the pitifully small skull, pushing a finger through one of the eye sockets.

'Really? Do you think somebody killed it?' His voice was almost gleeful, a suggestion of a smile on his lips.

'I've no idea. That's for the police to decide. But you must put the skull back and we'll go and phone the emergency services.' Flora watched despairingly as he made no attempt to climb from the hole. '*Now!*'

Still he remained where he was, a strange half-leer on his face, his full attention on his discovery. Flora couldn't bear to look at him. Brandishing the flashlight, she began to wend her way back up the dirt track alone as quickly as she could, playing the beam to left and right. A sickening fear had taken hold of her. Who could have done such a thing? And Hector's reaction was nothing short of bizarre; callous, even, whether he was of sound mind or otherwise.

'Wait,' called Hector. She could hear him stumbling behind her now, cursing from time to time as his shoes caught on half-buried stones and tree roots.

'Wait, will you!' He sounded angry now. 'What about the hare? About the bad luck?'

Before she could respond, she was pulled up short by the appearance of a shadowy, featureless figure on the path ahead. Pointing the torch straight towards it, she recognised Mr Homity, who raised a light of his own in her direction, dazzling her for a moment. She shielded her eyes with her forearm.

'Mr Homity, it's me, Flora. Can you – I can't see with that pointing at me.'

Ignoring her plea, he continued to aim the light directly into her face.

'Mr Homity, please. We've found something. Back there, in the woods. That is . . .'

'Found something?' His voice sounded sharp. 'What have you found exactly? And where is Hector?'

As if on cue, there was a yell from behind. Flora turned to see Hector waving his arms excitedly.

'Daddy, you must come and look. We were going to bury the hare and then I dug up some bones. Flora claims it's a baby, but I'm not sure. What do you think?'

'The hare? A baby? Whatever are you talking about?' Unblinking, Mr Homity stared beyond Flora, his pupils disturbingly dilated in the darkness. 'This is all most irregular. We should go back to the house. It's far too cold to be having this conversation out here.'

'But you need to come and see,' protested Hector. 'Flora says we should ring the police.'

'The police?' His father gave a derisory snort. 'Don't be ridiculous. Why on earth would we need to bother the police? I imagine you've found the pet cemetery next to the graveyard. All manner of animals have been interred there over the years. Yes, that's what it will be. Maybe even my boyhood companion, our spaniel Floss.'

He turned back towards the house, calling over his shoulder, 'Come along. There's no time for this nonsense. Mummy will be needing her supper soon.'

Flora was incredulous. His reaction made no sense at all. 'But the police really need to be informed – it's definitely not an animal.'

Mr Homity stopped suddenly, as though reconsidering. Flora could see the back of his head wobbling slightly in that way it did at times.

'Well, maybe you're right,' he said after a moment. 'But we'll have to use Hector's phone. The one in the library has something wrong with it.' His voice sounded suddenly distant. 'Yes. Yes, we must all go into the annexe.' The words had become slow and deliberate, as though he was reasoning something through. But then he seemed to check himself slightly. He rubbed his hands together briskly, licking his lips. 'And then we really must attend to poor Agnes, of course. It's getting late.'

His head juddering more than ever, Mr Homity led the way. The sound of rushing water grew louder as they neared the annexe. Sandwiched between Mr Homity and Hector as they approached the door, Flora began to feel more and more uneasy. She stumbled slightly as she felt the insistent pressure of a hand on her back, and shot a look over her shoulder to see Hector staring at her unnervingly, his face blank and unsmiling. It occurred to Flora now that she was actually being escorted, guided to the annexe. Her mouth felt dry. She thought of Mr Homity standing there earlier, staring down at her from the house. What had he been doing? Suddenly she wished she had said nothing about the skeleton; that she hadn't even drawn Hector's attention to the fact it was human, let alone his father's. It would have been far wiser to go directly to the police. Mr Homity exuded an odd tension, which made her question exactly what he had on his mind. Every one of her senses was heightened now. The thought flashed through her mind: *fight or flight*. She was a hopeless runner, but if need be, it would have to be the latter.

The building was in darkness, with only the porch light from the main house to their right offering any illumination. Mr Homity, leading the way, swept the beam of the flashlight ahead of them towards the entrance. Soon the light was on in the passageway, the door closed behind them.

After her last visit, Flora had sworn never to enter the place again. She would shudder every time she thought of Hector's surreal collection of dead animals. The fact that Mr Homity had indulged him and helped to provide the necessary materials was even worse. She felt Hector's hand grip her shoulder, steering her down the passage. Frantically, she darted a look at the door, planning her exit. The sooner she could get away from them, from Mill House altogether, the better.

The lobby felt cold, but as they entered the anteroom leading to the living room, the intense heat radiating from the log burner hit them at once. Everything looked unusually tidy and clean, despite Rita being away on holiday.

'Miss Lanyon, go and take a seat.' Mr Homity's voice had become forceful. There was a definite urgency to his tone. Flora's feet seemed to have turned to lead. He waved her towards the living room, spinning round to face his son. 'Hector, go down to the basement and fetch your cordless telephone, will you. Then we can call the police, if Miss Lanyon feels strongly about it.' His eyes flashed in the direction of the open door to the living room and the archway beyond, his head beginning to wobble once again. He stared pointedly at Hector, who seemed confused.

'But I didn't think you wanted . . .'

'Yes; well, maybe I wasn't thinking clearly before. If something untoward has happened in our grounds, I suppose we have an obligation to inform the appropriate people so that it can be investigated. Isn't that right, Miss Lanyon?' His eyes widened so much that he appeared almost demonic. 'We wouldn't want to fall foul of the law. Would we?' His mocking tone, his loose body language, told Flora that Mr Homity would have no qualms about breaking the law. In any way whatsoever.

A cold fear had taken hold of Flora. Her heart began to thud, so hard she could feel the rise and fall of her coat. Her gaze travelled from Mr Homity's simpering smile to Hector's bulging, questioning eyes; his perplexed expression. There was a sinister sort of undercurrent here; she wasn't sure what was going on between them, but knew that whatever it was, she wasn't intended to be privy to it. Trying to sound unperturbed, she began to inch her way back towards the lobby.

'Erm – if you don't mind, I – I'll just get back to my room. I've been out all afternoon and I feel shattered. Plus, the cat will need feeding. You – you carry on and make the call. I can speak to the police up at the house later, if they need to ask me anything.'

'One moment, please.' Mr Homity's voice was shrill. 'I think that perhaps the call might be better coming from you – since you are an outsider, you understand. Hector – *the phone*.'

Flora felt desperate. She turned to look at Hector, who hesitated briefly. Something indecipherable passed across his face as his focus shifted from his father to Flora, then back again. Without another word, he swept past them and disappeared through the archway which led to the basement. The sound of heavy footfall rang out as he descended the steps.

Mr Homity's tongue tickled his lower lip in that disconcerting way of his. Flora realised in horror that he had gradually manoeuvred himself so that he was barring her way to the door back into the hallway. There was an ominous click as it closed suddenly and he leaned back against it, both of his hands behind him. Flora felt a mounting sense of panic, as though she were about to explode.

'Do go through and have a seat. It won't take a moment. And then you'll have peace of mind that the matter is being dealt with.' His voice was even harder now, his eyes like flint.

Flora began to hyperventilate. Her head was spinning, blood rushing in her ears. All the while Mr Homity's cold, unwavering gaze was upon her, his mouth upturned into a peculiar leering smile, his head quivering. She felt like a wild animal, one of Hector's unfortunate victims, lured into a trap. Every instinct she had had screamed at her to run, but stupidly she had dithered. And now she was completely cornered.

'I – I really ought to . . .'

Hector reappeared from behind her. Everything seemed to happen very quickly. Before Flora had time to react, some sort of material had been clamped hard over her mouth and nose. Her hands scrabbled feebly to fight it off but it was useless.

The sound of voices around her became muffled and distorted as her vision blurred and she slid to the ground.

*

Blearily, Flora began to come round, confused to find she was unable to move her hands or feet. Everything was hazy initially, but as things came back into focus, she realised she was no longer in the lobby. A faint light shone down from somewhere above. Freezing air brushed her face as she felt herself bumped and dragged across cold, wet turf. Her limbs felt bruised and heavy; too heavy to lift. The sound of fast-flowing water gushed from below.

The mill wheel. She was being taken to the mill wheel.

Suddenly they stopped, somewhere near the water's edge. Flora was lying face down. She could taste earth and wet grass and wanted to retch.

'Should I untie her?'

She recognised Hector's voice; edgy, excitable. She winced as he gripped her arm, pinching the skin beneath her coat, then rolled her onto her back. Flora clamped her eyes tightly shut, praying they'd believe her still unconscious; give her a chance to regain her faculties.

'No. We can't risk her escaping.' Mr Homity's clipped response; icily detached. Suddenly his face was close to hers. She could smell his rancid breath as he leaned in towards her. He peeled back one of her eyelids with a slight, manicured fingertip.

She quelled the urge to scream, quickly rolling her eyes upwards into their sockets. *Play dead*, something told her. *Play dead and you might have half a chance of coming out of this alive.*

'She's still out. The other one was more of a challenge.'

Hector emitted a sudden, almost maniacal cackle. 'Yes, she put up quite a fight, didn't she! But she asked for it. All those lies she told.'

The other one? Flora's chest tightened. Could they be talking about Iola?

What felt like the sole of a boot shook Flora's thigh roughly where she lay. The sudden weight of Hector's thick hand was across her mouth and nose, feeling for her breath. She held it in, catching a whiff of sweat and soil, still ingrained in his palm.

'Do you think the chloroform has actually killed her, Daddy?'

Cold, bony fingers probed her neck. 'No. It's faint, but there's definitely still a pulse.'

Flora thought now of the friendship bracelet. Of the purple boot she'd glimpsed that day in the water. A monkey boot – Iola's signature footwear. Flora's instincts had been right. The barman's words had spurred her on even more. It had been ages since she'd seen Stevie, but the last time she'd bumped into him, he'd said Iola had been on a mission to find Warren:

'Another bloody wild goose chase, most likely. She's

booked herself into this B&B in some village in the back of beyond – the Cotswolds, I think she said. Something about a water mill? I was only half listening, to be honest.'

He'd sighed; a touch wistfully, Flora thought.

'I take it all with a pinch of salt. Too much wacky baccy over the years – it's addled her brain. But hey, if it keeps her happy . . .' Stevie had rolled his eyes in resignation. 'By the way, she said she'd been doing some thinking and she'll be writing to you soon. Wouldn't hold my breath though, knowing our Iola.'

No letter had ever arrived. Flora had been sad about that, although not entirely surprised. They'd parted on such bad terms. Even after all those years, Iola had never given up on looking for Warren. She'd been so sure there was still a chance of finding him alive. And it seemed her quest to find her baby brother had brought her here, to Little Hambley. To Mill House. And the warped little world of the Homitys.

What had happened to her?

*

They say that when you're dying, your whole life flashes before your eyes. Every single experience, the good, the bad; the sublime and the downright unpalatably hideous. That every hurt you've ever inflicted on another comes back on you a hundredfold. And once that ordeal is behind you, when you've received your just deserts and acknowledged your earthly transgressions with contrition, those loved ones who have gone before come to greet you; to guide you with renewed serenity on your way to the next life and into that soft, eternal light.

But none of this appeared to be the case. The shock

of being plunged into the icy water had revived Flora completely. It was as though she'd met with thousands of shards of glass, piercing her flesh from every angle. Apart from the pain, all she could feel was blind, indescribable panic. Her glasses had been carried from her face as she descended, blurring her vision. There was a quadrant of light coming from somewhere above. Something was wrapped tightly around her leg and she struggled in vain against its force. She was being sucked under by its weight and the strength of the current. As she fought to rise against it, she squinted up towards the light source and realised she was actually several feet beneath the transparent floor of the annexe, in danger of being pulled into the waterwheel. She writhed like an eel, lifting then lowering her arms, trying desperately to move herself back and upwards, away from the paddles. It was hopeless. She couldn't rise any further as the water chilled and engulfed her, bloating her lungs until she thought they might actually burst; drawing her down towards the silt and sinewy weeds that climbed from its depths.

As she scanned around helplessly, her eyes began to adjust to her surroundings. And it was then, stirred from the murky layer beneath, that she saw it appear once more. The boot. And then its counterpart. Flora felt her head shaking from side to side, her mouth falling open into a silent, petrified scream.

NO NO NO!

Because above the boots, trapped somehow behind the waterwheel, a partially decomposed corpse was beginning to emerge.

And she knew that it must be Iola.

To be confronted – and now trapped – with someone in such an appallingly real and horribly altered guise, all bare, bleached bones and grinning teeth; the gaping eye sockets that, though unseeing, seemed to bore into her very soul. In her worst nightmares, Flora could never have imagined anything so disturbing. Her arms, still bound, flailed in terror as she fought against the ghoulish vision, which loomed like the ancient figurehead of a ghost ship tethered to the prow. It seemed to be drawing her towards it as it pulsed with the movement of the current.

Flora could no longer feel her legs. With every terrified gasp, more water flooded into her mouth and up her nose, choking her, robbing her of every vestige of oxygen that remained in her system. The rush of fluid filling her ears grew fainter. As she slipped into oblivion, the last thing she saw was the distorted yet familiar face of someone else: someone very much alive, his bulging eyes wide and leering down at her through the glass as she reached out feebly one more time, before her arms grew heavy. As her strength ebbed away, she began to drift further downwards now; down, down into the deep, dark waters. A last feeble trail of bubbles left her mouth, rising to the surface beneath the glass as the cold, pitiless eyes continued to watch her demise; fascinated, devoid of emotion.

And then everything went black.

CHAPTER 44

December 2001

File: Roger Blight, Deceased

Transcript: Flora Lanyon's Diary Entry Extracts, 1975–2001

27 October 1975

Dear Ostara,

Mummy said something very strange today. She told me she knew I had bad dreams and if I was ever worried about burglars or anything, I could put my dressing gown across the bottom of my door at bedtime and it would stop them getting in. I tried doing it and it makes it really hard to open the door. It's quite clever really. I shall do it every night now. I wonder what made her say that though? I wonder if she knows?

Halloween 1975

Dear Ostara,

I saw something really bad this afternoon. I don't know what to do. Mummy sent me to the corner shop for a loaf after school. I saw Iola Chappell's mum over the road going in before me. I didn't want to bump into her on my own. She is quite scary-looking and sometimes she shouts. She left the baby outside in his pram. She often does that. Mummy says she shouldn't. I was waiting round the corner by the bins until she came out. Then I saw this man getting out of a big blue car. I thought he was going into the shop too. But he looked round to see if anyone was watching him. He didn't see me. Then he took the baby out of the pram really quickly and put him in the car on the back seat. He got back in and drove off very fast.

I remembered the number plate and I always keep a pencil and a little notebook in my pocket, just like Harriet the Spy does, so I wrote it down inside the back cover. Then Iola's mum came out of the shop and she started to scream. The shopkeeper came out to see what was going on. Then some other people came out of their houses because Iola's mum was getting louder and louder and waving her arms about. It was horrible.

I went back home and told Mummy a lie. I said they had run out of bread. I think I should have told her the truth. If I wasn't such a scaredy cat I would have just gone into the shop and I wouldn't have seen anything. I can't tell her about the man in the car now or she will know I am a liar. I don't know what to do about the number plate. A policeman came to the house but

I didn't say anything because I thought I would get into trouble. I hope the police find the baby very soon.

1 November 1975

Dear Ostara,

Uncle Roger has gone!! For good!!! Mummy told me when she picked me up from school this lunchtime. She says he won't be coming back. I think it must have worked, saying lots of prayers. I knew it would if I did it long and hard enough. This is the best day ever ☺.

I helped Mummy take some things to the Oxfam shop in town this afternoon. We went on the bus. She had put it all into plastic bags. He left his clothes and some other stuff in his room. Mummy says he told her to get rid of everything. Maybe he is going to buy some new things in his new house, wherever it is. We don't want his smelly old rubbish anyway. Tonight we are having fishfingers and chips for tea. I am so happy I could burst!

March 1977

Dear Ostara,

Mummy came out of hospital this afternoon. I was very sad to leave my foster parents. Today I had Golden Nuggets and orange juice for breakfast and Mrs Oakley made me a packed lunch with peanut butter sandwiches and a big piece of the lovely chocolate cake she baked especially for me. She hugged me hard before I left and said I had been the best daughter they had ever had. I cried a lot when Mr Oakley dropped me off this morning.

He was sniffing and said he thought he was getting a cold.

Mummy is much better but still not properly well. She was very tired and had to go for a lie-down after I got home from school. It feels strange coming back to this house. I have not thought about Uncle Roger for a long time and now I keep remembering what he did. It makes me feel funny and a bit sick. I hope things will get back to normal now. But I'm not sure what normal is any more.

November 1978

Dear Ostara,

I never realised how badly the baby being taken had affected Iola and her family. Now I feel worse than ever. I just had to do something, even if it is very late in the day. I hope my letter will help the police to trace the man with the blue car. I keep thinking about it all the time. If I had come forward when it happened, maybe they would have been able to find Warren. I feel so guilty. I can't tell Iola or she will hate me. I AM SUCH A COWARD.

November 1978

Dear Ostara,

The police didn't find the car or the man. Iola thinks they didn't even bother looking. I don't know if she's right or not. But she says she's going to find the car herself. I haven't said anything but I don't see how she can. I mean, where would you even start? And I know it's horrible to think of but baby Warren could even be dead and it might all be too late anyway. It's so, so sad.

January 1980

Dear Ostara,

Today started off badly but ended up being quite a good day in a way. I was waiting for Iola to bring her tray to the table in the canteen at lunchtime when three girls from 4B came and sat down on the bench a bit further down from me. I always try to ignore them – they're really horrible and always make comments about the way I walk, and my hair and other stuff. One of them knocked over the water jug. I think she did it on purpose, and it spilled into my holdall and all over my PE kit. They all laughed and Hayley, the one who'd knocked the jug, made some comment about it probably needing a good wash anyway. I felt like crying. Then Iola appeared with her lunch. Her face was chalk white and her eyes looked really angry. She put down the tray on the table next to me and walked over to Hayley very slowly. Then Iola picked up a cup and tipped squash all over Hayley's head. She said, "I think you could do with a wash now too." Hayley just looked totally shocked and her friends actually laughed. They aren't nice at all. None of them said a word to Iola, just got up and moved to another table. Hayley went off to dry her hair and her blazer. It's funny, because Iola's so tiny but they all seem scared of her. I saw them later in the corridor and none of them could even look me in the eye. Don't think they'll be bothering me from now on somehow. I am so lucky to have found a friend like Iola.

February 1984

Dear Ostara,

I am too upset to write much today. Iola found my diaries this morning. She knows everything now. She never wants to see me again and I can't blame her. I have lost the only friend I've ever had and it's all my own fault. My heart is broken. I wish I was dead.

September 1987

Dear Ostara,

I actually have a job!! Well only part-time, but that's probably for the best as Mum's so up and down. I can't quite believe they offered it to me – I really thought I'd fluffed the interview, I was so nervous. It's only a small business, repairing electrical appliances. Mr Jackson, the manager, seems very kind and there are only two older ladies working with me so I think that will be good. I will be based in the office and have to answer the phone, keep the files up to date and type invoices to customers, but it doesn't sound too difficult. At least the secretarial course came in handy in the end!

June 1992

Dear Ostara,

I have had to give up work to care for Mum round the clock. I'm a bit sad to leave as it gave me something else to do and a few extra pounds in my pocket, but I don't think I have any choice. Mr Jackson was very understanding. He said I don't need to worry about working my notice. He told me his own mum had been very poorly and needed a full-time carer towards the end of her life. That upset me as I don't want to think like that about Mum. After her fall yesterday, she is badly shaken. Thankfully she didn't break any bones but she has a nasty graze on her leg and a bump on her head. I don't think she's safe to be left alone now. But we will manage somehow.

December 2000

Dear Ostara,

There have been some bad ones in the past but this has been the most miserable Christmas I can ever remember. Mum's health is failing fast and she told me she doesn't think she will be around next year. She actually asked me, if things get too bad, to put a pillow over her face. I can't bear it. I know it's very hard for her but how could she expect me to do something like that? And when she is gone, I will have no one. I wish Iola was here. I keep hoping her letter will arrive in the post but it never does. I miss her so much.

October 2001

Dear Ostara,

I am terrified. I know it's only a matter of time for Mum now. She is growing weaker by the day. The letters keep coming from the gas people. The latest one said they have a legal right to access the property and that they'll obtain a warrant of entry and barge their way in if I don't open the door to them.

I can't risk being here when that happens. I know it's all sure to come out eventually but I don't know what will become of me when it does. I know she did it for me, but I wish Mum had never told me about what happened with Uncle Roger. After what he put me through, I suppose she thought I had a right to know. The thought that he'd been rotting down there all these years actually made me want to throw up. But now that I do know, I realise I've become a part of it all, keeping quiet about it all this time. Even if I wasn't the one who hit him and pushed him down the cellar steps. Or at least, that's how the police are sure to see it.

I have nowhere to go and no one I can turn to. I am in turmoil. I can't even sell the house now. Apart from Rufie, I'll have nothing. Once Mum's gone, I suppose I could blow it up, leave the gas on or something. But that would endanger the neighbours and they've done nothing wrong. What the hell am I going to do?

November 2001

Dear Ostara,

I can't quite believe it. And to think, if I hadn't bought that newspaper to see Mum's obituary, I would never have seen the ad! What an extraordinary coincidence! But then, you know I don't believe in coincidence. For once someone seems to be smiling down on me. The perfect opportunity to escape, to make a new life for myself.

I am devastated about poor Mum. Of course I am. But the worry of everything else has overshadowed my grief for the time being. At least she's no longer suffering. I just need to get away, get my head straight. I've bought my ticket and tomorrow I leave. My stomach is in knots. I must finish packing now. I have to travel light, so I need to be ruthless. And then I need to get some sleep so that I can focus. Because I feel it in my gut that Little Hambley has to be the village Stevie was talking about. And if it's the last thing I do, I need to find Iola and try to put things right between us before it's too late.

Just when it seemed that they hadn't a hope in hell of finding Flora, the officer allocated the delightful task of going through the household rubbish with a fine-tooth comb came across a newspaper from almost three weeks earlier with the 'small ads' page folded outwards.

Ringed several times in red biro was a request for a full-time, live-in carer. Coincidentally, on the same afternoon, another officer going through the telephone records discovered a lengthy call from a fortnight ago, between someone from 29 Ostleton Road and the same phone number specified in the job advertisement placed by an unknown person in the Gloucester area.

DS Kaur's heart sang. A solid lead. And one that would hopefully guide them straight to Flora Lanyon.

*

Mr Homity answered the door to Mill House in his usual, slightly imperious fashion. He stood with the front door ajar, half behind it and peering through the gap at the two police officers waiting on his step, one hand gripping the interior handle almost like a shield. He seemed irritated to be disturbed, professing never to have actually laid eyes upon the young woman who'd answered the job advertisement.

'So unreliable, a lot of people these days.' He rolled his eyes. 'Yes, I conducted a telephone interview with a Miss Flora Lanyon. I was looking for someone to care for my dear wife, and it seemed she had plenty of the necessary experience – after looking after her elderly mother for several years, or so she told me. I had high hopes – she sounded the ideal candidate. She was due to start a fortnight ago. But she never actually turned up. I did wait a day or so, to give her the benefit of the doubt. You know, in case she had been taken ill, or something unavoidable had occurred. I tried to call the contact number she had provided a few times, but there was no response.' He sighed wearily. 'Complete lack of common courtesy. One might have thought she'd at least have had the decency to let me know if she'd had a change of heart.'

'So, you never actually met Miss Lanyon in person, then?' DI Baines narrowed his eyes as he scrutinised the pompous little figure before him. He cleared his throat noisily. Sergeant Kaur detected the prickle of irritation in her boss's voice and smothered a grin.

Mr Homity shook his head. 'No. As I've already explained, she failed to show up. And now I have to start my search for an assistant all over again.' A noise from within caused him to glance sharply back over his shoulder into the hallway. He closed the door a little more so that half his face was in shadow.

'Erm – would you like to come in?' he said. 'Or will that be all? It's just that I have to see to my wife, you understand – I'm having to attend to her myself until I can fill the vacancy. It's not easy, as I'm sure you'll appreciate . . .'

'No, that's fine. You carry on, sir. Thank you for your help.'

The door closed abruptly. The two officers turned to one another with raised eyebrows.

'Charisma bypass or what?' Sergeant Kaur rolled her eyes.

'Hmm. You meet all sorts in this job. Ah well, back to the drawing board, then.'

Inspector Baines looked back as they crossed the slatted footbridge. He blew out his cheeks.

'Some place, this. Hell of a size for just one elderly couple. Must take some upkeep. Wonder if that mill is still operational? I'll have a quick nosy, if you don't mind – I love anything old and mechanical.'

The sudden blare of classical music boomed from somewhere to their right, stopping them in their tracks. A streak of orange and white bolted frantically across the lawn, heading away from the din and towards the trees surrounding the property.

DI Baines' mouth fell open. 'What the heck was that?'

'Looked like a cat. Bloody big one, though.'

As they headed back across the bridge, the sound of Tchaikovsky's *1812 Overture* grew louder, causing them to cover their ears.

'Jesus, that's deafening even from here. D'you think the old boy's hard of hearing?'

'I don't think *he's* the one playing it. Look.'

DS Kaur's eyes followed the direction in which the inspector was tipping his head.

Through the window of the annexe building, a young, dark-haired man could be seen, waving his arms earnestly as though conducting the booming symphony. He appeared, unsurprisingly, oblivious to everything else around him.

'There's the poor cat – up that tree.' Taking her hand from one ear, the sergeant gestured towards a huge oak, fifty yards or so from where they were standing. The creature looked terrified.

The music reached a crescendo as the cannons of the finale filled the air. And then mercifully, peace was restored. The officers dropped their hands, the noise of gunfire still ringing through their heads. The inspector stared up at the building open-mouthed.

'Christ almighty. What the *fuck* was that all in aid of?'

Sergeant Kaur smirked. She hadn't heard her boss swear like that before.

'Someone fancying himself as some sort of virtuoso, by the looks of things.' She stared up into the tree where the cat, its pupils dilated and fur on end, watched from a safe distance. 'Aww, poor thing. D'you think it's stuck?'

'Doubt it. Probably just waiting till the coast's clear.'

Sergeant Kaur approached the tree slowly, raising a hand gently towards the animal who was staring down at her warily through the foliage.

'Hello, puss. You can come down now.' Suddenly struck by the cat's distinctive two-tone face, her heart quickened. She called to Baines, who was making his way towards the annexe. 'Unusual-looking cat, this, sir.

And it's bloody massive. Didn't the Lanyons' old neighbour describe their cat as having funny markings?'

The inspector stopped in his tracks, turning to peer up into the tree. 'She did, yes. Ginger one side of its face and black and white on the other. A beast of a thing she said it was, too.'

The sergeant pursed her lips. 'Bit of a coincidence. D'you think we should have another word with the old boy?' She tipped her head towards the main house.

'Most definitely. And I'd like a chat with our budding maestro in there, too. I've got a nose for rats, and I can smell a rotting one here for sure.'

CHAPTER 45

Stretmore, December 2001

Detective Sergeant Kaur was finding it hard to keep her temper. After bringing Abraham Homity in, it had been agreed with the Gloucestershire Constabulary that it would be more convenient for them to take him back to the nick in Stretmore for questioning. But he was proving to be the most arrogant, infuriating man she had ever tried to interview. She wondered how long he'd continue to deny any knowledge of the two bodies weighted down beneath the waterwheel on his property. After their initial meeting at Mill House, the man had obviously panicked, realising he'd be found out, and had tried to make a run for it, but thankfully she and DI Baines had intercepted him as he was about to climb into a taxi down by the main road.

Even after they'd taken the statement from the Homitys' cleaner and established that he'd been lying about not meeting Flora Lanyon, Abraham Homity refused to answer any questions. And only that morning, the distressed family doctor had come forward with a letter he had just discovered, hand-delivered days earlier by Flora Lanyon but which had somehow found its way into his junk mail pile. The note, highlighting Flora's concerns about the medication Homity had been forcing on his poor wife and his dubious motives, was accompanied by a list of drugs, apparently annotated by Homity himself. There had also been a footnote about Flora's friend, Iola Chappell: that she'd found proof Iola had visited Mill House at some point in the recent past, but had been unable to find any trace of her. Yet *still* the man continued to deny everything. He sat bolt upright, with that smug, tight smile, refusing to make eye contact. It was frustrating beyond belief.

The son had been pretty hysterical and resisted arrest initially, but became more compliant when his psychiatrist, Dr Abercrombie, had been brought into the station. He'd given Hector an injection of something, which had calmed him down. Sergeant Kaur wasn't sure what the man's actual condition was, but it seemed he'd been receiving treatment and counselling since childhood.

The sergeant had paused the interview tape while they waited for Homity senior's solicitor to arrive. The man had been sitting, arms folded, tapping one foot and staring into space. He refused to speak to her and she was sure it was because she was a woman. Kaur had left him under the watchful eye of DC Moore while she went back to the office. She needed a coffee break before she swung for him. She thought of poor Flora, of everything she'd endured throughout her life. To think this miserable little man must have played a part in her death made her want to throttle him with her bare hands.

'How's it going?' Detective Inspector Baines was barging the door with one shoulder. He had just returned from Mill House, wielding a large cardboard box, piled with paperwork.

'It's not, sir. Homity's not admitting to anything. We're waiting for his brief. The son's going to be interviewed later with the support of his doctor, but he's away with the fairies at the moment. Had to be sedated.'

Baines nodded, raising an eyebrow. 'Hmm. Not surprised.' He dropped the box onto the nearest desk. 'This lot was found in the library at the house. All sorts of stuff in there.'

He gestured to one of the constables at the far end of the room. 'Got a bit of light reading for you here, Mike.' He turned back to his sergeant. 'How's the cat settling in?'

She smiled. 'He's a sweetheart. Left him curled up on my sofa. Lovely temperament.'

'Good job we found him, eh. In more ways than one.'

DS Kaur nodded. It had been fortuitous – if they hadn't spotted the cat, they might not have discovered the bodies. Not so soon, at least.

Baines studied her face. 'How much sleep have you had?'

Kaur felt shattered – and slightly fraught. She'd hoped he wouldn't notice.

'I'll catch a few hours later, Sir . . .' She dropped her eyes.

Baines sighed. 'Look, I'll take over with the old man if you want. Go and get your head down for a couple of hours. Not sure how poor the wife's mental state is, but maybe you could go and speak to her when you've had a kip. Hopefully she'll have improved a bit, now she's out of his clutches. She's been taken to a local nursing home – Treetops, I think it's called. Who knows – she might be able to fill in a few of the gaps.'

*

Sergeant Kaur had raised an eyebrow at her surroundings as she pulled up outside the home. Mrs Homity was sitting in an armchair, staring out of the huge window, when the young police officer entered her suite. Treetops was plush, beautifully maintained and languishing in acres of landscaped grounds – more like a hotel than a residential place. Nothing like the one her own grandmother had been taken into last year. No tacky floors or overpowering waft of urine. The rooms were large and expensively furnished. There was even a widescreen TV in one corner of the room.

'Mrs Homity, I'm DS Kaur. I'd like to ask you a few questions, if that's okay?'

The old woman looked up and smiled. 'Yes. I was wondering when someone might want to speak to me. Have a seat.' She indicated another armchair at the opposite side of the window. 'Where would you like me to start?'

*

Sergeant Kaur left with a slightly sick feeling in her gut. This was a complex tale and one that needed thorough investigation. But she had no doubt that every word Mrs Homity had told her was the truth. And it was nothing short of tragic.

The Homitys' marriage had been happy initially. But after the birth of their daughter, Xanthe, Agnes found her husband increasingly distant. One day, she'd confronted him and asked outright if he had fallen out of love with her. She was shocked when he broke down and confessed that he had been in love with someone else, but that it was all over. He vowed to try harder to make their marriage work, for the sake of their little girl.

Left in his care one afternoon while Agnes went into town, Xanthe had slipped out of the house and fallen into their millpond, where her lifeless body was later found. Agnes had returned home from her shopping trip to see her husband's friend, Kenneth Ogilvy, driving away on the main road. She realised Abraham had been drinking and that he hadn't been keeping a close eye on Xanthe. The pair were wracked with grief and Agnes could not forgive her husband.

Several years passed. Abraham was desperate for an heir to inherit the house which had been in his family for centuries. Reluctantly, Agnes had agreed to try for another baby and eventually fell pregnant. But shortly after their son, Hector, was born, she became severely depressed and had to be hospitalised, having no choice but to leave the new baby in her husband's care.

And it was here that the real story had begun.

'I knew, you see,' Mrs Homity had told the young sergeant. 'When I came out of hospital. Oh, I'd been in a bad way. I was in there six weeks, dosed up to the eyeballs on antidepressants and sedatives. But I still felt in my gut that the baby wasn't mine. It was the feet, you see. That was the first thing that made me think.'

'The feet?'

'Yes. You know, when a baby's born and they check they've got all their fingers and toes? I remembered lying in the labour room, looking at my baby's tiny feet. Just like Xanthe's. The second toe noticeably longer than the first. My mother's were the same. They call it Morton's toe, I believe. Of course, the baby had grown quite a bit while I'd been in hospital. And they do change a lot, even from day to day, in those early months. But his feet were totally different. Wider. The big toe much longer than the others.'

DS Kaur looked at her quizzically. She had neither experience of babies or podiatry.

'Feet might grow, Sergeant. But the shape of the toes . . . well, I knew something wasn't right. I asked Abey outright but he dismissed my concerns; said I was confused, that it was the medication. In the end, I had to let it drop when he said he thought I needed to return to hospital. But I just knew instinctively, even *without* the feet I'd have known, that this wasn't the baby I'd brought into the world. I nearly drove myself mad, watching that child grow up. His behaviour was erratic, often out of control. He looked nothing like me, nothing like Abey. But no one would listen to me. They thought it was my illness, my grief after losing Xanthe, skewing my judgement.' She shook her head angrily.

'And then, a couple of years ago, there was to be a charity auction in our village, raising money for a local hospice. I decided to clear out my cupboard. I had some beautiful cocktail dresses that might raise a few pounds. Abey and I had long had separate bedrooms. I preferred it that way and I think he did, too. He was out for the afternoon and I knew there were a couple of expensive coats hanging in his wardrobe that hadn't seen the light of day for years, so I thought I'd fish them out and ask later if we could donate them to the auction.' She put a hand to her throat. 'And it was then that I found it all.'

'I'm sorry – what did you find?' Sergeant Kaur looked up from her notebook sharply.

'A bag of baby clothes, amongst other things. Baby clothes that I didn't recognise. I thought at first maybe it was just my memory. I mean, I was pretty heavily medicated for some time after Hector was born. But then, when I found the newspaper, I began to piece it all together.'

'A newspaper, you say?'

'Yes. Abey had stuffed a pair of his dress shoes with newspaper. You know, to keep the shape. He hadn't worn them in years, so I thought I'd give them to the auction, too. But when I pulled out the paper, the headline caught my eye. An awful case – a small baby was snatched from outside a shop, somewhere near Rugby. About the time I'd been in hospital.'

'And the clothes?'

'There was a Babygro; mittens, a scruffy little jacket. But the picture of the baby boy who'd been taken – he was wearing the very same jacket.'

The sergeant sat forward. 'You're certain about this?'

Mrs Homity nodded hard. 'Absolutely.'

This felt momentous. Sergeant Kaur's heart began to pound. She tried to sound calm. 'So . . . you thought that the child you had raised – he might have been the same baby who was taken?'

'I was *certain* of it. I realised then that something must have happened to my own baby. I mean, it wouldn't be the first time that Abey had failed to care for his child properly, would it?' Her jaw clenched. 'I was going to confront him with it all, the moment he returned. But then I thought, he's had years to think this through: he'll have concocted some sort of story. I needed real proof. I wanted him to pay for what he'd done. To me; to the poor mother of that baby.'

'What did you do?'

'I decided to track down the family of the baby that was kidnapped. They can do tests these days, can't they? Prove people are related with a hair or a drop of blood.'

The sergeant nodded eagerly. 'DNA. So did you manage to find the baby's relatives?'

'It took me almost a year. The area where they lived was mentioned in the newspaper. I told Abey I was visiting a friend and caught a train, then a taxi. I found the little shop, near where the baby had been taken; went in under the pretext of wanting a newspaper, and asked the shopkeeper if he knew the family. The chap was just a child when it had all happened – he'd taken over the business from his father, apparently. But he told me that he knew the baby's mother had died and the remaining children had moved elsewhere.'

'So you drew a blank?' The sergeant felt deflated. She'd hoped that this was leading somewhere and it seemed now that the whole tale might just fizzle out.

'I thought I had. It was demoralising, having gone all that way. But as I was leaving, the shopkeeper called me back and said he'd heard that the older daughter, Iola, was running a market stall in Rugby, selling candles and crafts; that sort of thing. I hadn't time to go to Rugby as I needed to catch my train home, but I found a call box and was able to find her contact details from a list of local traders in the Yellow Pages. And so I wrote her a letter, telling her what I believed, and asked her to come and see me. At Mill House.'

'And this was when?'

'Last May. No – the May before. I forget.' The old woman closed her eyes as though finding it taxing. She seemed suddenly muddled.

'And did Iola respond?' DS Kaur tried to keep her tone measured, but was flushed with adrenaline now.

'Oh yes. After she'd arranged cover for her business, she booked herself into a guest house in the village.'

Mrs Homity dropped her head suddenly, clasping her hands in her lap. 'I wish I'd never contacted her now. None of this would have happened. I feel partially responsible.'

'Responsible for what?'

She lifted her face, her eyes moist with tears. 'For her death, Sergeant. And for poor Flora's, too.'

*

Iola sounded feisty. She had stood out like a sore thumb in the village, heavily pierced and tattooed with spiked, jet-black hair and colourful clothes. With Hector and Abraham out for the day, she and Mrs Homity had spent an afternoon together at Mill House, piecing together what the old woman believed had happened, to Iola's brother, Warren, and her own infant son. Iola had been angry at first; not with Mrs Homity, but with her husband. But she was desperate to meet Hector – or rather, Warren. She said she'd always known in her heart that he was still alive and had never stopped looking for him.

The following day Iola had returned to Mill House and gone straight up to the annexe. She'd told Mrs Homity she would know immediately if he was her brother and that she'd ask him to take a test to prove it. Agnes had been dubious, knowing 'Hector' could be volatile. But she had underestimated the strength of reaction this news would provoke in him.

'Hector went completely berserk, shouting at Iola, calling her a liar. I thought he might strike her. It was awful.' Agnes's face filled with anguish at the memory.

'Abey heard the commotion and went across to the annexe. I was watching from the kitchen window. He seemed to be calming the situation and then they all disappeared inside.' Mrs Homity covered her face with both hands. 'I don't know how I could've been so stupid. I didn't dare go over – I just waited, pacing up and down. I went upstairs, dug out the newspaper article I'd found, kept looking at the photograph, trying to reassure myself I wasn't mistaken. Abey came back to the house an hour or so later. He looked very pale and angry. He said that the young woman I'd invited into our home had left. That she'd said the most awful things and upset Hector. That I had done untold damage and what the hell had I been thinking of.'

She turned to DS Kaur. 'So I let him have it. Told him I knew he'd snatched the baby boy, waved the newspaper in his face. Said I knew something had happened to our own baby and I was going to ring the police.'

'And how did he respond?'

Mrs Homity shuddered. 'He went very quiet at first. Then he leaned in, very close to my face, a mad look in his eyes. I'd never seen him like that before. It was as if something had snapped inside him. And he admitted it. Everything.'

DS Kaur held her breath for a moment. 'That he'd taken Warren Chappell?'

The old woman nodded, her eyes welling once more. 'Yes. That he'd found our own baby dead in his cot. That he'd panicked, thinking he'd be blamed, especially after Xanthe. He claimed to have gone looking for a baby to take, so that no one would ever know . . .'

'And you were alone when this conversation took place? Just the two of you?'

'Oh, yes. The front went straight back up as soon as Hector appeared, though. Hector was ranting; incoherent. Abey got him to sit down, breathe deeply. Gave him one of his tablets. He told him they'd done nothing wrong and that the young woman had clearly been deranged. What did she expect, turning up at someone's door, making such outlandish allegations? And then I realised that something had happened to her.'

'So, did he actually admit that? That they'd . . . done something to Iola?'

'Well, no. Not in so many words. But from everything he was saying to Hector, it was obvious she'd been hurt, at the very least. And of course, now we know, don't we. Where the poor girl ended up.'

'Did you challenge either of them?'

'It would have been pointless saying anything to Hector. He is . . . disturbed, Sergeant, for want of a better word. And as soon as his medication kicked in, he sat staring into space as though he didn't know who he was any more, let alone what had just happened. But when I suggested to Abey that if they'd hurt Iola, I wouldn't hesitate to report them both, he turned on me once more.

'Was I so *stupid* to think anyone would believe a word I said? I had a history of mental illness. He'd express his grave concerns about my paranoia; my sanity, even – make sure I was sectioned and they'd throw away the key. He had friends, he said. *Influential friends*. I knew who he was talking about at once.' She gripped the arms of the chair. 'I realised what he was saying was true, that no one would take me seriously. I felt desperate.'

DS Kaur placed a hand gently on her arm. 'What did you do?'

'Nothing.' She gazed helplessly into space. 'We carried on as though everything was normal. But my thoughts started to get very jumbled in the coming weeks. And I felt so incredibly tired. It was then it dawned on me that Abey must be interfering with my medication. But I was powerless to do anything about it. All these things had happened, and here was I, confused and useless.'

Sergeant Kaur felt a rush of anger. The poor woman. Abraham Homity was even more of a piece of work than they'd suspected initially. Everything the GP had told them corroborated the old woman's allegations about the medication. But the more they could prove, the better the chance of him never seeing the light of day again.

She took a deep breath. 'And you're saying as well as everything else, you believe he disposed of your baby's body, Mrs Homity?'

The old woman buried her face in her hands and began to sob. 'Yes. And I have no idea what he did with it.'

'But what of Flora Lanyon? You said you felt responsible for her death, too?'

'It was when I saw the tattoo on her wrist – it triggered the memory. Of Iola. It must have been the medication Abey was giving me, you see – making me confused. Oh, I know my recall's not as it should be. And yes, there are days when everything is hazy and I can't think straight, even without my pills and potions. But sometimes everything was clear as crystal – and then I'd see things, imagine things. I wasn't sure what was real and what was in my head half the time. And when I *was* thinking rationally, I didn't dare say anything. I'd realised what he was capable of. I was frightened of him. I should have warned Flora – told her to leave. You see, I think one of the reasons she came to Mill House was to look for her friend.'

'But you can't be held responsible, Mrs Homity. Not when you've been a victim in all this yourself.'

'A victim? Is that how you see me?' She smiled sadly. 'I can never forgive myself, Sergeant. I wish it were me at the bottom of that pond. I wish it was all over and I was with my Xanthe again. My life ended a long time ago.'

DS Kaur rose to leave. She wasn't sure there was anything left to be said. There would need to be a thorough excavation of the grounds to see if the baby's body could be found. What a grim one that was going to be.

'Sergeant?'

She paused at the door, looking back as the old woman raised a hand, shifting forward in her seat.

'You might want to question a man called Kenneth Ogilvy. I think you'll find he and my husband were lovers.'

CHAPTER 46

Tuesday 7 January 2002

Cotswold Herald

More Shocking Revelations in Mill 'House of Horrors' Trial

New evidence has been brought to light in the grim case of two bodies discovered beneath the waterwheel at eighteenth-century Mill House, just outside the picturesque village of Little Hambley. Wealthy mill owner Abraham Homity, 76, stands accused of double murder in a case which has rocked the local community. His son, Hector Homity, 26, a keen amateur taxidermist, was also remanded in custody, but after extensive questioning has now been transferred to a psychiatric hospital under Section 48 of the Mental Health Act.

On 21 December of last year, police discovered the remains of recently deceased 36-year-old Flora Lanyon, weighed down beneath the ancient mill wheel visible through the glass floor in the renovated annexe to the impressive property, along with another initially unidentified female, now known to be Iola Chappell, believed to have been in the water for more than twelve months. Ms Chappell was reported missing last year after failing to return numerous phone calls from her brother, Steven.

Ms Lanyon is thought to have been employed as a live-in carer to Abraham Homity's wife, Agnes Homity, 72, who has suspected dementia and has now been transferred to a local nursing home.

In a further twist, shortly after Ms Lanyon is believed to have left her home in Stretmore, near Rugby, badly decomposed human remains, now known to be those of Roger Blight, Lanyon's uncle, were discovered wrapped in a rug by shocked gas board officials attempting to obtain a meter reading from the basement of the house Flora once shared with her now deceased mother, Sheila Lanyon. Police are treating the death as suspicious, although it is as yet unclear whether this has any connection to the current investigation.

We can now also reveal that the discovery of the skeleton of a male infant buried within the extensive grounds of Mill House was made on Sunday. After further interrogation, police have obtained a full confession from Mr Homity senior. This morning they issued a statement saying that they now believe the baby's remains to be those of the real Hector Homity, claimed by Mr Homity to have died of natural causes aged only six weeks, in 1975. Mr Homity insists that the baby was under his sole care and was a victim of Sudden Infant Death Syndrome (cot death) shortly after his wife was hospitalised only weeks after giving birth while suffering post-natal depression. He maintains that his wife had no knowledge of the baby's demise and that, in order to spare her the pain of the infant's loss, he kidnapped a child to replace their dead son with the intention of passing him off as their own.

Homity claims that the boy he and his wife raised is actually Warren Chappell, snatched in 1975 from his pram outside a corner shop just yards from his Stretmore home. The investigation into Warren's disappearance has now been reopened and police are in contact with his two surviving siblings, Steven, 34, and Carly, 32, who are co-operating fully and awaiting results of DNA tests to confirm Homity's claims. In connection with the kidnap, police would also like to speak to Abraham Homity's close friend and confidante, Kenneth Ogilvy, a retired solicitor from Cheltenham. They have been unable to locate him so far and are appealing for anyone knowing of his whereabouts to come forward.

Tragically, Warren's mother, Doreen Chappell, died from alcohol poisoning in 1980, aged only 33. Her body was found by her eldest daughter, Iola, aged only 15 at the time. The identity of Warren's father is unknown.

Iola, who would have been 37 later this year, was last seen by her brother Steven in May 2000. Steven has told police that Iola had always been obsessed with finding their lost brother and said she had been following up a new lead.

The case continues.

Epilogue

39 Ostleton Road, Stretmore, 7 January 2002

There had been much speculation about what had happened to Flora Lanyon, and with everything that had come out in the last week on the news and in the papers, it was the first topic of conversation on everyone's lips, in Stretmore and beyond. *What* a way to finish up. And a decaying body in her basement to boot. *Eugh*. Molly Baxter found it both thrilling and horrifying, in equal measures.

But above all else, Molly was kicking herself. If she'd come forward sooner, she might have been in the papers herself; achieved her fifteen minutes of fame. Even made a few quid out of it. She'd considered taking it to the police, saying she'd just found it. But they had ways of finding these things out, didn't they? No, she couldn't say anything now. It would reveal her for exactly what she was: a nosy neighbour. And a thief.

When the letter had arrived that warm spring morning almost two years earlier, she should have taken it straight round to number 29. She knew that. But she hadn't. It was addressed to number 39, even if it didn't have her name on the envelope. So she had opened the letter; read it, and read it again.

She'd been intrigued at the time. Well, well. Mousy Flora actually had some sort of past, then. She vaguely remembered her mum mentioning something about a baby called Warren being snatched when she was little. She'd wondered who this Iola was; what her relationship with Flora had been. Why they had fallen out.

But she couldn't really have gone round to Flora's with it after that. Not when the envelope was torn and Flora would know she'd had a sneaky look. She'd heard it wasn't strictly legal to open someone else's mail, too – she could have dropped herself right in it.

So there it sat, in her kitchen drawer, sandwiched between the pages of Molly's Jamie Oliver cookery book, where it would have to stay. Because she didn't want to bin it.

After all, it was a little bit of history now.

Postscript

Lime Tree Lodge,
Little Hambley,
Gloucs.

Tuesday 16 May 2000

Dear Flo,

I hope this reaches you okay - I forgot your house number so I'm taking pot luck! I saw our Stevie a couple of weeks ago and he said your mum was in a bad way. I'm sorry to hear that. She never liked me but I know how close you two are. I've often thought about writing before but I'm not great with words. I just wanted to let you know I've thought a lot about you since we fell out. I was hurt and angry you never told me - or anyone else - that you saw that man taking Warren. I was in a bad place anyway and that just tipped me over the edge. I realise now you were a scared, screwed-up kid. Just like me but without the big gob - ha-ha. We all do stupid things when we're young - I should know that better than anyone. And now I'm older and wiser (ho ho!!) I've realised life's too short to bear grudges. So there you go.

Remember Jez - from the squat? I saw him last month getting out of a Bentley outside the town hall. He's something high up on the council apparently. He did an interview with the local rag about this drive to clean up the city centre. No dreads and all suited and booted these days. Looks like he sold out. Maybe he changed when he got his hands on his grandad's dosh. I wonder if he'd even remember me? Doubt it somehow.

What I really wanted to tell you was that I got this weird letter last Friday from a woman in the Cotswolds saying she thinks her husband took Warren and all these years they've been bringing him up as if he was theirs. It all sounds very fucked up. She reckons she was taken ill not long after her own baby boy was born - about the same time Mum had Warren - and had to leave the kid with her husband when she had to go into hospital. Anyway sometime last year, she found some awful cheapo baby clothes (!!) in a bag stuffed into a cupboard or something that definitely didn't belong to her own little prince. And then she saw a picture of our Warren in an old newspaper and recognised the blue jacket - even in black and white you could still see the big stain on the front - the same one Mum used to put on Stevie when he was a baby. This woman says she never felt like the baby was hers. She says a mother can sense these things. I wouldn't know.

The long and short of it is I'm booked into this B&B in the Cotswolds (address at the top - and guess what - there's a pub called The Jack and Jester in the village! WTF!! I thought our local was the only one in the whole world! I'll have to check it out before I go - looks a bit posh - bet the bogs actually have seats and loo rolls, ha-ha) and I'm going to meet the woman tomorrow at their house.

I spoke to her on the phone this morning. I reckon she's a bit scared of her husband to be honest. I don't think he knows anything about her contacting me. He sounds like a control freak. They live in this bloody massive mansion. It's an old water mill or something. I hope if it does turn out to be Warren they haven't turned him into some sort of poncey Little Lord Fauntleroy! But he'll be grown up now anyway, won't he. I keep forgetting that. I told Stevie I was going to the Cotswolds to look for Warren but not the rest. I reckon he thinks I'm barking mad. I haven't told the police or anything yet either. I'll make sure I've got enough proof before I go in all guns blazing.

Anyway watch this space. I'll keep you posted.

Bye for now.

Iola x

PS Maybe we can meet up for a few bevvies when I get back? Defo not in The Jack though - somewhere with a bit more class! Wonder if you've changed? I'm a bit fatter these days but you'll still know me - I'll be the one with the purple boots ☺.

Speak soon.

PPS Here's a little hare just for you x

Acknowledgements

First and foremost, huge and grateful thanks to my wonderful editor, Rachel Hart. Her patience, support and guidance throughout have been invaluable and greatly appreciated. A big thank you to Thorne Ryan for her enthusiasm about the book's premise. Thanks also once again to Rhian McKay for her meticulous copyedit and helpful suggestions, and to Raphaella Demetris and Lottie Hayes-Clemens for their input. Many thanks and a big shout-out to the lovely wider team at Avon Books. There is so much going on behind the scenes to bring the reader the final polished article and all credit to those unsung heroes working away in the background who help this happen.

As always, huge gratitude to all the bloggers and reviewers who are so incredibly generous with their time – we authors have so much to thank you for. Also to all the lovely writers and Twitter friends who are unfailingly supportive and encouraging – writing can be a solitary pursuit and it's comforting to know we're all in a similar boat!

Thanks as ever to the people central to my existence, my wonderful family: to my husband, Mark, my children, Gemma, Natalie and Christopher, and my grandchildren, Olivia, Josh, Isaac, Noah, Oliver and Gracie. You all help to keep me sane! A special nod (and a pat on the back!) to (then five-year-old) Oliver, who came up with a brilliant idea for a plot point!

Finally, a massive thank you to every reader who has bought and read this book – your support is invaluable and I'm eternally grateful to you all. I really hope you have enjoyed the story.

A mysterious figure.
A whispering community.
A deadly secret . . .

A haunting, twisty story about the power of secrets and rumours, perfect for fans of Ruth Ware's *The Turn of the Key* and Lucy Atkins's *Magpie Lane*.